IN THE BLOODSTREAM: AN ANTHOLOGY OF DARK FANTASY AND HORROR

I0641346

Compiled
with an Introduction by
Eden Royce

Edited by
Michael LaRocca

Copyright Notice

"Watching the Eater" copyright © 2013 by Shaun Avery

"The House on the Corner of Brim and Stone" copyright © 2013 by Marcia Colette

"Moonsbreath" copyright © 2013 by J.H. Fleming

"Fifty-five Shades of Green" copyright © 2013 by Ross Baxter

"Movement" copyright © 2013 by Laura DeHaan

"The Tome" copyright © 2013 by T.C. Phillips

"The Light of a Beautiful World" copyright © 2013 by Josh English

"The Thing Within" copyright © 2013 by Erin Eveland

Editor: Michael LaRocca   Proofreader: Nicole Kurtz

Cover Artist: Nancy Grayson Donahue   Published by Mocha Memoirs Press, LLC

Publisher's Note

This is a work of fiction and may contain descriptions of adult situations, explicit language, and scenarios. These stories are for adults only. Please keep this out of the hands of people under the age of 18 years old.

Table of Contents

Introduction

On my list of favorite horror movies, the original *Psycho* is securely at the top. While watching this first part of this movie, you may wonder when it's going to show any real signs of horror.

I agree; *Psycho* starts out as a thriller.

But when it shifts to horror, it does so with a skill and finesse that leaves me amazed at this movie's relevance over fifty years after its release.

Moving from a visual medium to the written word, horror changes. Within the visual realm, the camera coaxes the eye into deceiving the brain. Little is needed to create an uneasy atmosphere: a bit of music in a minor key, some mist and ambient creaking sounds. For additional visual interest, add a few jump scares and the artistry of arterial blood spray.

In fiction, the writer is faced with a challenge of how to create chills and disturbia without special effects. Here there is no visual shorthand to rely on. Whether the author intends to instill fear, revulsion, or awe, they must do so with the proper choice of words, crafting the scenes they've chosen into clear pictures for the reader.

Nowhere is this truer than in short fiction. Less space means more decision, more honing, more editing down to the bare essence of what must be kept to tell the story best. What doesn't add to the story is struck down, ruthlessly cut out. Only keep what cuts closest to the bone.

This anthology is our homage to the short horror form. It consists of thirty-one tales of dark fantasy and horror written by authors from across the world. We welcome you to "In the Bloodstream".

Eden Royce
Charlotte, NC

The Skin Thief
by Kierce Sevren

Tonya woke to her daughter's screams and to Barley's ferocious barks and growls. Abigail had nightmares on occasion, like all children her age, but Tonya had never heard her daughter shriek like this before. She made her way to her daughter's room, tripping over toys lying in the hallway.

"It's okay; Mommy's here," she whispered as she turned the last corner. "Shh, shh, Barley."

"Mommy."

Tonya pulled the string on Abigail's side table lamp and light streamed through the pink tutu shade. Barley stood half on the window sill and half on Abigail's bed. His hackles were raised and teeth bared at the dark glass. He didn't register that Tonya was in the room. His attention was fully on the window.

Tonya sat on the edge of the bed and wrapped her arms around her daughter's shoulders. "Barley, that's enough," she said and patted his rump.

Only then did he turn, licking his chops and nervously checking the window one last time. He huffed and jumped off the bed.

"What's wrong sweetie? Bad dream?"

Abigail shook her head. Her eyes were wide and soaked in fear. "I saw him."

Tonya's heart jumped. She looked to the too thin glass that separated her daughter's room from every danger outside. "Who? Who'd you see, honey?"

Her small daughter shook her head and huddled against Mr.

Big, her oversized plush teddy. "He told me not to tell."

"Who told you not to tell?"

"Johnny did, Mommy. He said you wouldn't understand."

Tonya paused a moment, thankful that the 'he' was her son and not some predator. "Was Johnny telling you scary stories again? Monsters?"

Abigail nodded.

"Which one this time?"

"Skin-walker," she whispered.

Barley whined and pawed at Tonya's leg.

"Skin-walker?"

Abigail nodded again.

Tonya looked at Barley, Abigail's self-appointed protector. He gave her big wet eyes as though pleading with her to make the big scary something go away. It made her smile a little, to think that the brave Barley got sucked into Abigail's hysteria. "You know that Johnny likes to scare you sometimes. I'm sure he just made up this skin-walker thing."

Abigail shook her head and buried her face in her stuffie. Indistinguishable mumbling escaped the toy.

Tonya stroked her daughter's hair.

Abigail turned her head. "It's real. Johnny swore it. And I saw him, Mommy. I saw the skin-walker out there." She pointed to the dark glass.

Barley whined and jumped up onto the bed. He looked out the window.

Tonya's thoughts churned. She should drag her son out of bed to make him explain himself. But then, it's been a difficult week already. Getting them both up in the morning after losing however much sleep this was going to take wouldn't be a good option either. She would have to talk to him tomorrow. Again.

"It's not real. Johnny is just trying to scare you."

Abigail turned to look at Tonya, giving her glossy, wide eyes. "You promise?"

"I promise. Now, how about snuggling back down? Mr. Big here looks really sleepy."

A small grin lit up Abigail's face and, after squeezing Mr. Big, she nodded slowly.

Barley turned in circles before settling down to lie against Abigail's legs. Tonya stroked his head, scratched behind his ear, and got up.

She hugged Abigail and helped her settle back under the covers. She kissed the top of her head. "Would you like me to put on some music?"

With one last nod from Abigail, Tonya got up and turned the radio on to the classical music station.

She pulled the lamp string and made her way back to her room. Checking the clock as she settled under her covers, she noted the time, 12:21 A.M.

#

"Mommy. Mommy." Abigail's soft voice and small hand pulling at her shoulder woke Tonya.

"What is it, sweetie?" Tonya said as she turned over.

"I can't sleep."

Tonya groaned as she saw the time on the clock. 1:10 A.M. "I'm sorry, but you have to try. It's going to be morning before you know it."

"I did try. But...."

"But?"

"He kept looking at me," Abigail whispered.

Tonya searched her daughter's very serious face to see if there was a joke in there somewhere. She looked down at Barley who stopped panting momentarily.

"He was growling at *him* but *he* wouldn't go away."

She looked at her daughter and tried to force her brain to make some sort of sense of what she was saying. "The skin thing?"

"Walker, Mommy. The skin-walker."

Barley whined.

Tonya sat up. "Abi, that's not possible. Okay? It's just something your brother made up to –"

"No, Mommy. He didn't make it up. He said it's real. And I saw him."

This is ridiculous, Tonya thought. She shouldn't have to deal with this at this hour. Johnny is really going to get an earful tomorrow. Maybe no video games for a week.

"Sweetheart, I promised you that there is no such thing as a skin-walker, didn't I?"

Abigail nodded and clutched Mr. Big.

"Would Mommy lie to you?"

She shook her head.

"That's right. Now you need to get some sleep or you're not going to have a good day at school tomorrow." Seeing Abigail squeeze her plush, she sighed. She didn't really want to get kicked on and rolled on by her little restless sleeper. But... there would come a day, one day soon, where her darling little girl wouldn't need her like this anymore. She scooted back and patted the bed.

Abigail smiled and climbed in. Tonya folded the blankets around her, holding her tight.

Barley took the invitation too.

"No. Barley. Down. There's not enough room in this bed for three of us."

He huffed but jumped down as he was told. After a minute of trying to find a comfortable spot on the floor, Barley lay down.

Tonya listened for Abigail's breathing to grow deeper and more evenly spaced before she gave in to sleep herself.

#

Barley's growl ripped Tonya from her dreams. "Shush, Barley. You're gonna wake Abigail," she whispered as firmly as she could.

He didn't stop. She cracked an eye open and watched Barley's tail bobbing beyond the foot of the bed as he made his way to the window. His growl deepened.

Tonya turned over. She saw... something... dip out of sight. *A face?* She shook her head. No that couldn't be, she assured herself. She was still half dreaming, she told herself. This had to be something her mind made up after the commotion earlier.

She got up and looked through the glass to the dark night outside. The yard beyond was barely lit by the sliver of moon in the sky, but it was enough to see that there was nothing moving in their small back yard. She scanned what she could see of neighbors' yards. No movement there either.

A branch full of thick dark leaves waved in front of her. Tonya's heart jumped. The moving limb was unexpected and her brain made more of it that it should have. Barley barked. Tonya jumped back. "Dammit, Barley."

He gave her what looked to be a grin. His tongue flopped loosely out one side of his mouth.

"Funny guy, you got me. I nearly thought there was something out there too."

Tonya looked at Abigail who was, thankfully, still asleep. And then, to the clock. 2:20 A.M. She groaned. "Is this night never going to end?"

I have to get up in a little over four hours, she thought, really feeling the achy fatigue consuming her head. *Tomorrow's going to be a nightmare.*

She picked Abigail up and moved her back to her bed. Barley followed, climbing on the bed as soon as Tonya pulled the sheet and blanket up. She gave him a firm glare and tapped his snout with her finger. "No barking until the morning," she commanded, though she had no confidence he'd understand let alone obey what she was saying.

"Sleep, just a little more sleep," Tonya said to herself as she climbed back into bed.

Rather than falling back into sleep, she stayed awake. Her mind raced at every small noise, inventing images that should have been there. Her bed developed a mass of uncomfortable spots, and her pillow seemed determined to stay too warm. She tossed and turned for what felt like hours, but every time she checked the clock, only minutes had passed.

She began to feel her body giving in to sleep once her mattress and pillow ceased conspiring against her. Her eyes caught the red glow of her clock, claiming it was close to 3:20.

Finally.

#

Abigail's screams jolted Tonya from her dreamless sleep. Harsh red numbers blared on the clock face, 3:30 A.M. "Ten minutes. Ten freaking minutes."

Tonya got up, her head swimming in the foggy haze between dreaming and reality. "She's too old for this. I'm too old for this," she mumbled as she stumbled down the dark hallway.

She was barely into Abigail's room when she saw what looked like a pale, lithe man, barely clothed, crouching just outside the window. Tonya blinked and he was gone. She raced to the window and looked around. There was nothing there. Nothing in the dark, empty air just outside of her daughter's window. No branches to crouch on, not a tree for branches to even grow on. There couldn't possibly have been anyone outside of her daughter's second story window. She shook her head again and tried to recall what she saw, but it was so foggy now. Was there even anyone there at all?

Abigail had stopped screaming and was sobbing. She buried her face against Mr. Big.

Barley barked incessantly.

"Shh-shh-shh." She wrapped her arms around Abigail and tried to soothe her.

"You saw him Mommy, didn't you?" Abigail pleaded.

Tonya looked at her daughter's tear streaked face and fumbled for words. Her mind failed to find answers. She gave the only one she could. "I don't know what I just saw." She hugged her daughter and headed out of the room.

Abigail followed, as did Barley.

Tonya headed across the hall to Johnny's room. She knocked. "Johnny, wake up." Pausing only for a second to listen, she knocked again.

"Five more minutes," Johnny's voice called out.

"I'm coming in."

Johnny sat up and rubbed his eyes as Tonya, Abigail, and Barley came in. Barley jumped on Johnny's bed and licked his face.

"What's the matter?"

"You need to tell your sister it's not real."

He furrowed his brows and pursed his lips. "Huh?"

"The skin-walker story you told your sister. She's been up all night scared to death. Tell her the truth. That it's not real. So we can get some sleep."

Johnny was slow to respond.

"Tim said it's real."

"Johnny!"

"What?"

Abigail's soft sobs became wails. Tonya turned around and scooped her up in her arms.

"What?" Johnny repeated. "What's going on?"

"Your sister thinks she keeps seeing this skin-walker standing outside of her window."

Johnny's posture straightened.

"You saw it too, Mommy." Abigail said between sniffles.

"I don't know what I saw, sweetie."

Johnny stood up and walked behind Tonya. "I'm sorry, Abi. I made it all up just to scare you. It's not real."

"But I saw it. It was outside of my window. Barley saw it too. So did Mommy."

"Sometimes when people aren't quite awake yet, they see things, honey," Tonya said, hoping she sounded more sure of the fact than she felt. "I'm sure there was nothing there."

"Yeah, Abi. That's happened to me before too."

Tonya felt Abigail's grip around her neck loosen, and her little body relaxed. "All right now? Johnny said he made it up, right?"

Abigail sniffled against Tonya's neck and nodded.

#

"Aren't you going back to bed?" Johnny asked Tonya as she made her way from the bathroom back down to Abigail's room.

"No, I think it'd be better if I slept in your sister's room for the rest of the night."

"Oh. Okay," he said and looked down at his hands.

Tonya could barely see him in the dark hallway but noticed he seemed hesitant. "Something wrong?"

"No. No, um, I was wondering if I could stay in her room too?"

"Scared?"

"No," he answered a little too quickly. "I just feel a little bad."

Not too old to get scared? Tonya thought with a little humor. It'd been a long time since he'd wanted his mommy to save the day. "Sure. Come on, grab your pillow and blanket. We'll camp out tonight."

Abigail joined them on the floor as well. Barley paced around them for a minute, seemingly unsure of what to make of this or where he should lie. He finally settled down to lie along Tonya's legs and at the bottom of Abigail's feet.

Tonya lay there listening to her children drift off and tried not to think about how hard the floor was. She tried to not look out the window. Her brain couldn't make up any more monster sightings if she didn't look. But occasionally she did give into the impulse and was happy to see nothing beyond the dark glass except for the edge of the moon hanging at the top of the window.

She hadn't realized she had drifted off until she woke up to a soft growl. Tonya moved her leg to nudge Barley who had to be growling in his sleep. He wasn't there. She cracked her eyes and saw him standing at the door with his nose in the crack.

"Need to go out?"

He looked at her and wagged his tail. She moved her foot and he wedged his muzzle in the door to open it.

She couldn't help but feel it was a godsend that this house already had a doggy door installed by the previous owner. She used to hate getting up in the middle of the night to let him out.

Tonya sat up straight as though an electric current ran through her. Fear, worse than she'd ever experienced, broke her body out in chills. *If there had been something lurking around outside...*

She didn't let herself finish the thought.

No, that's silly. It's just paranoia. There was no creature squatting in midair looking into my daughter's room. There is no such thing as a skin-walker, she thought. She wanted to laugh, but something in her body, buried deep beneath her brain, told her it not only wasn't funny, but was deadly serious.

Tonya got up, careful to not wake her children, and crept into the hallway. She closed the door with minimal noise. As she got to the hallway, a clattering noise came from downstairs. She strained to listen and she thought she heard muffled whines and stifled barks. "Oh God."

She ran into her room and reached for her cell phone on her nightstand. It wasn't there. She searched her bed covers for it, but it wasn't there either. Panic washed through her brain as she realized that she'd left it on the kitchen counter. If there was someone in the house with them, she'd have to get to her phone to call for help. She grabbed the aluminum bat that she kept behind her bedroom door and started down the stairs. The carpet muffled the sound of her footsteps. The clicking of Barley's nails scraping against the linoleum and more pronounced whining grew louder. Tonya's heart raced. She held her breath fearing that whatever was attacking her dog would hear her. She hoped she could sneak up and knock him out before anything could happen to Barley.

Tonya paused on the bottom step. The noise had stopped. Fear mixed with dread.

She raised the bat to her shoulder and took a couple of shallow breaths. Indecisiveness gripped her as she considered her next move –

stay on the stairs and surprise the intruder, or continue with *plan A.*

A shadow moved against the wall removing one of the two choices. They were coming around the corner. Flexing her fingers, she tightened her grip. She raised the bat above her head.

The floor groaned under footsteps. Tonya braced herself and held her breath.

A mass jumped out in front of her. She was in mid-swing when she stopped herself. The bat was inches from Barley's head.

"Shit, Barley! What the hell?" She slapped a hand over her mouth. There still could be someone there.

Barley stood there between Tonya and the front door, his tongue hung out of one side of his mouth. His tail wagged. Tonya watched him for a minute while she strained to listen for any signal that someone was still coming. Barley panted and cocked his head at her.

He barked.

"Shh, Barley," Tonya whispered. She was starting to feel unsure. Silly. Perhaps there wasn't someone in the house after all. "Is there someone here, boy? Or were you getting into something you shouldn't have?" she said softly, as though some intruder wouldn't hear her.

Barley barked again.

Tonya took a deep breath and steeled her resolve. She jumped and twisted to face the hall which led to the kitchen, and waited. She waited for any movement. For any sign at all that someone was there. But, nothing moved.

She looked down at her dog, suspicious that her overactive imagination had gotten the better of her.

He returned the look and trotted off into the kitchen.

Tonya lowered the bat, but didn't put it down. Just in case. She followed Barley and flipped the light on.

A bloody mass writhed on the floor behind the legs of the closest chair. The unexpected movement made Tonya jump back and raise her bat once more. She couldn't make out what it was. Taking one step at a time, she carefully crept toward it. It made a high-pitched whine and writhed frantically. A segment of Tonya's mind told her it was Barley, that he had been skinned alive. The rest of her mind couldn't believe it. He was just there, perfectly fine. It wasn't possible for him to have been skinned in the time it took for her to turn on the light.

She turned to look at her dog. And he *was* Barley. His sweet chocolate eyes looked up at her. His tongue hung to the side of his muzzle, bobbing with each breath. Not one piece of his fur coat was out of place, matted, or otherwise disturbed. His tail waved lazily behind him.

He stood tall, proud. The same way he looked when he chased off that burglar who broke into their apartment years ago.

Maybe, the thing on the floor is a trick, Tonya thought and spun around. Her muscles clenched, prepared for the blow the monster would surely inflict.

There was nothing behind her.

She exhaled and tried to get a better look at the bloody thing on the floor, but to do so would have required her to get closer. That wasn't an option.

It let out a high-pitched cry. Pleading. Confusion washed over her. It sounded like Barley. But what if it was the skin-walker? What if he was lying there hoping to draw her closer?

Then why is Barley not trying to attack it? The question rang like a bell in Tonya's mind. "Dear God," she said.

"God had nothing to do with this," a deep voice rumbled behind her.

A coldness she'd never felt before swept through her. Her

nerves erupted in electric sensations. Nearly every hair on her body felt as though it stood on end all at once.

She raised the bat above her head and spun around.

Her dog hadn't moved. He stood there panting. His tail wagged. She stole glances around the room hoping to catch the source of the voice in something other than Barley.

"You know it isn't true." His mouth moved to form words that weren't possible.

Tonya tried three times before her voice caught up with her moving mouth. "What isn't?"

"God. That's just something people made up to sleep better at night."

"I-I don't believe you. Of course there's a God."

"But there's no such thing as a skin-walker?"

"N-no, I, uh...." Tonya tried but couldn't finish the thought. Her mind scrambled to make sense of what she couldn't.

"No? You believe in a mythical being who couldn't stop your husband from dying in an accident with a drunk? Who did nothing to help while you struggled to raise your kids? Who will do nothing to protect you now? But you won't believe that I exist?"

Tonya shook her head. Tears rolled down her cheeks. "You're not going to take my daughter. I won't let you hurt my kids." She tightened her grip on the bat and took a step forward.

He stood up on his hind legs. His mouth twisted into a smile.

"Who said I was after your kids, Tonya?"

'Twas The Monkey Killed The Medium
by Adam Millard

The medium was dead, her head caved in with her own crystal ball. I wasn't the one to discover her lifeless corpse, but I was there when the accusations began to fly, and let me put it this way: it wasn't a safe environment in which to find oneself.

"Somebody must have seen something," Miranda, the bearded lady, sobbed. She was trying desperately not to look at the pool of blood or the shattered skull from which it had leaked.

"Did anyone see anything?" I asked, already knowing what the response would be. A cacophony of frantic and defensive voices told me that they had seen nothing, heard nothing, and hoped to God that the murderer responsible was long gone, for the mere notion that the same fate would befall them before sunrise was harrowing.

"Who was the last to speak with her?" I asked. For the life of me, I didn't know why I had opted to put myself in charge.

"Casper," the bearded lady said, pointing an accusatory finger towards the giant, whose countenance changed to one of utter panic.

"I saw her *hours* ago," Casper said, his voice sonorous, deeper than a bottomless ocean. "She was alive when I left her to count her pennies."

Hilda had a thing about pennies. She would count them for hours, stacking them in neat piles of ten or twenty – depending on how brave she was feeling. It was a harmless trait that had endeared her to almost all the carnies. All except one, apparently.

I could see from the solemnity in Casper's eyes that he had not caved the woman's head in. His gigantic frame belied his gentleness, and I didn't for one minute believe him capable of such an atrocious act.

"Oh, this is terrible," Cassandra, the contortionist, said. "Hilda was like a mother to me. When I find out who did this I will make sure they follow her into the afterlife." For a woman of such slight stature, I must say I believed her conviction. I'm not a detective, not like the great Holmes or Marlowe, but I'm a good reader of faces, and I could immediately exonerate the contortionist of any blame.

"Can we all just calm down a little?" I said, stepping over the strewn medium. "I have a splendid headache, and the last thing we need is chaos." I crouched, examined the old lady, searching for any evidence that might provide us with answers. I could feel eyes burning into me, watching me anxiously, either waiting for a response that would see us to the perpetrator, or ascertaining I wasn't tampering with the scene or removing vital clues from the dead medium's personage.

At first I saw nothing. Most of the old dear's face was spackled with blood; her silver hair was drenched in crimson and peppered with brain matter that would, under other circumstances, cause me to gag. I fought the sickness down, though, just about managing to maintain an air of professionalism. To vomit all over the poor medium, therefore tainting the body, would almost certainly put me in the frame.

"Anything?" Bob-Bill, The Two-Faced man, asked. I hadn't been anticipating the interruption, so found myself slightly startled at the sound of his voice.

"Give me a minute," I said, trying not to sound irked. "There's a science to this." I was starting to sound like a fictional detective, or at least I *hoped* I was.

The first real breakthrough I made was the position of Hilda's corpse. She was almost at the entrance to her tent, which meant she had either made a run for it, attempting to flee her attacker, or crawled there while whoever held the crystal ball pulverised the back of her head. "You see the blood trail?" I said to the rest of the carnival, all of who were now in attendance. They parted and glanced down at the smeared stain leading back to the medium's table.

"Was she dragged?" a heavily tattooed woman said as she lit her pipe.

I shook my head. "Not dragged, no. Not unless our killer wanted to remove the body from the scene, only to discover the woman weighed half as much as Casper." I sighed. "No, she was trying to escape the clutches of her attacker when the final, and most powerful blow, struck home. One might deduce that this attack lasted longer than a second, but no longer than ten." I realised that all eyes were on me, their owners probably trying to figure out what *deduce* meant. "Let me put it this way. Whoever assaulted, and subsequently killed, our wonderful Hilda did so with full intent and, even when the chance to change their mind presented itself, they did nothing of the sort. This was cold-blooded murder."

Muted voices and suspicious gasps filled the tent; the carnies glanced around at each other's faces as they formed their own conjectures.

One of them had killed her. I scanned the faces of those present for any variations, no matter how insignificant. The Bearded Lady looked apt to pass out, as did Cassandra The Contortionist. Casper The Goliath was scratching his head, obviously puzzled by the whole affair. The Tattooed Lady puffed nonchalantly on her pipe, filling the space on either side of her head with blue-grey smoke. Bob-Bill was arguing with himself over where they were respectively at the time of the medium's death, though two faces – unless in cahoots with one another – was obviously enough to absolve them from the crime. The sword swallower and fire eater, Heather, hadn't moved since the corpse's discovery, though I know she couldn't have done it as she was with me, and had been since the curtain fell almost three hours prior. Which left Terrence "Ratboy" Malone, Hadji "The Great Regurgitator" Abu, whose capuchin was perched upon his right shoulder, The Hermann Twins – who I was able to discount since the crime in question would have required the use of arms, or at least limbs, and Hank and Henrietta Hermann had none to speak of – and Josef "Cannonball" West. To know that one of them had killed Hilda, and was now partaking in the investigation, caused the hackles to rise on the nape of my neck.

I turned my attention back the body beneath me and, more importantly, the blood-stained crystal ball beside her head. I was loath to pick it up, and so lowered my head to within an inch of it. Upon its reflective surface I could ascertain no prints, but there was a solitary brown hair. I was, to say the least, very pleased by the appearance of such an incriminating clue, and made my feelings known with a guttural exclamation that I could neither control nor explain. "Eureka!"

"What?" The Ratboy asked.

"Has he found something?" Hank Hermann said, shuffling across the floor, wormlike.

"Indeed I have," I said, hoping that by the end of the night the people of the carnival could sleep safely in the knowledge that the perpetrator had been captured and would soon face the full force of the British judicial system. "There is a hair upon the ball. A single hair that will identify the medium's butcher."

I hadn't expected a pat on the back at such stellar detective work, and so wasn't disappointed when none came.

"I'm not sure I want to know," The Great Regurgitator said. The monkey sitting on his shoulder squeaked in concurrence.

"What colour's the 'air?" The Tattooed Lady asked, tapping the spent tobacco from her pipe before refilling the barrel.

"Brown," I said. "Which eliminates you, Cassandra, Terrence, Casper and Hank." The ones I hadn't mentioned recoiled in horror; that they should still be under scrutiny was borderline offensive.

"Well I *know* it wasn't me," The Great Regurgitator said. "I would most certainly remember something so brutal."

"Well, it wasn't me, *neither*," Josef said. "I've spent the hours since the show chasing oblivion in my tent." He raised a glass of tarry liquid; The Cannonball's own brand of illegal moonshine.

"Maybe you did it pissed," Ratboy said. "You could've caved her head in and not know a thing about it."

Josef, not believing a word of it, took a long hard slug of the fluid. Wiping the residue from his chin, he said, "It's good stuff, but it's not *that* good."

"This is getting us nowhere," The Contortionist said. "Somebody did it, and it terrifies me knowing that it was one of you."

"Me too," Henrietta said, squirming forward so that she was once again level with her brother.

"You're still in the frame," Casper said, tapping the limbless girl with his gigantic right foot.

In the meantime, I'd managed to pluck the solitary hair from the crystal ball and hold it up to the nearest candle for closer inspection. What I noticed, however, only confounded me further.

It *was* a hair, but a lot coarser and nothing remotely human. As I twisted it between my thumb and forefinger, my mind whirred inexorably towards a suitable explanation. While I considered this new evidence which might lead to the identity of the assassin, the carnies talked amongst themselves, pointing the finger at each other, trying to explain where they were at around the same time poor, old Hilda was being thrashed by an instrument which should have foretold of the attack. It was an irony that was not lost on me.

"Everyone quiet," I said as the origins of the mysterious hair finally dawned on me. "I think I have it."

The carnies fell silent, anticipating the next words to pass my lips. If I knew then what I know now, I might have chosen to remain silent.

"This hair is not human," I said.

"What makes you say that?" The Great Regurgitator asked.

"It's plain, see." I held it up to the candlelight; the carnies grouped closer, inspecting the single hair a little less intently than I had. "I would say this belongs to an animal. A creature that had no real motive to murder the medium."

"I don't understand," The Tattooed Lady said. "You think something – an *animal* – came in here and smashed Hilda's head in with the crystal ball."

"Maybe it's from a fur coat," The Ratboy said. "If the killer was wearing a stole, maybe some of it came loose."

"No, this is from an animal," I said, sniffing the hair. I knew the smell that met my nostrils, and immediately turned my attention to the perpetrator. "This hair belongs to Pip."

Truth be told, I didn't believe the creature capable of such a malicious act, not without guidance from its trainer.

"You think my *monkey* killed the medium?" The Great Regurgitator asked, slightly flabbergasted by the accusation. "That's ridiculous." He plucked the capuchin from his shoulder and began to stroke and nuzzle it in a tender display that was on the boundary of decency.

"It would make sense," The Contortionist said. "I've always said that you can never completely tame a wild animal. It's in their blood–"

"Killing old ladies is *not* in Pip's blood," The Great Regurgitator interjected. "He is completely tame, and more harmless than any of you." The monkey squawked in agreement, though I could sense something amiss, and what the creature did next confirmed my suspicions.

Pip leapt from its handler's grasp, scampered along the ground, and snatched up the crystal ball. Raising it, he brought it down in a savage arc and proceeded to do it, over and over.

The Bearded Lady gasped. "Oh my! He's *right*. It was the monkey killed the medium!"

"*Impossible!*" The Great Regurgitator snarled. "I will not have Pip blamed for such a heinous crime."

"Neither would I," I said, taking the blood-smeared crystal ball from the frantic capuchin. "In fact, I would go so far as to suggest that this monkey was *taught* just what to do."

All eyes turned to the capuchin's handler, who suddenly looked as guilty as sin. "I didn't teach him any such trick," he said. "And I will not tolerate this nonsense any longer."

He turned to leave, but for some reason I opened my mouth and – as I said earlier, if I knew then what I know now, I would perhaps have let him leave the tent.

"Nobody's leaving this tent until we get to the bottom of this."

"What motive would Hadji have of offing the old dear?" Hank Hermann asked.

"It makes no sense," Henrietta opined, shuffling a few inches forward.

"Then perhaps we should ask him," I said. Once again, all eyes fell upon The Great Regurgitator, who I could see was now sweating despite the cold, mid-October chill. "What reason did you have to murder Hilda?"

The man glared at each of the faces imploring him to respond. His scowl reminded me of those ancient Japanese masks; such terrifying artefacts that had the propensity to turn one's blood to mercury. The effect was only exacerbated by the terrible silence.

"No," he said. "I will not be held accountable." He paused, ran his fingers through his glistening hair. "Pip was taught to kill the medium, but not just by me." He scanned the tent, intimating that each and every one of those present – except for me, of course – had had a hand in Hilda's demise.

"Don't listen to him," The Tattooed Lady said, though I could tell by the way she now chewed upon her pipe that his accusations held some truth.

"*All* of you?" I said, incredulously. "But why?"

After a moment of painful silence, The Ratboy said, "She *knew* things."

"Well of course she bloody *knew* things," I said. "She was a medium, and a damn fine one, at that."

I felt something brush past my foot, and glanced down to find the Hermann twins had shuffled up to me. "She was going to tell you about...well, she had seen in that stupid ball of hers something..." Henrietta wasn't making any sense, but then her brother finished her sentence for her.

"Henrietta and I have been mating," he said. "We don't care how disgusting you think it is. We're very much in love, and the old bag was going to try to ruin it for us."

As sickened as I was, I already knew about their incestuous behaviour. "That was no reason to kill her," I said. "What about you?" I asked The Ratboy, who began to pick at his protruding front teeth as if it would somehow distract me.

"I didn't have a problem with her until she caught me...stealing from the pockets of the audience. She said she was going to put me out of a job unless I confessed to you. Well," he grinned; his stained, yellow teeth seemed to extend even more. "I guess this is my confession."

Stealing I would not tolerate, especially from those kind

enough to attend our shows, without whom we wouldn't be able to continue as a traveling carnival. I would have had no choice but to cancel the boy's contract.

"And *you*?" I asked.

The Tattooed Lady sighed, draped her arm across The Contortionist's shoulder. "Cassandra and I are lovers," she said. "And that old biddy was praying to God that we would go to Hell for it."

"But you don't *believe* in God," I said.

"Best not to take any chances," she replied.

As I went around the tent, each of the carnies revealed their reason for killing the medium. The Cannonball had attempted to rape her, and failed; The Bearded Lady had witnessed the attempted rape, and had chosen to remain silent; the fire eater, Heather, had been caught in a very compromising situation with one of the midgets at a show in Dorchester a year prior; Casper – who had been so convincing – had a thing for Heather, who had visited him one night, maudlin and confused, asking for his help; Bob-Bill had returned to their cannibalistic ways and had been caught devouring a severed hand; and The Great Regurgitator, whose monkey had carried out the devilish deed, simply hated the way she counted pennies. "As if she's some sort of Fagin," he said.

I was shocked at each of the revelations, and soon found myself wishing things back the way they were the previous day. Life as a carny is never boring, but the events of that night had crossed a line that we could never go back to. I knew, as soon as Casper stepped forward, that things were a-changing.

"Now, I don't want any trouble," I said, holding aloft placatory hands that trembled beyond my control. "Listen. Come to your senses before it's too late."

"It's *already* too late," The Tattooed Lady said, lighting her pipe once again. "We thought the monkey would take the fall for us, but it appears that some things are best left to us humans."

They crowded me, and I – terrified and somewhat resigned – fell to my knees, landing atop the medium's corpse with such force that a ghastly sound erupted from her throat.

It might have been Casper that manhandled me into the cage, which is where I have spent the last three days. They're feeding me, and giving me water whenever necessary, but I believe their only reason for doing so is to prolong my agony. You see, I've heard them yelling and repeating things, though not to each other. They're teaching Pip new tricks. Occasionally, the monkey ambles past the cage, and I can see a glint in its eye, as if it knows what's coming. Just yesterday it sliced a banana in front of me using such skill that one could quite easily mistake it for a trained chef.

Today, I watched Casper and The Great Regurgitator paint a target upon a huge board, which I'm certain I will be strapped to for the next show. And the monkey? Well, he's been throwing knives for two days now, and what terrifies me is that he's not too good at it. Though, I guess he doesn't have to be.

Sacrifice
by Jay Wilburn

He was not sure how his ankle was sliced through, but he was sure it was deep and he was sure what would happen should they be caught. He leaned on the guide's shoulder as they plowed headlong through the savage forest. The other soldiers were not within sight and were beyond earshot. The branches whipped across his face and over his breastplate in the darkness. His face was scratched and his armor sounded back with dull rings from the impacts.

He could hear the sounds of pursuit behind them. The bodies traveled close to the ground through the underbrush instead of the higher branches. The soil thudded with paws or claws or some other formation not seen in the civilized world across the ocean.

No one will ever know what became of me, he thought.

He tried to run, but his severed tendon would support no weight. He nearly brought the guide down with the attempt. The savage blurted something in his alien tongue. Clovis assumed it was a curse. He let it pass as the guide continued to drag him away from the inhuman sounds closing in behind them in the blind wilderness.

They left the trees and opened into the tall grass and starry sky of a field.

This is death, he thought.

He begged. "Por favor, otra vez ... No vamos aqui."

The guide responded in his own tongue as he pulled Clovis farther into the open. The sounds of coarse fur or rough scales against the brush and tree trunks behind them became the swish from the grasses. He dared to look over his shoulder as they hobbled forward. The grass ripped in deep furrows behind them in at least a dozen paths.

Clovis looked forward again in the endless night.

It will surely end soon enough.

Clovis saw the mound in front of them in the pale light of the stars and sliver of moon. It was too smooth and rounded to be either natural or real. The mirage did not waver as the guide steered them toward it. He could hear the grass being parted close behind them. He feared to look again, but he felt sure the monsters would catch them before they reached the mound.

And what difference does it make if we reach the strangely rounded hill? Clovis thought.

The guide began pumping his naked legs as they mounted the steep slope. Clovis could feel the blood draining into his boots through the fabric of his pantaloons. As he felt the flesh of his ankle slide apart around the wound, he felt ridiculous in his formal armor fleeing New World monsters slicing through the grass. The guide pulled him up into the air above the field.

They collapsed on top. He heard the howls below and behind them. He waited for the creatures in the grass to expose themselves and climb the hill to feast. The howls bled into hisses and roars.

The guide said something as he stepped away from Clovis lying on his stomach on the short grass of the mound. Clovis pushed his gloved hands into the dirt and lifted himself to see the guide running down the other side of the mound.

"Que … No vas … por favor," Clovis reached out and dropped back on his breastplate on the ground.

The guide shouted in poorly formed Spanish. "Espera agui … aqui solo … sacro … sacroisima."

Sacred? Clovis thought. *What is sacred?*

The guide ran back into the grass on the flat ground and charged through the field with real speed without the Spaniard to hold him back. The furrows in the grass cut along the base of the mound on both sides. Clovis watched as the shadows passed below him and whipped out across the land after the guide. Even with his additional speed, the hidden creatures still moved faster.

Clovis looked the way they had come and considered going back to the woods.

I could reengage the expedition and fight these beasts with modern weapons and soldiers. Maybe even our savage allies will help us.

Something hissed and turned in the grass along the bloody path that dribbled down the mound into the disturbed grass. He saw a flash of orange eyes and the shadow of a ridged back and then the creature circled around the mound under the line of the tall grass.

Clovis turned in time to see the guide plunge back into the far tree line. The furrows crashed through after him, whipping branches and brush in their path.

He waited to hear the scream of the savage being brought down by the beasts. He heard a hiss and growl in the grass beside him. He looked as the shadow slithered through the grass away from the mound.

"Sacro … sacroisima," Clovis whispered as he lay on his stomach trying to spot the shadow that would not climb the strange mound where the guide had left him.

His vision blurred as his hands and arms collapsed under him.

I need to bind my wound before I bleed out on this most sacred place.

Clovis blacked out.

#

He awoke in daylight looking over the short grass at the trees at the edge of the field. He jolted and tried to rise up from the ground. Bitter pain laced out from his ankle. His other limbs went weak and he rolled to his back over the ungiving metal of his breastplate. The light flashed up from it into his eyes, dazzling him a moment before he could see the sky.

"Ayudame ...ayudame," he shouted over his dry throat.

Then, he remembered the monsters and he did sit up. The furrows were gone and the tall grass waved slowly in the breeze. He scanned around the trees, but saw only trunks. He looked for broken branches and clawed bark, but saw none. He glanced behind him and spotted the blood trail leading down the smooth slope. The hill sat perfectly curved as if formed by a sculptor. He followed the line left by his blood back to the trees. There was no sign of blood in the tall grass and nothing unusual about the woods other than he was alone in them and thousands of miles from his real home across the ocean.

Clovis looked at his ankle through the wide tear in his clothing and boot. It was deep and infested with sickness. He was not sure if it was natural or supernatural from the venom of some savage world monster. Red lines traced his veins in both directions from the wound.

It used a sharp claw or tusk, indeed, Clovis thought. *I will walk as a cripple for life.*

"Quedo lisiado de por vida," he muttered.

Clovis drew his dagger and began cutting strips of cloth away from his pants.

It's too deep, he thought.

The wound opened and bled again as he tied the bandages tighter against the cut. He continued to bind the wound tighter despite the dizziness and nausea. It was worse when he tried to look down at his work. It felt as if the mound under him would twist right off the Earth from the spinning.

He needed sticks to brace the damaged ankle. He looked out across the grass at the closest trees.

"Oye," he shouted.

His voice echoed back at him. Insects and birds continued their chirping.

He tested the ankle with the slightest pressure and felt it turn with agony.

"No ... no," he whispered.

He dragged himself down the steep slope. Each move brought a hiss from his lips and more pain from his ankle. He heard a growl from the trees. Clovis looked toward the sound and lost his balance. He rolled down the hill screaming in pain. The tall grass did not brace his fall well.

He heard them before he saw them. He pulled himself up to look across the top of the grass. The furrows approached again. They were more terrifying in the light. Shadows rose above the whipping grass and then dropped back down as the creatures raced to the mound from the trees again.

Clovis tried to push himself back up the slope, but his ankle refused. He dug his fingers into the sculpted earth of the hill. The creatures roared as they tore along the ground after him. He inched his way up the mound as the creatures converged. He clung only a few feet up the slope when the orange eyes flashed from the edge of his imprint in the grass at the base of the mound. The creatures hissed and gurgled before fanning back out in the grass. He continued to drag himself upward as the shadows disrupted the grass circling one another. He would lose them in the growth and then get a flash of darkness between the blades.

He reached the top of the hill covered in greasy sweat. He looked down and saw the blood soaked through the poor bandaging around his wound. Clovis unfastened the leather straps of his armor and cast it aside on the ground beside him.

The monsters hissed below him.

They won't step up the hill to put me out of my misery, he thought.

I will have to go to them once I am ready for that.

He closed his eyes and groaned.

"Sacro."

The monsters growled after he spoke. The sound rolled through the forests. The birds and insects went silent.

"Sacroisima."

He opened his eyes and watched the furrows spiral out in the field from his tiny island of short cropped grass. The monsters reminded him of sharks. He had seen them when he came over with de Soto the first time. He feared them when he nearly died in the hurricane on the ill-fated founding of the De Luna colony hundreds of miles south.

I will vanish into the jaws of grass sharks in the year of our Lord 1560 and no one will know I was ever here, he thought. *The chiefdoms of the godless savages will not miss me or search for me either.*

The furrows spiraled near the tree lines again, but did not reenter the forests.

Maybe not entirely godless.

He looked back over in the direction the guide had left the previous night. Clovis hadn't heard him scream. Perhaps he had escaped the monsters.

If he wanted me dead, he could have dropped me in the woods and escaped while … they … ate me.

He drew his dagger again and carved into the dirt next to his armor.

1560 Angel Clovis De Luna

#

The dark field was full of them. He clasped his hands over his ears. They crowded the space between the sacred mound and the trees. Orange eyes flashed over and over. He rolled so that his face planted in the dirt.

They clicked instead of hissing or growling.

He rolled to his back and screamed. "Ayudame … ayudame."

His voice barely carried over the clicking monsters and the night sky did not answer. He tasted blood in the back of his throat.

#

He awoke feeling his face burning. The flesh was blistering on his cheeks from the sun. His hand came away wet.

Angel Clovis heard the birds and insects again. The sounds of the bugs made him shiver. He heard buzzing. He sat up slowly and saw them crawling over the bloody rags around his ankle. He swatted the flies away and then groaned in pain.

"Agua," he whispered. "Por favor, mi Dio … Christo … por favor … no mas … no mas, mi Dio."

He pulled his dagger and stabbed it into the dirt below his name that he had scratched out the previous day.

Clovis slid slowly down the hill. The bandages pulled loose and dirt caked in the open wound. He continued to slide down. As the wound was exposed, he saw the black and green flesh below the cut inside his torn boot and he could smell it.

I will not survive another night.

He landed in the tall grass and began crawling forward on his belly much like the monsters that infested this field and forest. He heard the swish as the creatures approached from the woods. Clovis continued dragging himself forward to meet them.

We left disease behind us when we came the first time, he thought. *Perhaps the monsters will save me from my diseased flesh now.*

The noise stopped. He paused and listened, but nothing came.

He continued to crawl. He started to rise up on his elbows to see how far he was from the woods and he met the orange eyes.

The black claws seized him and pushed him backward. He closed his eyes and waited for the teeth to sink into his flesh. Then, he was airborne. He landed hard on his back knocking the wind out of him.

As his vision cleared, he sat up and found himself back on the mound near his armor and speared dagger. The furrows circled in the grass near the base.

He tumbled back into the grass. "Por favor … Dio, por favor."

The orange eyes narrowed at him. The black claw locked on his throat and lifted him out of the grass. He tried to see the monster, but his head was twisted painfully toward the bright sky. He felt bites on his arms and closed his eyes waiting for death.

Again he was thrown upward on the slope. He opened his eyes and saw deep slashes in both his bleeding biceps.

Clovis gritted his teeth as he bled into the hillside.

They are toying with me. These creatures bat me about like a cat with a rodent.

Clovis used his good foot to drag himself back into the grass.

"Soy raton, los diablos. Comeme ahora."

He closed his eyes and waited for the game to continue. He heard the growl and felt the shadowy claws close around his legs. Clovis braced himself. Then both his legs snapped through the bone. He opened his eyes and screamed up at the sun. He clawed at the sacred hill trying to pull himself back away from the tall grass. Then, the claws grabbed his arms.

"No, no, no … por favor, no."

Both arms snapped under the grip tearing through the flesh in shards. Clovis screamed until he blacked out.

#

He drifted awake shaking. It was either still daytime or it was daytime again. He was back on the mound. He tried to move, but he was numb and his limbs wouldn't respond. He tried to speak, but his throat wouldn't open.

He heard scratching to his right.

He moved his eyes slowly and saw the guide. He tried to speak again and failed. He turned his head slowly and saw the savage was using the dagger to mark out and obscure Clovis's message in the dirt.

The savage stopped and turned his head slowly to meet Clovis's gaze. The guide lifted the Spaniard's knife and pointed it at him.

The savage spoke. "Yo … No, tu …tu muerto … mi familia … tu diablo … tu tiene muerto con tu Dio … dibloisima muerta lentmente."

Clovis tried to speak again. His throat was too dry to open. The savage gathered Clovis's armor lifting the gear and stood over him.

Why does he think I killed his family?

The savage pointed at the ground with Clovis's dagger. "Sacroisima … espera aqui … mi familia … comer … tu …vida esa noche … lentemente."

The guide stared at Clovis a moment longer and then walked out of his line of sight down the slope of the mound. Clovis listened to him walk away until the sound of his feet was lost in the sounds of the circling monsters.

Why does he want me to wait? Clovis thought. *How will his family "eat my life?" What happens tonight? Why slowly? Why?*

He tried to move again, but his limbs were broken and

unresponsive.

He begged the monsters with a hiss, "Ahora … por favor, ahora. No … lentamente … ahora, por favor."

They continued to circle in the tall grass without responding.

Lady of the Manor

by Jim Ryan

When I met Grom-Githick, he changed my life forever.

My cruel brother Charles chased me with a pair of shears that day, threatening to cut off all my hair. I hid from him in the forest behind our manor's apple orchard, where Father sometimes hunted. I knelt on the ground there and rocked slowly back and forth, overwhelmed by feelings of rage and helplessness.

In that moment I forced myself to accept the fact that Charles and I despised each other and that we would never be reconciled. Charles took every opportunity to belittle me and turn anything I accomplished to ashes. Long ago he'd established himself as the one in the family whose deeds would be met with praise and support, and Father had gone along with him. I think Charles did this because he was always fearful that I might steal Father's affections. He need not have worried on that count, since I no longer sought them.

Having now fully realized the loss of both my Father and my brother in my heart, I wandered the forest aimlessly until the shadows became long and sunlight was scarce. It was then that I found my way into a clearing full of saplings and found Grom-Githick there.

He was a small, shriveled creature then, no bigger than one of

Father's hounds. His skin was a very pale grey and covered in bark like that of an ancient oak. Small branches and twigs intertwined like hair all the way up and down his length. At first I thought he was an old log that had fallen to the ground. But then he groaned and rolled over, and I saw his pale, yellow eyes looking directly at me.

I was frightened at first, and backed away. Then the creature spoke to me.

"Don't... go..." he said, his gravelly voice barely above a whisper.

Every instinct told me to run, but instead I stopped, transfixed.

He raised himself, coughing, on a gnarled elbow. "Do not... be afraid. We'll not harm ye."

The creature needed my help. This was something special. This was something only I had seen. This was something I could do to be helpful to someone, and the task could be mine and mine alone. There would be no need for Father's approval, nor Charles's.

As I approached, I saw that there was a sadness about him, and that he was very ill indeed.

"What has happened to you?" I asked.

"We have been harmed, we have," he said. "Our heart torn out and shattered."

With difficulty, he moved some of his wooden tendrils aside and I saw a deep dark hole that burrowed into his chest. It looked old and rotted.

"How can you live without a heart?" I asked him.

"Many humans do," he said. He chuckled for a moment, then stopped and shuddered when it became too painful. "We must grow a new heart. Ye can help us, ye can." He moaned painfully and lay back down.

"Why should I help you?" I asked.

He turned his head to look at me. His eyes seemed to stare into my very soul.

"Ye have a desire. A deep desire. One ye dare not speak. We shall make it so."

A raven flew overhead, cawing down at me. It was nearly dusk.

"I have to go. My family is waiting for me." I knew this to be a lie – Father and Charles cared not one whit for me – but they would grow suspicious if I stayed out too late. Father had made no secret of the fact that all of his affections belonged to my brother, and that I was no more than an asset to be controlled. I hated my Father for that almost as much as I hated Charles for twisting him into the kind of monster that would do such things.

"I'll be back," I said, but before I drew back to leave, he reached forward and gently took my hand.

"We are Grom-Githick," he said.

"I am Agnes. I am pleased to meet you, Grom-Githick," I said, a smile coming to my face. It was the first time I'd smiled in longer than I could remember.

#

That night, after the servants had put out the lights, I crept from my bedroom, left the house and returned to the clearing. On my way, I heard a soft keening that was at once mournful and enchanting, as though a chorus of fairies were singing a funeral dirge. It grew louder as I approached, but fell silent when I entered the clearing.

Grom-Githick was still there, looking pale as ever in the moonlight.

"Were you singing?" I asked. I sat down beside him, still gazing upon him in wonder.

He nodded his wooden head. "We lament that we are brought low. We were great once, but now... so very lost."

I found my heart aching in sympathy. I carefully extended my hand and laid it on the side of his face. The bark tickled my fingers.

"Don't worry," I said. "I'll take care of you."

He smiled. His teeth were yellowish green and came to very sharp points.

"Thank ye, lady."

I found that he was very light, as though he were almost completely hollow. I gently picked him up and carried him back to the manor house.

#

No one used the cellar anymore. It was empty save for discarded crates and old, rotted firewood and cloth sacks. Charles and I had stopped playing down there after I turned twelve. I hid Grom-Githick there, and brought him a cot to lie upon. I set light to a brazier to keep him warm, but placed it away in the corner lest it set him alight as well.

"What do we need to do?" I asked.

"Life. We need life to grow a heart."

"What kind of life?"

He hesitated, then said, "Life's blood restores us."

I thought about it. "We have animals. Will that work?"

"Aye, a wee bit at a time."

I nodded, knowing what I must do.

#

Every night for weeks after, I brought Grom-Githick mice or rabbits or anything else I could find in the lands around the manor house. We bred pigs, horses and other livestock, and I would sometimes steal away with the odd runt of a litter that I felt would not be missed. At first Grom-Githick would not allow me to watch him consume them, but my curiosity was too great. Eventually he showed me how he would slice the beasts open with the sharp, twig-like points of his spindly, multi-jointed fingers. Then he would pour their life's blood into his open wound and absorb their essence with a low, sung prayer whose words I could not quite grasp.

I would go to Grom-Githick whenever I could. I had never had a true friend before. Mother had died when I was very young, and ever since that time the only ones allowed in the manor aside from Father, Charles and myself were the servants.

Grom-Githick recovered slowly. He grew larger and turned a darker, healthier shade of grey. Soon after he was able to sit up on his own. And yet, his wound was still there and his heart had not yet regrown. Whenever I came to visit him, we would sing songs and play games, to the extent that he was able. He did not fully understand the ways of humans, so I taught him what I could.

I told him of life at the manor, and of Father, who was Lord of these lands. I told him of the selfishness of my brother Charles, who would one day succeed Father, though he did not deserve it. In turn, Grom-Githick told me of his mother, whose name he said must not be spoken aloud. He said that long ago she bore a thousand children, of which he was one. I wasn't sure I believed him, as he told many a tall tale, but I was rapt with attention.

#

One evening, Father made a pronouncement that made me feel very sad and alone. I went to the cellar to seek comfort.

"What vexes ye, lady?" Grom-Githick asked.

"Father has said... he has said that he will begin bringing Charles with him when he sees to his business. Charles is to learn how to be head of the house."

"It is a grave thing, then?"

I nodded. "He will not bring me. I am to remain nothing but a prisoner in this house until the day Father marries me off to someone."

"Is there naught to be done?"

"No. I wish Charles would just disappear."

Grom-Githick gave me a look that I could not completely fathom. In it I saw a great deal of concern and perhaps just a hint of hunger.

"This is ye're heart's desire? Ye wish to be rid of Charles?"

"If it weren't for Charles, Father would care for me again. Like he did in the old days before Mother passed away."

Grom-Githick leaned toward me, the twigs near his face bristling with an aura of extreme seriousness.

"It is a grave thing ye do by wishing this. It cannot be undone. But if it is truly ye're heart's desire, we shall make it so."

I hesitated for only a moment. "Yes," I said. "I do wish it."

"Then by your Ladyship's will, it shall be done," said Grom-Githick. "He will bother ye no longer."

#

That night, I went to bed feeling very uncertain about the situation. But when I awoke the next morning I discovered that Grom-Githick had been as good as his word. Charles was nowhere to be found.

Father was up in arms and had the servants searching everywhere for my brother. As the day grew longer and there was still no sign of him, I became concerned. What if they searched the cellar? Surely, they would find my friend there. I would have to warn him.

After breakfast, I made my way down to the cellar. Grom-Githick was there, and this morning he looked better than he had ever before. He was a much darker shade of grey, like the color of ashes. His wound was still visible, but it looked as though it had partially healed. He was now so tall that when he stood to greet me, the twigs springing up from his head brushed the ceiling.

"You're better!" I said.

"Aye, lady. We have ye to thank for it."

"But I came to warn you," I said. "Charles is gone, just like you said. And now Father is searching the whole house. We must go."

Grom-Githick shook his head at me, smiling. "Let him come. We cannot flee, Lady Agnes. We have much to protect, now. Thanks to ye."

I heard a high, keening sound that was very much like the song I'd heard in the forest the night I rescued Grom-Githick. I looked around, confused, for he was not singing.

He pulled back the blanket that lay across his cot and revealed what was beneath it.

Springing up from the dirt floor under Grom-Githick's cot were what appeared to be several tiny, grey, leafless trees. The keening was coming from them, I knew immediately, for they swayed back and forth in time to it.

"We have become strong enough to spread our seed, lady. Behold ye're manor's new subjects! Bow down, childlings, to the new Lady of these lands."

The tiny trees bent forward, as though trying to bow. I felt honored, but also bewildered and a little frightened. Something was very wrong.

"How... how did you recover quickly enough to do this?" I asked.

I greatly feared the answer I might receive, but at that moment we were interrupted.

"Agnes!" my father's voice boomed from the stairs behind me.

"Get away from that abomination!"

Father strode down the stairs, his face a mask of rage.

"No, Father!" I said, turning to meet him. "You don't understand. He's my friend!"

"It is a creature of evil," Father said. "I hunted this monster in the forest weeks ago. I tore out its vile, wooden heart, and clearly I must do so again!"

Father shoved me out of the way and moved to the woodpile, where he picked up a rusty axe that sat atop it.

"YE!" Grom-Githick bellowed, pointing a long, twisted finger at Father. "Murderer! Blight! It is ye're neglectful rule that has darkened the land." Grom-Githick's eyes blazed with an intense hatred. He gnashed his sharp, wooden teeth.

Father seemed taken aback, but not by what my friend had said. He was instead staring into the woodpile. He looked suddenly very distraught, and had tears in his eyes. He moved away, raising his axe defensively as he did so. He nodded briefly back to the woodpile.

"It is this beast that is the murderer. Look, Agnes," he said as he came to stand between me and Grom-Githick. "Look and see what your friend has done."

I dreaded greatly what I might see in the woodpile, but I had to look. I already suspected what lay there. When I reached the pile, my fears were proven correct.

Deeper into the pile, underneath several logs, was Charles. He lay dead. His skin was as pale as a sheet, and it looked as though his body had been sliced open across his belly. With mounting terror I realized what Grom-Githick had done.

With an enraged cry, Father stepped forward and lunged at Grom-Githick with his axe. Grom-Githick nimbly dodged out of the way and grabbed Father's wrists, wrapping his twig-like fingers around them.

I backed away from the woodpile, my mind a whirlwind of fear and anguish. I had been betrayed, not only by Father, but by my only friend in the world. Watching the two of them struggle only reaffirmed how much I hated this manor and the situation it had put me in. I hated fate for giving me a friend for the first time in my life and then cruelly taking him away from me. I hated Father even more now for being the one responsible for the loss of Grom-Githick's heart, and yet I could not bear to see the creature at his throat. In that moment I hated Grom-Githick too, for what was he but a teller of tales and half-truths? I'd wished only for Charles to be gone, not for his death. But the fact that I knew what I'd see in the woodpile before I looked told me also that deep down, I had known what my wish had truly meant. So most of all, I hated myself. For this was all my fault.

I lashed out in the only way I could. I knew now that Grom-Githick and Father were both monsters, and I had no hope of overcoming either one of them, let alone both of them. But I knew it must all stop now. They should not be allowed to continue roaming the world, each twisting and corrupting it in his own particular way. I could let neither of them escape.

I pushed over the brazier I'd set in the corner of the room. The brazier's flames had not yet fully died out from the night before. Now those flames spread to the cloth sacks on the floor nearby, and from there they quickly ignited the crates and the rotted wood in the pile, making an instant funeral pyre for my hated brother.

As I fled up the stairs, I heard father's howls and the terrible, screaming voices of Grom-Githick's children as they burned.

I dashed from the house and out into the orchard. I watched as the house in which I'd lived my whole life smoldered and was set ablaze. Some of the servants made it out of the manor before it burned to the ground. Others were not so lucky.

But my concern for the servants was driven from my mind when a new keening song arose. It sounded once more like a mournful dirge – one tinged not only with sadness, but also with clear overtones of anger. And vengeance.

But it was not coming from the house. It was coming from the forest, behind me.

I sank to my knees as the keening drew nearer and the truth of the situation dawned upon me. There had been nearly a hundred little grey saplings in the clearing where I'd found Grom-Githick, and

I knew from my explorations that there were likely thousands more in the forest itself.

And for the first time, I understood why Grom-Githick referred to himself as "we." Grom-Githick was not the name of the creature, but of his entire race.

I had truly inherited Father's legacy. I was now the Lady of these lands, Lord help me, and just as Father had, in one terrible act I'd aroused the ire of its inhabitants. I had forsaken Grom-Githick's friendship, just as he had forsaken mine.

As Lady of the manor, I owed the land my life's blood for my betrayal.

When they came for me, I did not resist.

The Bottle Tree

by Lizz-Ayn Shaarawi

Blue dots danced across the ground as WillieMae Ceaton smoothed her blazer over her ample bosom and waited for the young couple to arrive. With a quick glance she ensured the grounds were immaculate and no stray dandelions or dog bombs had snuck their way onto the property. When Katie and Dennis called her office and expressed their concern about finding adequate housing, WillieMae did get a smidge offended by the northerners' preconceived notions about what they should expect.

"Now, we'll need someplace with indoor plumbing," the husband, Dennis, informed her.

"All due respect, Mister MacAfee, but it is illegal to have an outhouse within city limits," WillieMae explained. She emailed them information on the numerous available houses in the area, much to the couple's surprise. ("They have the internet down there?" the wife, Katie, exclaimed.) The couple sifted through the prospective dwellings and narrowed it down to a handful, all which were found lacking the moment they set foot on each property.

The Tudor on Elm Street was too old, despite having been built in the 1980s. The Victorian on Church Street was too big, while the ranch style on Harper Road was too small. Katie couldn't stand the rose-covered trellis of the modern three-two on Larch Lane. The cars in front of the houses didn't measure up to Dennis's standards when they visited an Edwardian house on Adams Drive. They didn't want a McMansion in Daughtry because the commute would be too long. The houses closer to the tire plant Dennis was hired to manage were too run down to even consider.

After a fruitless day of searching for the perfect home, the group returned to Sunnyside Realty so the young couple could pick up their car. Leaving Dennis in the lobby, Katie slipped off to use the restroom (indoor plumbing in the office, surprise, surprise. Air conditioning, too!) As Katie stopped by WillieMae's desk to say good-bye, she noticed a listing for a 1940s bungalow atop a stack of papers.

"The Buckman house on Mill Road? Oh, you don't want that old place," WillieMae assured her, sliding the listing out of reach.

Katie leaned across the desk and snatched the paper back. "I might. It's cute."

"It's an older house. It needs some maintenance. "

"A fixer-upper might just be what I need to keep me busy while Dennis is at work. I can't imagine there's much to do around here," Katie said with a smile.

WillieMae mirrored Katie's pleasant expression though she mentally ticked down a list of popular local events and activities. "I think it's more suited for a local family. Old Mrs. Buckman wasn't quite right in the head. There are certain... nuances that houses of particular families acquire. They need to be handled in a specific manner."

A flush of anger blossomed on Katie's cheeks. "Isn't that discrimination?"

"No, ma'am. It's common sense," WillieMae replied. "As you and your husband so astutely pointed out during our lovely afternoon together, things are different down here."

"We're going to look at that house," Katie insisted.

"I sincerely suggest we not."

Katie stood straight-backed and glared down at the realtor. "If you won't show us the house, we'll find a realtor that will."

WillieMae suppressed a sigh and grabbed her blazer.

They met Dennis in the lobby. Katie bounded over, full of excitement, and told him about the house. As it was late in the day, the couple offered to meet WillieMae at the house so they could head over to Greenville for dinner without returning to the realty office.

A flash of blue blinded WillieMae, snapping her out of her thoughts and back to the situation at hand. She glanced at her phone and realized that she'd been standing there for fifteen minutes, waiting. The young couple was late. Hadn't they been behind her when she pulled off at Jefferson? She shook her head and punched in the security code for her phone. Just as she scrolled through her contact list and stopped on 'The MacAfees,' she heard the groan of an engine as it navigated the twisting gravel road. The couple's SUV rounded a corner and, spraying gravel, slid into the driveway. Dennis leapt from the car. "Where are we? I couldn't even find the road on our GPS."

"I printed out directions for y'all," WillieMae said as Katie wandered past them, her mouth agape.

"They don't help if you're already lost," Dennis growled.

WillieMae pointed to a thin line in the distance. "That's the highway right there. It'll take you straight to town if you go east and on to the plant if you go west."

"Oh, Dennis," Katie gasped.

Her husband ignored her. "Well, it's damn near maze-like back here. How are we supposed to find our way around?"

"You're right," WillieMae replied. "It's too remote. I'll find you more listings tomorrow. Perhaps out near Chapman?"

"Dennis!" Katie called. Dennis followed his wife's gaze to the small, storybook cottage in front of them. His anger drained, his hands unclenched.

The well maintained lawn, dotted with the occasional maple and spruce to shade the house, swept up to a wrap-around porch that the previous owners had fitted with a wooden porch swing.

"Can we see inside?" Katie asked.

A high pitched tone issued from the WillieMae's phone as she held it up to the front door. The key box on the door popped open. With a smooth click, the front door's lock opened.

Grins spread across both of their faces as the young couple stepped into the house. Hardwood floors gleamed. Crown molding edged the walls and ceilings. Custom-made stained glass sparkled in the setting sun. "It's perfect."

The couple wandered through the rooms, smiles growing wider with each discovery. The kitchen had been recently remodeled. The appliances were relatively new and top of the line. Katie ran a finger across the built-in breakfast nook. A flash of color caught her eye. She peered the through the bay window. "What's that?"

WillieMae didn't have to ask what Katie was looking at. A dead tree stood in the yard. Blue glass bottles threaded through the leafless limbs. The spreading dusk made the sky golden, causing the bright color of the bottles to glow.

"Local superstition is all. They call it a bottle tree. You see them here and there. It's a form of protection," WillieMae said.

Katie's eyes widened. "Protection from what?"

Dennis's deep, booming laugh broke the tension. "Who cares, it's just a stupid custom. We can take it down later."

"I wouldn't recommend that. In fact, I'm sure I saw a couple of new listings come into the office today. They're closer to town, to shopping, to the interstate."

"I want this one," Katie said, her eyes locking onto WillieMae's.

"As a professional realtor, I will sell you this home. But as a citizen of Beaubelle, Mississippi, I strongly recommend you look elsewhere."

Dennis's face turned ugly. "We want *this* house. Where's that Southern hospitality we always hear so much about?"

"Who was that guy whose picture we saw on the bus bench downtown? He's with a national realty chain, isn't he? Maybe he'd like the commission more." Katie spoke to Dennis but glared at WillieMae the entire time.

WillieMae's shoulders slumped in defeat. "I'll draw up the paperwork. If you need a good mortgage broker, I can give you a list to choose from."

Dennis's face relaxed. "That's more like it."

#

A month later, Katie and Dennis drove down from Boston. Their belongings followed a few days later by truck. After the last box was unpacked, Dennis settled into his job as the manager for the local tire plant and Katie set about decorating the house.

One morning, just after Dennis had left for the plant, Katie dragged a sealed box from the garage into the kitchen. Her fingers danced across the handles jutting from the knife block until she chose a short one with a sharp, squat blade. It slid from its place with ease. Gently, the blade skimmed the top of the box, severing the packing tape. A loud pop sounded as she tore the box top open the rest of the way.

Smothered under layers of plastic were light mesh curtains. Katie freed them from the confines of the box and headed for the laundry room.

The stepstool was rickety and Katie had to balance to prevent it from rocking. She held the clean curtains, still warm from the dryer, in front of her and threaded the tabs through the metal rod. As she released the curtains, allowing them to drape to the floor, she heard a low groan. Her skin crawled at the sound. She pushed the curtains aside with trembling hands and followed the sound into the yard. It looked empty. A quick glance ensured her cell phone was just a few feet away, charging.

Phone clasped tightly to her chest like a talisman, Katie crept through the house, but all of the rooms were empty. The moan slipped through the air, causing the hair on the back of her neck to prickle. She crossed the foyer, opened the front door, and peeked through the crack.

Trees bent in the wind. Leaves on shrubs trembled. The porch swing squeaked softly as it rocked back and forth. Katie could feel a hot breeze ruffle her hair. The sound came again, low and deep. The bottle tree.

Katie crept across the yard toward the dead tree. The wind blew across the bottles and the groans sighed from the phials. Katie laughed at herself, embarrassed. She reached for a bottle on the lowest branch.

"You ought to not do that, Miss."

Katie spun around at the sound of the voice and found a small girl, barefoot and coated in a layer of grime, watching her from across the road.

"And why not?" Katie responded.

"My granny says them bottles keep bad spirits in." The girl wiped her nose on her arm.

"I'm sure your granny means well," Katie said in an indulgent tone. Her fingertips brushed the blue glass and a dark mist swirled at her touch. She stepped back.

"Told ya." The little girl shook her head and disappeared into the woods.

Katie staggered away from the tree and raced into the house as fast as her feet could carry her. The moment she crossed the threshold, she slammed the door closed and locked it. The lock on the knob and the small deadbolt seemed insufficient protection.

The wind outside died down. After a few minutes, Katie began to feel foolish. Her gaze wandered over to the bay window. It's only a tree, she told herself. That stupid old lady spooked her with stories about protection. And that girl! Who lets their child run around the woods?

She realized she had forgotten to eat lunch. That was it. It was just low blood sugar combined with spots in her vision from the heat. How could she have been so silly?

After a couple of hours of talking to herself, she was convinced that she hadn't seen anything in the bottle. As she stood at the stove making dinner, she snuck a peek at the tree through the bay window.

The bottles, each impaled by a single branch, sparkled. Not only did the tree no longer give her a sense of danger but it was actually quite pretty. She watched the last of the sun's rays reflect off the glass. Calm descended over her. She stared out of the window as the sky grew darker and darker.

Water hissed as it boiled over the pot, snapping Katie back to reality. She rushed to mop up the spill before it crusted onto the stovetop. The door to the garage flew open and she jumped. Dennis chuckled as he entered the kitchen. He wrapped an arm around her, giving her a peck on the neck in the process. She squealed and pushed him away.

"Go wash your hands. Dinner's almost ready," Katie said, giggling.

Steam rose from the plate of spaghetti as Katie placed it in front of her husband. She filled his wine glass and sat down opposite him at the nook. "How was work?"

He frowned as he slurped the noodles, talking between bites. "Still getting used to the workers. They really are a different breed down here. Got no respect for authority."

"You just have to prove yourself," Katie said as she sipped her wine. Her gaze drifted to the bottle tree. She could just make out its shape in the darkness.

"I'm the boss. I shouldn't have to prove anything," Dennis snapped. Katie glanced back at him. As he sucked a strand of pasta into his mouth, it whipped around like a tentacle and left a red smear on his chin.

Katie frowned. She turned back to the window. Dennis gulped his wine and held the glass out for more. With a sigh, Katie rose to get the wine box from the fridge. A low groan rolled over the house.

Dennis's head whipped suddenly to the side. "What the hell was that?"

"Oh that's just the wind against that tree." She refilled his wine glass. "You want some parmesan?"

His brow furrowed, but he nodded. Katie picked up the wine box, planning to put it back in the refrigerator when she got the parmesan. Dennis grabbed her wrist. "Leave it."

Her hand released the box but Dennis didn't loosen his grip.

"It's making my hair stand on end," he said.

"It's white noise. You'll get used to it. By tomorrow you won't even notice it." She pulled away from his grasp.

They ate in silence. Dennis fumed while Katie pushed the food around her plate. The moans intensified. Dennis slammed his fork down with a clang. "Dammit, that sound's driving me crazy!" He leapt to his feet, dashed past Katie, and into the garage. Katie heard the rumble of the garage door opening. A moment passed, and then the sound of breaking glass filled the air.

Katie peeked out of the front door. "Dennis?" Another crash echoed through the darkness. She slipped on a pair of flip flops and trotted out.

Dennis stood at the end of the property. The groans grew louder as Dennis smashed bottle after bottle into a glass recycling bin.

"Dennis, stop! What are you doing?"

Glass shards exploded as the next bottle hit the bin. "I should have taken care of this on the first day. Stupid thing. Stupid, backward people. We should've never moved down here," Dennis snarled as he reached for the next bottle.

The groans rose to a crescendo. The hairs on Katie's arms stood on end. Something felt off. She glanced around at the still trees. "There's no breeze."

Dennis glared at her. "What are you babbling about?"

"The wind isn't blowing." A tremor crept into Katie's voice.

"So?"

"What's making the noise on the bottles?"

Black mist swirled around Dennis. It slid over his skin and into his clothes. "What the hell?" It was all he could manage before pain clouded his face. He screamed, his eyes bulging, as the mist ripped him apart.

Tiny droplets of blood rained down on Katie. Mouth agape, her body shook as her mind struggled to comprehend the carnage before her. The mist gathered in the air like a swarm of bees. She stumbled backward, tripping over her own feet as she fled towards the house. The moan rang in her ears but the front door seemed so close. If she could just manage one last burst of speed, she knew she could reach the house. Summoning all of her strength she pumped her legs as fast as humanly possible. The moan receded. Her feet slapped up the steps to the front porch. As her fingers closed over the doorknob, an involuntary sigh of relief escaped her lips. She turned the knob but it wouldn't budge.

It was locked.

Katie jiggled the door knob, frantic. The lock wasn't automatic and she was positive she hadn't turned the lock on her way out. She banged on the door.

The house lights dimmed as if it was staring down at Katie through narrowed eyes, disappointed.

"Please," she begged. "I'm sorry. It wasn't my fault. It was Dennis."

A light *snick* sounded as the lock disengaged.

"Thank you," she cried. "Oh, dear God, thank you."

Her hand tightened on the door knob. The moan, loud, close, came from behind her. Her entire body trembled as she slowly glanced over her shoulder. The mist reared back.

"I'm so sorry," she croaked.

In one large burst, blood droplets sprayed across the front of the house.

#

As the sun broke over the trees, the dirty little girl threaded the dead tree limbs with blue bottles. She marked each one with her finger, a circle with a cross in the middle, as she mumbled "aroshna" under her breath. Each incantation met with a quiet screech as black mist appeared in the glass. "There sure are a lot of angry souls, Granny," said the little girl.

WillieMae struggled to pull a FOR SALE sign from the back of her car. "Yes, sugar. There sure are." The rubber mallet made loud thwacking noises as she hammered the sign deep into the dirt of the front lawn.

"I tried to tell them not to mess with the bottles." The girl picked up another blue bottle from the crate. "Aroshna."

"I warned them, too. But sometimes people get so caught up in what they want they don't listen to what they need." One final *twack* and the sign stood tall and straight. WillieMae wiggled it to check for any give but it remained still.

"Them northerners just don't listen do they, Granny?" The girl picked up another bottle.

"No, sugar. They sure don't." WillieMae turned her attention to the blood and tissue that splattered the porch. "Lord have mercy, I think I'm going to have to get Hank out here with the pressure wash."

"Best get the big chunks before the crows come," she said as another bottle slid onto a branch. "Aroshna." Circle. Cross.

"I suppose you're right." WillieMae grabbed a large black garbage bag and rubber gloves from the back of her car. The FOR SALE sign rocked in the breeze as a gentle moan came from the bottle tree.

Lammers' Atoll

by Kieran Daly

Inspired by H. R. Giger's *Hommage a Bocklin*

Note: The VOC mentioned in the story stands for Vereenigde Oost-Indische Compagnie (Dutch East India Company)

When they came across Lammers he was clinging to a piece of flotsam, his head resting against the timber, his eyes closed. Vejerin called out to him but no answer came from the figure bobbing up and down in the water, its eyes remaining shut. Only when they were dragging him on board did the man show a sign of life, groaning weakly. They laid him on the deck at Clemens's feet, Vejerin going to Clemens's side as they did so. The Captain and his Chief Officer regarded the prone form beneath them.

"Seaman," Clemens addressed the drenched figure.

The man moaned, moving his head a little.

"Seaman," Clemens said again.

The man's eyes fluttered open and regarded the Captain's. Then their owner turned his head to the side and weakly vomited out some water.

"Take him to the galley," Clemens ordered. "Get some sustenance into him."

Lammers' exhausted eyes looked directly upward into the sky, blinking as they rested on the black flag billowing from the mast high overhead. Then he was being lifted.

\#

Clemens and Vejerin entered the galley about half an hour later to find the new arrival eagerly wolfing his way through a piece of pineapple, a small plate of yams before him. The diner looked up, the workings of his jaws gradually slowing as he watched the two pirates move along the opposite side of the table. He wiped juice from his chin as Clemens sat before him. Vejerin remained standing, a little behind the Captain's right.

Clemens took in the disheveled figure before him, its food-streaked, drawn, exhausted, sun-burnt face. Nothing remarkable. What *was* noteworthy was up further. The man couldn't have been more than thirty years old but his hair was completely white. The man cleared his throat.

"Thank you for your hospitality," Lammers said.

Clemens betrayed no recognition of the gratitude. "You're Dutch," he eventually said.

"Yes."

"You work for the VOC?"

Lammers nodded. "Yes."

"What ship?"

"The *Coen*."

Clemens blinked. He said nothing for a few seconds. "Tell us what happened."

#

With a total of 355 persons on board, including 215 crew and 140 soldiers, the Dutch East Indiaman *Coen* had set sail from Rotterdam for Jakarta. Packed with building materials, paints, guns, wine and domestic goods, it was to deposit this cargo upon arrival at its destination and load up with spices from the VOC's warehouses before returning to Holland.

The outward journey had been uneventful until just after they had passed Christmas Island, when with only a little over 200 miles between them and Jakarta a powerful storm blew the vessel off course to the west.

It was a day and a half before the storm dissipated and the *Coen*, her sails badly damaged, could redirect herself toward Jakarta. The ship had only been limping eastward a few hours when the... "singing" reached the crew's ears. A hypnotic, ethereal oo-ing spread throughout the boat in seconds, weaving its fairy-tale like spell upon every single man on board. If he was not already there, he made his way up on deck where he stood silently, listening.

The ship was approaching a triangular-shaped atoll. However, not one soul on the *Coen* was interest in this uncharted landmass. One side of the atoll was partially obscured by three "islands" of sorts, and it was these islands that were the focus of attention. Or rather, their inhabitants. The islands were roughly circular and varied in size, the biggest being about 250 feet in diameter. The second largest was maybe half the size of the big one, with the smallest of the trio covering maybe only a fifth of the big one's area.

The islands' features were bizarrely identical, the only differing factor being the size of said features. At the centre of each island was a clump of palm trees, beneath whose fronds stood a group of three women, naked as the day of their birth. The producers of the singing, these dark-haired, olive-skinned beings of incredible beauty varied in size with each island, the trio on the small island being little taller than pre-pubescent children, though their state of feminine development was that of a mature woman.

The *Coen* dropped anchor and Captain De Groot assembled a landing party to investigate the islands, able seaman Anton Lammers being among those selected. The *Coen*'s longboat was lowered into the water and headed for the medium-sized island, the closest one to the ship. The short journey to the shore was a silent one, the only sound to be heard apart from the singing being the rhythm of the longboat's oars in the water. Looking about, Lammers noted every pair of eyes on the boat fixed straight ahead upon the island women. Glancing upward at the *Coen*'s thronged deck Lammers regarded the similar sight there.

The longboat ground softly ashore and the landing party disembarked. After reaching the dry sand and walking a few steps on the beautiful white grains, Lammers felt a knot of concern in his stomach. He slowed to a stop. Something was not quite right. With the sand. It felt as though...*the sand were moving ever so slightly up and down*. Or something beneath it was. Lammers looked up ahead at the landing party which was moving further away from him. Obviously none of them had noticed this...anomaly. Just as he was beginning to worry if maybe his mind were failing, Lammers heard a voice snap at him to rejoin the group. Looking up to see the stern eyes of the boatswain fixed upon him, Lammers jogged after the party, scolding his eccentricity as he reached his comrades.

As the band neared the women, the knot in Lammers' stomach made its presence known once again, and his heart picked up speed. By the time he halted before the singers, the women mere feet away from him, his heart was racing in his chest. There was something terribly wrong with these women. But then of course, they were *not* women. Real women blinked occasionally. Their throats moved when they sang. Their mouths closed every now and then. And their chests moved for breath.

Despite the fact that alarm bells were ringing in Lammers' head and a mental voice was telling him that this island was a horribly dangerous place and that he should turn and flee at once, Lammers had to *know*. He had to *find out*. He had always been curious, impetuous.

Aware that the ground was rising and falling beneath his feet again, and with greater intensity now (was it *breathing*? Breathing *excitedly*? With *expectation* perhaps?) he reached a quivering hand out toward the woman on the right. No-one commanded him to desist. Maybe they were all too entranced by the spectacle before them or were curious to have the mystery solved themselves and were content to have Lammers volunteer to answer it for them. Whatever the case may have been, Lammers' enquiry went uncommented upon.

Lammers' extended finger impacted the form beneath its left shoulder. Encountering the resistance of neither bone nor muscle it kept going. With a cry of revulsion Lammers yanked his hand backward. Holes flashed open all over the women's bodies: on their faces, torsos, arms, legs. No area was spared. Each of the holes was about a quarter-inch in diameter, making the women look as though they had endured a particularly horrific medieval-style torture involving nails. Some of the men returned to life at this sudden, shocking development, startled grunts escaping them. A few backpedalled a little.

Lammers had had enough. He turned and burst through the men behind him, racing for the longboat. A few steps into his sprint the air filled with bloodcurdling shrieks and screams. Though he knew that what was happening behind him was terrible beyond imagination and that he should simply keep running, his curiosity won the day once more.

He turned to witness an unspeakable nightmare. Most of his comrades lay writhing and shuddering on the sand, in various stages of disfigurement. The majority of their clothing had disappeared. What remained gaped with huge holes, exposing melting, boiling flesh. Plumes of steam rose from their squirming, liquefying forms. It was the clear fluid jetting from the holes in the women's skin that was causing the atrocity, Lammers saw. Whatever it struck, it consumed.

One of the men still standing collapsed to the sand and the lines of spray that had been dissolving him were now free to leap toward Lammers, who darted to his left to avoid the dreadful substance. He escaped all but two of the deadly jets. He cried out as burning pains bloomed at the side of his right knee and at the tip of his right little finger. Instinctively he snatched at the aggrieved digit (the stricken flesh was already bubbling) with the fingers of his left hand. The pain lessened there somewhat but also began to speak from the thumb, index and middle finger of his left hand. His eyes flashing momentarily upon now unidentifiable puddles where the bone and musket barrel of two soldiers were being quickly devoured, Lammers turned and ran.

The moans and whines of the dying men receded quickly behind him as he galloped toward the water, but the terrible singing remained, strong and clear amidst the charnel house. The ground beneath him was panting now, its eager rhythm almost sexual in intensity.

Lammers blazed into the water at speed, tumbling beneath its surface. Oblivious of the relief this afforded his burned fingers and knee, he scrambled into the longboat and began rowing. He had only performed two frantic strokes when the front of the boat began to rise up out of the water. A huge, reddish-pink flat shape was lifting it higher and higher. His stomach a wretched cauldron of panic and terror as he tilted backward (what new horror was this?), he noted similar mysterious giants emerging from the brine on both sides of the ascending boat. Water coursed down the bizarre shapes in floods as they climbed into the air, with Lammers observing vein-like lines streaking the highly-coloured, parabolic-shaped bodies.

His helpless craft almost perpendicular to the water, Lammers spilled from it into the shallows. His head emerged from the water just in time to witness the longboat thumping back down onto the surface a mere foot away from his skull. He looked up to see the shape that had lifted it, now free of the longboat's weight, flick into line with the rest of its incredible brothers. A set of these shapes was ascending from various underwater points all around the island, all of them rising at exactly the same speed, curving as they ascended, the tip of each one arcing forward to meet an opposite number in the circle. To Lammers it was like watching some incredible corolla of petals coming together about a flower. When the orb was complete (it must have measured fifty feet from summit to base, Lammers surmised) the petal-things began to pulse softly as a unit, the gigantic pink bulb contracting and relaxing horribly, no doubt in sync with the loathsome throb of the sand concealed within, Lammers' belaboured mind speculated.

Arrhythmic movement caught the corner of Lammers' eye and his gaze descended to the base of the bulb where the skin of one of the petals was bulging outward sharply and intermittently, as though it were being struck from inside by something. There was a shape behind the sporadically appearing bulge, Lammers saw. Suddenly the blade of a dagger appeared through the pink wall, slicing a line downward to the water. A quivering hand appeared through the newly-created tear, its steaming skin burnt down to the bone in places. Its blasted fingers let the dagger fall into the water before it shakily pushed at the sides of the flap, widening it. A head, which was little more than a feebly-covered skull, appeared. A few tufts of hair sprouted oasis-like from a few random locations in the sea of hideous burn tissue above a shocking landscape that had once been a face. The liquefied contents of one eyesocket clung to a cooked rag of flesh adorning the demon's cheekbone. Its remaining unharmed eye shone brightly at Lammers, full of some terrible emotion that Lammers had never witnessed in a human being before. The entity's scalded, haphazard mouth opened and it emitted a few terrible raspy, guttural utterances before its head dropped forward and the dreadful apparition was still except for the flesh-coloured fluid dripping from its crown into the water which hissed and steamed upon receipt of the liquid. Only then did Lammers see the large signet ring on one of the ghoul's fingers. He had seen that ring before. Captain De Groot had been wearing it.

There was the crack of musket-shot and Lammers looked up to see the curved pink wall soaring over him billow as holes appeared in its skin. (Was skin the right word? Yes he thought it was, this circular pink ball was the protective dermis of some terrible sea-plant monster, pulsing as it digested his comrades inside its bulb.) Looking behind him Lammers saw a line of soldiers and some sailors at the bow of the *Coen*, each with a musket pointed at the throbbing abomination before him. Lammers' stomach pitched horribly upon noticing the anomaly immediately beyond the ship. The biggest island was now much closer to the *Coen* than it had been when the unfortunate landing party had boarded the longboat. Had the ship moved? Lammers doubted very much that it had; it had been anchored securely. No, it was the *island* that had moved, demented as such a scenario may have sounded.

Lammers jumped to his feet and began shouting and screaming at the men by the *Coen*'s bow, gesticulating wildly as he tried to get them to move the ship away from the bizarre approaching danger. When nothing changed on the deck Lammers sat back down and began paddling frantically toward the *Coen*, the singing of the "women" on the two remaining "open" islands and the thunder of musket-shot providing a fittingly deranged soundtrack to his desperate little voyage of warning. He had almost reached the vessel when the hugely depressing sight of it beginning to rise from the water greeted his eyes. The same pink petal-type things that had closed over the middle-sized island ascended skyward before him on either side of the ship, only these were truly huge, maybe twice as massive as the ones that had trapped the landing party. Up and up the 1200-ton *Coen* went, its terrible lifters quickly becoming visible to a demoralised Lammers as the ship left the water. Climbing much slower than the ones not bearing any load, there were three petals raising the *Coen*, which stopped ascending suddenly.

Lammers spotted the reason. The anchor chain was pulled taut, the timber cat-head beam supporting it pitched at an angle from the ship it was never intended to endure. A few seconds later the resistance the anchor was encountering gave and the *Coen* resumed its ascent. Lammers watched helplessly as it was borne upward, beginning to angle away from him as the colossal petals beneath it began to turn inward.

When the ship was about thirty feet above him, the cat-head, damaged in the unorthodox raising of the anchor, came free of the ship. Seeing it hurtling directly toward him, Lammers leaped from the longboat. When his head re-emerged from the water he found the longboat in pieces. Grabbing hold of a long piece of flotsam he looked upward to see the *Coen* about fifty feet above him, perched at a perilous angle on the curving petals. Then it slid off them into the centre of the forming bulb, multitudes of screaming men spilling from its deck as it went.

Then everything was gone. The vast pink orb, fully formed before Lammers, was pulsing unspeakably. Looking toward the island he had escaped from, he saw that the terrible bulb there was still doing likewise. On the third island its singers sang, calling him. Immobilized with fear and shock, Lammers gazed at the beautiful girls beneath the palm trees on its sands. Then the tide had him and swept him out to sea, the sirens receding into the distance.

#

From the journal of Will Clemens, Captain of *The Black Zephyr*:

25 October 1750

Lammers has been asleep for a little over six hours now. The man's mind is undoubtedly broken, what with his fantastical tales of wax-women and giant sea-flowers. The sinking of his ship and the loss of his shipmates has clearly taken a terrible toll on him, compromising his sanity.

We have just passed Christmas Island, headed west. Finding Lammers' atoll would be like stumbling upon a needle in a haystack but both Vejerin and I know that the prize could be immense. The Coen was the flagship of the Dutch East India Company's fleet and has always carried a huge cargo. Many pirates have taken her on but all have failed to best her. And now she lies in the shallows of an atoll! May fortune smile upon us and bring us to her!

26 October 1750

Upon discovering our intended destination today Lammers flew into a demented frenzy. Four men were needed to take him to his quarters where he screamed and sobbed for over an hour before abandoning his theatrics. The poor wretch, he is completely mad.

27 October 1750

The women, they are so beautiful! Their singing so sweet, so entrancing!

I must send some men to Lammers' quarters to silence his pitiful shrieks.

And then to the longboat!

The Madness in Her Eyes
by Rie Sheridan Rose

It started so innocently. We were all drinking one night over at the Twisted Lizard – a typical college hangout selling cheap beer and jacked-up soft drinks. Since the beer was cheaper, we'd all learned to like the taste. Maria and I had only been dating for a couple of weeks, though I'd cast dewy-eyed glances her way the entire Spring term. The Two T's – Tom and Tabitha – had apparently been going steady since Junior High, and we all expected they'd be married after graduation. Whit and Sammy were always together, and, in retrospect, there was probably more to their relationship than I realized at the time, but I was just an Iowa farm boy, and I didn't really give it much thought.

The point is, in essence, there were three couples sitting in the Lizard bored with cramming for finals and on the last edge of each other's nerves. When Sammy piped up with "Hey, guys – I got an idea–" Maria jumped on the interruption.

"What have you got in mind, Sammy? This place is really dragging me down tonight."

Sammy flushed. When Maria turned that molten grin on a fella, it was hard to keep your equilibrium. Much less be coherent.

"Well…I was talking to one of the pre-law guys yesterday, and he was telling me that him and his buddies get a real kick out of playing hide-n-seek–"

Tom made a rude noise, and I thought Whit was going to go over the back of the couch to get at him. I waved him back.

"Ain't that a little tame for college students, Sammy?" I asked. "I mean, I gave up hide and go seek in fifth grade, and *I* was a late bloomer."

"Lemmee finish. They play hide-n-seek in Moonlit Acres."

"Ain't that...?" All the possibilities coalesced at once, and I felt a huge grin crack my face. "That would be awesome."

"Is that legal?" asked Tabitha nervously. She didn't talk much, so when she did, people listened. "I mean, isn't it desecration of some kind?"

We listened...but this time no one paid attention. Too bad.

"C'mon, Tabby – it will be fun," said Tom.

And, being Tabitha, she was easily swayed, particularly when Tom gave the idea a thumbs up. She was probably the only one who could've talked us out of the whole thing, but we were beyond rational, and caught up in the thrill of perceived adventure.

Piling out into the sweet summer night, we headed for Whit's van. It made most sense to take one car. Less likely to attract unwanted attention that way.

"This will be *amazing*, guys," Whit enthused. I don't think I'd ever heard him so excited by anything – which was saying a lot. He high-fived Sammy.

Tabitha shivered, and Tom hugged her tighter. "I'm still not sure about all this," she said softly.

"It'll be fun, sweetie," Maria assured her. "I wouldn't go if I thought anything could go wrong."

Maria was the sensible one of the bunch, and her calm seemed to seep into Tabitha. Tabby smiled tentatively. "You're right," she murmured. "It is definitely better than sitting in the Lizard all night."

Whit and Sammy began to sing every verse of "Dem Dry Bones" at the top of their tone-deaf lungs. By the time the "knee bone's connected to the thigh bone" rolled around, we'd all joined them, and the van fairly rocked with sound as we wound through the streets to the far edge of town.

Moonlit Acres was the oldest cemetery in the county. It had originally been connected to the old Spanish mission that was the local tourist Mecca. It had continued to expand for a while after the mission crumbled – after all, people were always dying, but religion ebbs and wanes. The tombstones ranged from illegible bits of broken granite to handsome marble edifices housing some of the richest families in the state. I guess, when you think about it, it was a pretty small cemetery compared to more modern ones. Perhaps one hundred graves at most lay within the fence line, and they were neatly laid out with a path circling the outer perimeter. A high wrought iron fences surrounded the entire thing, but the chain on the gate was cursory at best, and we were in our wiry phases. It was easy to slip through.

The cemetery lived up to its name. The full moon flooded the area with light, limning the white marble and granite like a black and white horror film. Everything stood out in stark relief. Giggling like schoolkids, we huddled around an obelisk in the center of the graveyard.

It seemed colder somehow, within the fence, as if we had left summer outside the gate and stepped into October. The smell of flowers was in the air, sweet, and yet subtly wrong – the dying gasps of faded bouquets.

"You be It, Sammy, since this was your idea," Tom ordered, taking charge, as he usually did. "This will be Base." He slapped the monument beside us. "If you can get here without It touching you, you will be Safe. Now, to make it more interesting, Paul – you go with Tabby. Whit, you go with Maria, and I'll be on my own. That way, neither of the girls have to go it alone, but there won't be any mushy stuff slowing things down." He winked. "This place is weird enough as it is."

Tabby looked like he'd drowned her puppy. I smiled down at her and took her hand. "Don't worry, Tabs. I'll make sure the ghosts don't get you."

I saw the barest trace of a smile flit across her face. She'd be all right.

"Let's hide!" Tom yelled, clapping his hands together. In the still night, the sound cracked like thunder.

Adrenaline shot through me, leaving the taste of metal on my tongue. Tabby and I raced away from the obelisk, hands threaded tightly.

"Slow, down..." she gasped when we hit the outer path. The shadows enfolded us like a cape. "Please. Paul, I can't...run...anymore."

I stopped. "Tell you what. Let's just walk the path. This is a silly game anyway."

I could tell from the grateful squeeze she gave my hand I'd hit on just the right thing to say. And it was true – I *did* think it was a stupid game. I'd been swept up in the moment at the Lizard, but now that we were here, I really didn't want to play.

One eye on Sammy, who was easy to see in his white t-shirt as he crept through the tombstones, we chatted softly about school as we walked. Tabby was studying to be a nurse – Tom was pre-med.

"Haven't you ever wanted to do something else, Tabs? Something for yourself?"

"When I was little, I used to tell stories," she said softly. "I thought it would be fun to be a writer."

"Why not? That would be so cool – I would tell everyone I knew you when."

She ducked her head. "It was silly. I wasn't any good."

"Practice makes perfect, they say. Give it a shot."

She slipped her bangs behind her ear with her free hand, the gesture self-conscious as she shrugged. "Nah, that was kid stuff. I'll be able to help Tom in his practice. It'll save us money in the long run."

"But what do *you* want, Tabby? Your life is important too."

"I don't mind."

A shriek split the night, and a burst of movement caught my eye. Maria was sprinting toward the obelisk, Sammy hot on her heels.

"Surprised he didn't come for us first," I told Tabby, leaning down to whisper in her ear.

"The shadows are pretty thick here," she answered. "If we stick to the path, he probably won't even see us at all." She ducked her head shyly. "Sammy's never been too observant."

I laughed. "True."

Maria made it to the Base safely and sank down upon the border of stone at its base. I was glad she'd made it without being caught.

"He'll probably go after Whit next. See, he's right over there." She pointed across the graveyard. Sure enough, Whit was easy to see against the moonlit sky.

A rustling sounded in the trees behind us, and a stench assaulted my nose – fetid and rank, with a hint of damp earth. "What the hell is that?"

Tabby glanced behind me, and her face froze in an expression of sheer terror.

"Tabby? What is it? What's there?"

I started to turn, but she screamed, shaking her head wildly. She nearly jerked my arm out of the socket as she turned and bolted, not for the obelisk, but the gate.

Her urgency infected me, and I bellowed to the others. "Let's get out of here!"

I could hear crashing behind us, and heavy, shuffling steps. I didn't want to know what was gasping and snarling back there.

Tabby's eyes were glazed as she stared back over her shoulder. She moved slower and slower...dragging to a halt.

Now it was I tugging her hand. "Tabby, come on!"

She didn't move, and I could hear the thing behind us getting closer.

I finally grabbed her around the waist, resisting the urge to look back as I lifted her off her feet and carried her toward the gate.

The others pounded across the cemetery, dodging or vaulting graves as we tore toward the exit. "Get the van started!" Sammy yelled at Whit as he waved his friend through the fence.

Whit fumbled open the driver's door to the van, and I could hear the gears grinding as he tried to turn the engine over. Sammy held the gate open as far as it would go, and Tom slid through, throwing open the back door of the van. Maria was right behind him.

"C'mon, Paul! Hurry up!" she yelled.

I could feel my heart pounding in my chest as I ran. Tabby was getting heavy, but I didn't dare let go of her.

I thrust her through the fence to Sammy, who took her from me and bustled her into the rear of the van. The footsteps behind me were closer yet. I shoved through the gap in the gate, tearing some skin off my back, but considering it a fair price.

"Go, go, go!" I shouted, diving into the van.

Whit took off with a squeal of rubber as I slammed the door shut.

"What was that thing chasing us?" Tom asked.

"I don't know. I didn't really see it. Did anybody?" I glanced around the van. Everyone shook their head – except Tabitha.

Tabitha's eyes were dark holes in her white face. She huddled into herself, rocking back and forth. A high-pitched keen stuttered from her pinched lips.

"Tabs, are you okay?" Tom asked, laying a hand on her shoulder.

She jerked away from him, her rocking never varying.

"Baby...?" The pleading in his voice was heartbreaking.

She never even blinked.

Whit drove straight to the nearest hospital. We all piled into the emergency room, Tom carrying Tabitha in his arms.

"We need a doctor!" he yelled.

"Please, sir. You'll be seen as soon as possible." The nurse on duty was firm but soothing. "What seems to be the problem?"

"My girlfriend is in shock. Her pulse is thready, and she's non-responsive."

The nurse sighed. "Medical student, are we?"

"What does that matter?" Tom growled, close to tears. "She needs help."

"She'll get it. Now, you can stay with the girl, if you are her significant other. The rest of you, go home. Your friend here can notify you of the diagnosis when we have one."

She was right. There was no need for us all to be here. She was so calm and sympathetic. Just like Tabby would be when she became a nurse...

...Only, she never did. That night in the graveyard was twenty years ago. The gang drifted apart, but I still keep in touch.

Maria and I never did date much after that. We tried a couple of times, but it felt wrong somehow. She's a lawyer in LA now, married with two kids.

Tom stuck by Tabby for over a year, but she never even recognized him after that night. Eventually, he gave up and went on with his life. He became a psychologist, specializing in trauma victims.

Whit and Sam opened a deli in New York City. Like I say, there's probably more there than meets the eye – but who gives a damn anyway?

And I...I spend at least one day a week beside Tabitha's bed at the asylum, holding her hand and talking about my day. It doesn't make any difference. She doesn't see me. She doesn't hear me. But, I keep trying...hoping someday to get through to her, find out what she saw that night...but I cannot pierce the madness in her eyes.

Named for a Lion

by Stephen McQuiggan

Back in the day he had formed The Laughing Club, and being the sole member had elevated himself to President. There was nothing to laugh about in the office though; work was a joyless grind, a sucking bore. At least it was until the glorious day that Harold arrived, coughing and wheezing. Straightaway he knew Harold was the new Adam. God, he missed Adam, missed his pleading voice: 'Why do you do it, Leo?' *Because I'm named for a lion!*

Things had been funnier at school. The squints, the warts, the lazy eyes that tickled him so much had grown stale, but in high school he had discovered a world of ailments guaranteed to make you wet your pants.

A girl with a giant head that flopped precariously to one side, several kids in clunky wheelchairs, and a whole herd of faces devoured by greasy, volcanic explosions – you could actually feel the heat from those babies when you walked by! There was even a lady teacher with a harelip and, best of all (he'd laughed so hard he thought he'd have to go to the Nurse's Station), Debra Randall let out a shriek in French class and ran out with blood streaming down her legs.

But, far and away, Adam had been his favourite.

A living skeleton, a boy so frail the teachers whispered to him lest he buckle under their breath. You could blow on his head and it would sail away like a dandelion clock. Adam had something called leukaemia. Leo Googled that to see what it meant; it meant he had to enjoy it whilst he could because Adam might not be around much longer. Leo began to follow him, bumping into his skinny body as often as he could, marveling at how easily he bruised.

He never thought he would find another to take his place.

So, when Harold showed up for his first day at work, bent under the burden of his hump, his spindly limbs barely strong enough to carry his meagre frame to his desk, Leo felt his heart skip a beat. Here were all his childhood victims reborn in one feeble, eminently punishable body.

Harold was so weak, so delicate, so perfect.

As the rest of the staff hurried to welcome him, bombarding him with handshakes and smiles, Leo watched him carefully, sure that Harold's straw like fingers would snap off at any moment. He watched him all that day, keeping his distance, relishing his quarry. As Production Manager (he preferred the term *Overseer,* and often fantasised about bringing a whip into work) it was part of his job remit to survey, after all. Hell, it was a vocation.

He uttered not a word in case he seemed too eager. He sat calmly, trying to still his racing heart, unable to believe his unexpected good fortune, as Harold fretted and sweated over reams of paperwork, picking at his eczema that fell like albino cornflakes onto crumpled invoices. Leo watched, studied, bided his time. *You've stumbled down to the wrong watering hole, Harry Boy,* he thought, *once I begin my campaign there will be no easing up.* He would not make the same mistakes he made with Adam, not this time. This was his second chance.

He was named for a lion, and a lion was made to devour with impunity. This time around he would make damn sure to savour every last morsel.

He started by berating him at every opportunity. 'You're slacking, Harold,' he would say. It became a mantra those first few weeks, until even the rest of the staff began to pepper their pity with sniggers and refer to him as 'Slack Harold'. Leo kept him working late as often as he could, burying him in paperwork, just to see his head bob up and down on that pipe cleaner neck, as the sweat pooled alarmingly under his arms.

'You *disgust* me,' he told him, usually as Harold's tongue started to loll, blanched and wormlike, as he tackled the last bill of sale.

Harold would just smile his thin smile – an action that made Leo think of diluted milk – then redden slightly (there wasn't enough blood in the aberration to facilitate a full blush) before returning to his work.

Leo's favourite thing though, better, more satisfying than any of the verbal volleys he served from behind the desk, was to *smell* him. He would hover over him, placing his arm on the desk (and how strong that arm looked in juxtaposition, how manly) as he leaned over him in a proprietary manner and bathed in his foul waft. That odour was an elixir to Leo, intoxicating him, tearing away his inhibitions until he felt drunk on his physical superiority.

And on his moral superiority too, yes, because anyone that weak, that sickly, must surely be paying the price for past grievous sins.

'You disgust me, Harold. You really do.'

From this vantage Leo could see every crumb of dandruff (icing sugar on the bully cake), see how the blotches extended to the scalp in motley profusion, and the bald spot cratered by scabs and bony protuberances. It looked just like a landing pad, and Leo couldn't resist dangling a long pendulum of saliva over it, rejoicing as it splashed home in a glutinous puddle; he was only mildly irritated it didn't sizzle.

Harold recoiled as if from acid. His top shirt button was fastened but still his collar was too baggy, his head swiveling like an angry tortoise. 'I-I-I don't wish to complain,' he sputtered, 'but I will if you persist with this b-b-bullying.' He actually puffed out his pigeon chest.

Leo laughed, placing his hand (his mighty paw) right around that spindly neck, his fingers almost touching. 'You make one squeak to Personnel and I will kill you,' he whispered. 'You believe that, Freak?'

Harold nodded his head like a dashboard ornament, and as he did so Leo was convinced he heard something jingle. 'I-I-I really need this job.'

Of course you do, thought Leo, *who else would employ you?*

'Patience is not my forty, Harold. Remember that.'

'Forte.'

'What?'

'Patience is not your –'

'You correcting me, gimp?' He squeezed harder, until spit bubbles formed on Harold's wormy lips. 'Just do exactly as I say, when I say, and we'll have no problems. We're going to be close you and me, cheese and crackers. You're mine, Harold, all mine.'

Leo was careful to wash his hands afterwards (you just couldn't leave things to chance), but they still felt slimy with whatever residue that freak was secreting. What if he was contagious? The next morning however, Leo felt his usual dry-palmed self, thriving with energy. The same could not be said for Harold.

As the days crawled by, Harold's skin grew a brighter yellow. Leo began to ponder the possibility that he would croak right there in the office; it was hard to concentrate on work now, so intent was he, so eager to hear that final rattle. It got so bad that Sandra from accounts, and a few of her office acolytes, had taken to gathering around Harold and clucking over him, looking over at Leo with wide beseeching eyes that pleaded, *Send the poor man home.*

Leo pretended not to notice. He knew those tutting bitches would never dare actually ask out loud; pity did not make you brave. Let them talk behind his back, let them call him callous and cruel. It was what women did – their very own version of The Laughing Club.

How *could* he possibly send him home?

What if Harold died there, denying him the bravura encore he had dreamed of witnessing since he was a boy? No, they must all soldier on through this difficult period and hope for the best – there was every chance Freaky Harry would expire in their midst; patience was key.

And after that final, and long desired, full stop?

What confections would be so sweet, what ailments and afflictions rise above pale shadows of this humpbacked and crumbling colossus before him – would everything after this be anti-climax? Leo didn't like to dwell on that, though he had an inkling, one that both scared and excited him, that perhaps he could inflict his own maladies on even the most robustly healthy if he only dared.

I am tough of sinew and nerve. I am named for a lion and my will shall be law. I am king of the urban jungle.

Yet even a king's will is powerless against the march of time. One day, Harold didn't weigh in at all, had managed only a brief gasping phone call to Sandra, who informed Leo 'that poor, poor man' was just too ill to make it in.

Leo bit his lip, finding no solace in her tears or her trembling voice. Whatever was wrong with Harold was getting worse. The twisted little bastard was circling the drain, no doubt about it. He would have to be quick if he was to wring out every last dreg of enjoyment from that bony shell.

First he had to deal with Johnson, the Area Head – and he was so smug, so superior, mused Leo, his head could cover an entire area, and a vast one at that. Johnson perched himself on the edge of Leo's desk, a casual reminder of his status, a vulture vantage point to peer down on his prey (hadn't Leo adopted this tactic himself?), brushing non-existent lint from his immaculately pressed trousers.

'This Harold character, he's a liability, no? I think, in all good grace, you should put together a severance package for him. Something generous enough to take the sting out of it, enough to make the firm look caring but not a charity.'

Sandra fumbled a coffee cup in the background, then busied herself with a phone call to compensate; Leo noticed she hadn't hit the extension button, so the line was dead. She was talking to no one, a feeling he could relate to when he raised his eyes back to Johnson's easy grin.

'I thought I was in sole charge of hiring and firing in this division,' he said pleasantly, but inside he growled.

'Of course you are,' said Johnson, as to a wayward child. 'No one's being fired. Harold's not well. It is in everyone's interest that we come to an arrangement. I'm sure you'll do the right thing.'

But he's mine, Leo wanted to say, *all mine.* He counted to ten to regain his royal composure.

'Harold's fine. He'll be back at his post before you know it. I don't feel it is in the company's interest to be seen to discriminate. We don't need bad press, or worse, a lawsuit, over something as delicate as this.'

'I think an amicable settlement would negate any –'

'Harold's not going anywhere!' Feral, risky, but he could not lose him, not now he was so close.

Johnson regarded him coolly, then left, slamming the door behind him in an unaccustomed show of irritation.

Sandra was staring at Leo, her make-believe call forgotten, and was that...Yes, it was adulation in her eyes. Leo, more used to fear and pleading, squirmed.

'I'm just nipping out for an hour,' he told her beaming, mawkish dial. 'Refer all calls to Head Office until I get back.'

He had to pay Harry Boy a visit, get him back in to work as soon as possible, carry him in if need be. Johnson must be shorn of any and all ammunition. It would be a tragedy to lose him now, just as the Reaper's hand was tightening around his scraggy throat.

He parked in a secluded cul-de-sac and grinned to himself. *Perfect,* he thought. It was exactly the house Leo would have picked for him, a little pensioner's bungalow painted in sky blue and off white; it resembled an Eastern Bloc health centre. Leo felt his hair (his *mane*) tingle with excitement; he had hit pay dirt here, struck the proverbial mother lode. There were ramps to the door, and cripple grips on the wall. He instinctively knew that the interior would reek of urine, coupled with that indefinable essence of putrefaction common to the terminally, hilariously, ill.

'Crip Grips,' he said in an awed whisper; he couldn't believe his luck. This was even better than his tenth birthday, the one where Uncle Marty took a stroke and spewed jelly all over his own shirt.

He considered knocking (*Open up little pig, or I'll huff and I'll puff*) but just pulled his jacket sleeve over his hand and opened the door, waltzing in to what he fervently hoped was decay central.

He found himself in a chintz wonderland populated by decorative porcelain figurines, and antimacassars draped over armchairs like the skins of long dead cats. The air was awash with lavender, but the *Undersmell* was here too, refusing to be dressed up or disguised.

This must have been his mother's house, thought Leo; would he find a double whammy and discover Freaky Harry cosied up in bed with Mommy Dearest's desiccated corpse? Or would the Freak be a flyblown cadaver himself, mouth frozen in a rictus grin that said, 'I beat you, Leo. I escaped.' The thought brought a pulse of panic. He had to hurry.

'Harold!' No answer, just dust motes dancing on the heat of his breath.

'Harold, you need some help?' *Do you need a push, Harold, do you need a heartless shove into the Great Beyond?* Leo made his way into the kitchen, where the table and chairs were still wrapped in shop plastic. *This is not a home, this is a showroom, a façade. No one actually lives here, no one…*

'Harold!' He heard a pained grunt from down the hallway and followed its echo to the bathroom door.

He's dying on the toilet, just like Elvis, dying on that scaffold-like contraption above the pan, the one all mutants like him have to use just to have a dump. I should have brought my phone, I should be able to video this, I…

Another grunt, then Leo burst in, his exclamation of 'Surprise!' dying on his lips. Harold stood before him, naked, his body writhing, forming a new alphabet of itself as it elongated, bubbled, and the bones cracked like shotgun blasts.

'Jesus,' whispered Leo. He felt he had reached a mocking zenith, one that few others could even have imagined. It was as if Adam had returned from the grave to show him all the wonders of a deformed hell. 'You are *one* sick puppy.'

Harold began to shed his skin, the hump on his back bursting wetly as huge wings spread forth, flapping languorously. He looked down on Leo with triumphant eyes (*they are a façade, no one lives there either*). 'I'm not sick,' he hissed on a belch of flame, 'I'm getting stronger.' Then he lunged, clamping his massive jaws over Leo's mouth.

Leo fell away, crawling back to consciousness with slow treacle steps. He awoke in a soft white room that stabbed at his eyes, unable to touch his face because his arms were strapped behind his back. He flinched every now and then as the light changed, convinced Harold was about to swoop down and carry him off in his talons to some distant nest of bone.

Time passed slowly. He rocked back and forth, chewing on his lips. He felt so weak, so delicate. His mind felt scorched; he couldn't tell up from down, the moon from Monday. All he could do was stay awake, keeping his ears peeled for the soft whoosh of leathery pinions.

And sure enough, they came.

As his unblinking eyes dried to molten rivets in his burning skull, he heard their dolorous beating outside the door. They flapped awhile, crackling gently, until they transformed themselves into muffled voices. Then the door opened, and Leo tried vainly to burrow into the unyielding cushions that padded his room. When he dared to look it was not Harold that loomed above him, fiery slaver dripping from his gaping maw, but two burly men dressed in coveralls. One wore a smile, but it was really just a mask; Leo knew appearances counted for nothing anymore.

'Hello, Leo,' said Smiler, making a feint with his fist that caused Leo to scream out loud like a little girl.

'This one's totally unshelled,' Smiler said to his partner. 'They found him gibbering about monsters, babbling about dragons. Isn't that right, Leo? What's wrong, big lizard got your tongue?'

The two men laughed; Leo's tongue was highly visible, lolling from his mouth like a Jack In The Box on a broken spring. Smiler leaned closer, putting his face directly into Leo's, placing a proprietary hand on his shoulder.

'Benson retires next month,' he said, and on his breath was the unmistakable graveyard waft of the Undersmell. 'And when he does, I get this ward all to myself. Know what that means, Freak? It means you're mine, all mine.'

Leo felt something within him give seconds before his bowels let go. Smiler wrinkled his nose, putting a hand to his face to hide his grin.

'You disgust me, Leo,' he said. 'You really do.'

From the ruins of his mouth, Leo roared.

Shunned

by John Grover

Elijah sat on his bed and waited. His bedroom door was locked from the outside. Through the door he heard the voices of his parents. They were distraught. His mother Anna and his father Jamie were discussing his fate for hours, and he was fearing for the worst. He was sorry for his crime. He hadn't meant for it to happen but it had. Now, all he could do was wait for the Elders to pass judgment.

He got up from the bed and approached the door. He tried the doorknob one more time, just to see. Yep. Still locked. Elijah crouched by the door to listen to his parents' exact words and hopefully find out what would become of him.

"How long will they deliberate?" Anna asked.

"You know it is not for us to question the Elders," Jamie answered. "Time is of no consequence to them."

"It is to me. This is unfair. He's our son. It is cruel to keep us waiting so long."

"Anna, do not question their wisdom."

"You don't think they'll decree *that* punishment, do you?"

"I cannot answer that."

"Jamie, they can't. He's only fifteen...just a boy. He didn't mean ..."

"Anna, please, no more. You will only drive yourself mad."

What was his mother talking about? What punishment? Surely it couldn't be that bad. He didn't mean to do what he'd done. It had just happened. It wasn't as if someone had died or was hurt. This was all a little much. Inside, he'd always questioned his family's ways, the ways of his people and the town. A town isolated, a town rife with secrets and rules. A town in fear. Of what? What were they all so afraid of?

He got up from the door and paced around the room. He saw the moon shimmering through his window. He wasn't sure how late it was because they'd taken his clock from him, along with all the other timekeepers in the house, for that matter. It was part of the Elders' way. No one was to question how long it took to consult. How long it took to make rules. To answer pleas, to conduct business, to moderate disputes, to regulate the affairs of the people or...to pass judgment.

Elijah felt guilty for what he had done, but did not regret it. He was only sorry it hurt his parents and that the Elders' eyes were turned toward them. But if he had a chance to do it again, he would.

He thought about sitting on the bed again but changed his mind. He slid his hand along his bed sheets and the quilt his mother had knitted him for cold nights. Both felt so comforting. A fly landed on the quilt, rubbed its legs and crawled along the bed. It buzzed briefly before taking to the air and gliding by Elijah's head.

"Trapped in here too, buddy?" He watched the fly circle his lamp then head off to his closet, probably to nestle in his flannel shirts or maybe the mud-caked boots he wore on the farm.

He sucked in some air then let it out slowly. He brushed his fingers through his curly hair. He noticed sweat dampening his fingers. Was he nervous? Guess he was. Funny, he didn't feel anxious before he got up from the bed. Perhaps he should have stayed there. *That punishment.* That was what his mother had said. What struck terror deep down inside her? He sensed it in her voice, how frail she'd sounded just then. Small. Helpless. Hopeless. Such dread in the very words, almost as if she'd had a hard time even uttering it. What could it be?

Back at the door. He stood this time and pressed his ear against the wood. They hadn't given up their discussion - well, at least his mother hadn't. He listened more intently this time.

"We could say that he escaped," Anna began. "Open the window for him and send him away. He could make his way over the Briar Hills."

"Have you lost your mind?" replied Jamie. "Do you want them passing judgment on us? We will surely receive that punishment."

"He's our son!" She raised her voice at him. Elijah had never heard her do that before. Never. She would have never dared. "I would do anything not to forget-"

"Enough. Someone might hear you. I will listen no more. Pass the time another way."

"I can't. He didn't do anything wrong. He didn't know…he didn't know. My baby. We can't let this happen, Jamie. Please."

"Anna, be strong. We know nothing until they've made their decision. We don't know what they will do. For now, we must be solemn and faithful."

"No one will help us. All of our friends will remain silent. They all know what the Elders' punishments are like. They've seen it before. You've seen it. How can you sit idly by?"

"I do not sit idly by!" Jamie roared. "I obey! I get down on my knees. I read the Good Book. I trust in our Elders. They have seen the God made flesh. They have witnessed the miracles. They are the Word. We obey. Do not bring their wrath upon us. The law is the law. He broke the law. Stop questioning the ways of things or I will have to take action."

"But, Jamie…"

"Push me no further, woman."

An image of his father raising his hand against his mother filled Elijah's mind. His heart raced. His throat went dry. Fingers trembling, he brought his hand up to the door. He knocked, softly at first. "Mother, Father, please let me out. I don't understand what's going on. Please, I'm afraid."

"Elijah," Anna wept.

"No," Jamie said. "Do not answer him. Get away from the door."

"Mother, let me out!" He knocked harder now, a moment away from pounding.

"Say nothing." His father's voice lowered into a hush.

He heard them whispering to one another, still arguing.

"Let me out! I want to get out." He pounded and yelled. "Don't let them hurt me. Please!"

He pushed himself away from the door and jumped onto his bed. Tears flowed. How could the punishment fit the crime? He hadn't even known what he was doing was wrong. This was inhuman. How could the Elders say that they loved and protected the community when they behaved like this? His own parents were too terrified even to talk to him.

"Why is it wrong?" he asked. "Can someone tell me why?"

There was no answer. He knew they were still there, whispering.

The moon drowned in a pool of clouds and the light was gone. He got up on his knees and tried to push his window open but it wouldn't move. Not a budge. Elijah stared into the yard, recalling its shape from memory since the inky darkness obscured everything. If he were able to get out there, could he run as fast as his legs would carry him to the hills? Navigate the fences, watch for trees and their gnarled roots? What about the briar patches, the sinkhole somewhere near the edge of the woods? Then there were the dogs. They would surely bark and give away his escape.

Briar Hills. Another rule. No one had ever been to the top of them. No one was allowed. There were fences erected. The hills were dangerous, the Elders said. Hungry things waited there to devour human flesh. Rumors ran among the kids in town. It was said that on the other side of the hills other children played, children happier than they. Teenagers, too. Different from him and his friends. They belonged to big families that played music and sang songs. There was laughter there. Joy. Banquets with sweets and pies and fresh fruits and vegetables. Elijah had always wanted to see for himself. He wanted to meet them and sing. He hoped someday he would. If it weren't for this town and the Elders, he would–

Elijah broke down in howling sobs and sank onto his bed. His chest heaved and tears soaked his cheeks. What were they going to do to him? Silence greeted him from the other side of his door. He no longer heard his parents' whispers. Eventually, frustration and fatigue took their toll and he fell asleep.

He didn't know how long he'd slept, but it felt like hours. Elijah opened his eyes. When his murky vision cleared, his gaze settled on a spider web in the corner of the ceiling. The fly he had observed earlier was caught in the web. He watched it struggle, tiny legs wriggling in the gossamer strands.

Elijah's heart fluttered when he spotted the spider climbing onto the web. It stalked the fly slowly. Eight legs of death crawled in rhythm, spindly and sleek, calculating with utter precision.

The spider drew nearer and the fly's wings fluttered madly. Silk entwined the prey and there was no escape. Friction led to exhaustion. Fighting was fruitless. The hungry predator took its time. Elijah lay frozen on his bed, mouth agape, eyes jutting, unable to look away. His limbs felt glued to a glittering web. He tried to move his legs, to jump up and save the fly, but they felt like lead.

He watched, helpless, as the spider reached its prey. It flitted over to the fly and eased itself on top of it, devouring it with ferocity unmatched.

That's me! Elijah realized. *I am the fly. Trapped in here. Waiting for the end to come. Are they going to kill me? Is that why Mom is so upset?*

Elijah jumped from his bed and rushed to his bedroom door. It was still locked. He curled his hand into a fist and pounded on it. "I'm still here! Do you hear me? Mother, Father! I am still here. Let me out. Please, let me out! I know you are there and I know you hear me. Let me see you. Look at me. This isn't right! You can't keep me in here forever!"

His cries fell on deaf ears. Nothing answered beyond the door.

Moments later, footsteps reverberated. He listened. Feet shuffled. A crowd entered his home, and, slowly, his bedroom doorknob turned.

Elijah pushed away from the door and dashed across the

room. He shoved his bed between him and the door and braced for the worst.

The door glided open and two men and a woman walked into the room. They all wore black. The men had long white beards; the woman had a tuft of snow-white hair atop her head. They glared at him with accusing eyes. Their faces were flushed with red.

"Elijah," the tallest man said. "Your crime must be punished. Your offence is a grievous one. Ignorance will not save you from judgment."

"Let the punishment fit the crime," the woman said.

"We have meditated and conferred on this more than on any other issue," the tall man continued. "Our decision is not made lightly." He lifted his arm and pointed at the boy.

Elijah's heart sank. His throat went dry. He felt a thousand eyes on him. He stood alone, darkness gathering around him, threatening to swallow him.

"Elijah, you are hereby *shunned.*"

"No!" his mother wailed from the next room. It startled him. "Not my child...I beg of you!"

The tall man continued, his eyes full of rage. "Your name will never be uttered again by anyone in the community. Your name will be erased from all records. Our ears are stone to you. Our eyes are blind to you. You are not here. You have never been here. You have no existence to us."

With his last word, the tall man turned his back on him. The other man and woman followed suit at the exact same moment.

Elijah walked up to them. They didn't move. "You won't speak to me?"

No reply came.

"Or look at me?"

None of them moved. They were as still as the mountains.

"Hello? I am here," he said. "I am Elijah."

He went to place a hand on one of them when he noticed it looked a little transparent. *What's this?* Could it actually be that he could see through it? Panic swept through him. His entire body trembled. "Mother!" He ran into the main room of the house. A small fire crackled in the hearth.

His mother stood with her back to him. She wept. Her shoulders shivered.

"Mother," he called to her. "Mother!" he yelled. "Mother!"

She remained, unflinching. Made of stone like the hills they were not allowed to climb.

"Mother, please... I'm afraid. Please, hold me." He stretched his arms out to embrace her and saw right through them. A moment later, they started to vanish.

Elijah dropped his arms. He backed away from his mother and saw his father at the table, sitting with his back to him. "Father, what's happening to me?"

Only the silence answered him.

"Please...Father, I'm sorry. I didn't know. How could I know? What's going on?"

He spotted a looking glass across the room on the north wall. He stepped in front of it and caught a fading image of himself. A hollow man. A ghost staring back at him. What horrified him the most was that this ghost was vanishing into nothing.

Elijah turned and ran from the house. Everyone in the road stood with their backs to him. They were as still as the mountains.

"Can't you see me?" he yelled at them. "Any of you? Can't you hear me?"

None of them replied.

"Please, someone!" he called as he ran. "Someone, please help me! I don't understand. I–"

He couldn't hear his voice. Although he screamed at the top of his lungs, nothing came out. His footsteps left no marks in the dirt.

He decided to head toward the hills – the ones he'd been forbidden to climb. He ran as fast as his legs would carry him, but now he could no longer see them. He did not have to climb the fences that blocked the forest; he went right through them.

The briar patches did not cut him. The gnarled tree roots did not trip him. And the dogs did not bark at him.

It was when he reached the foot of the hills that darkness crept into his sight and the silence took him. Guess he would never see what was on the other side of those hills, after all. Before he faded away, he heard the last remnants of a song and some laughter resonating from the top of the hill.

A Christmas Carnage

by James S. Dorr

While otherwise in all respects entirely normal, I had possessed from my childhood a nature overly sensitive to phenomena not ordinarily perceived by the general run of human beings. Therefore I was not extraordinarily surprised when, upon returning one cold winter's evening to my apartments, I saw, glowing green at me from beneath the door knocker, a pair of eyes.

Aha, I thought, perhaps the ghost realm intends to play the Marley-Scrooge game on me. I, having read the Charles Dickens epic, had always wished for just such visitations upon my own self, aiming to demand of the specter of Christmas *Present*: "Just can the speeches and make with the gifts."

Alas, as I was to learn to my horror, those who inhabit the world of spirits don't appreciate puns.

But I am, too, a realist. My thought, as I prepared myself for slumber – "early to bed and early to rise," as was my motto as well as that of the illustrious Franklin, "that's what brings in the Benjamins" – was that what I had seen was no doubt the mere result of a bout of indigestion. An underdone potato, perhaps.

I slept through the warning, *à la* Dickens, of rattling chains, only verifying their presence the following morning through scars left on the threshold of my bedchamber door, and some flecks of rust beneath. The subsequent tour of Christmas Past I also put down simply to a dream – a student of history in my college years at Miskatonic U. (I still hum the team fight song, *Roll On, Roll On, Cthulhu, Down the Field*), I have often enjoyed such sleep-induced reveries of long gone worlds and times.

But when the next apparition appeared, ah, *that* snapped me to immediate alertness.

I recognized who she was in an instant, even if she had been dead in her grave for at least the past century. I had seen her pictures in my family's album when I chanced upon it once during my teenage years, on a rare occasion when it had been left out unlocked in my father's room: Ancient sepia-tinted *Daguerreotypes* made into postcards. She had in her youth, according to family legend, been an artist's model in Paris.

And indeed such photos they were, to one as I then, as even now still, a virgin! Fully awake, I attempted to speak. "G-g-great Aunt Carol," I managed to stutter.

"Your umpty-umpth-great aunt Carol, actually," she replied with a smile – and what a smile it was, exactly the same as on the eighth in that set of postcards, the one where the only garments she wore were a pair of fishnet hose and a fur Santa Claus hat. "But I don't feel so old, so perhaps I'll accept just being your 'great aunt.'"

And yet here she was in my bedroom in the flesh. Lots of

flesh, in fact, in that she now wore precisely the same garb!

"But to business, umpty-umpth-great nephew. I am the Ghost of Christmas – do we really have to go through the whole routine?"

"I-if that's 'Christmas Present,'" I managed to get out, "may I have –"

"I know," she said. "I've always known, ever since that time you sneaked into your father's den, just what it is of all you might think to ask for, that you've wanted most."

To get laid! I thought. But –

"It's one of the perks that comes with being deceased," she said, her breath like perfume, both sweet and sexy. "Just as I could anticipate your predilection toward wordplay." She frowned at that, for a moment perhaps, but then went on, her lips forming a *moue*. "But as spirits, you know, we *do* have limitations."

"I-I-I-I-I," I stammered.

"I wish to help you." She pouted again. "I *am* the Ghost of Christmas Present – and it's been long enough since my death that I could use a little lift myself. A sort of a treat for 'Santa,' if you will." She took her cap off, letting raven hair cascade down over smooth shoulders, alabaster white, gleaming with only the slightest sheen of sweat. Brushing her rounded thighs. "But, alas, I am a ghost only. The flesh we must leave behind."

"I-I-I-I-I-I-I," I stammered.

"But," she said, brightening, "there may, perhaps, be a way."

Once more she smiled, squirming seductively, sitting now, next to me, on the side of my bed. Leaning, her lips touched mine –

But all I felt was air!

"You see the problem," she said with a slight moan. "To regain our bodies – our *corporeality* – there must be a sacrifice made with human blood."

"Y-y-y-y-you mean I've got to cut my finger or something, like that early scene in that movie, the one back when everyone's still in the van, *Texas Chainsaw Massacre*." Memories flooded into my head – it had been a seminal moment for me when I had seen that film. Just like, in its way, with Aunt Carol's French postcards. One that had stayed with me.

"Actually more like toward the end of the movie," Aunt Carol murmured. "You realize, it's been a huge number of years. It's going to take *lots* of blood."

This time it was *I* who grinned, realizing, suddenly, that there were certain advantages to being of a possibly overly-nervous nature. I motioned for her to stay on the bed while I hopped out myself, throwing on a robe, and opened my closet door, drawing from it the implement I had been moved to buy as a protection against burglars: A 28-inch Black & Decker chainsaw.

Now Aunt Carol grinned with me.

"How many do you think it will take?" I asked.

She held up her fingers, then wiggled her toes as well. "One victim for each half-decade?" she said. "I think that might do."

I checked the tank to make sure it was gassed up, when, once again, Aunt Carol pouted. "Is it going to be *very* noisy?" she asked me.

I shook my head. "It's top of the line – it has a muffler. Why don't you just wait for me? It shouldn't take long."

Aunt Carol just nodded.

#

It is here that my memories become somewhat unclear, only that I went, stealthily, from door to door in my building, starting on the very top floor and working my way down. A quick, circular cut let me through each locked door, then – the rest, as I say, seems to blend, room to room, as if cloaked in a red fog. I do not know even how many I visited that late, moonless night, before my saw finally ran out of fuel. Only that I had left the building altogether, and was down the block having just left another.

I thought of Aunt Carol's words, whispering them to myself. "I think that might do."

No fool I, I carefully wiped the chainsaw's handles clean before abandoning it in a dumpster. Then, realizing that some other late walker might yet come upon me, practically naked beneath my gore-soaked robe, I made haste to skulk back to my own rooms as unobtrusively as I was able.

Once more memory shifts and slides, as if I experienced all that came after in some kind of dream. But a wonderful dream! A dream surpassing all others, exceeding even that which I had imagined.

Suffice to say Aunt Carol *had* waited. And this time, when she kissed, it was with lips of solid flesh!

How can I describe it? The taste. The touch. The waves of pleasure. The sheer sensuality that washed my body, over and through it, and every nerve ending. I, whose nerves were sensitive anyway! A nagging thought came: with my neighbors all slaughtered, I, alone, in my building – my block – having survived this *holocaust*, might not the police find in this an excuse to consider me suspect?

But, even if so, would it not have been worth it?

"Shhhh," Aunt Carol whispered.

And with that, another thought – that of that tiny frown Carol had flashed when she recalled my wordplay. And was it not selfishness that the spirits, at least in the story, were committed to *punish*?

"*Shhhhh!*" she whispered again, her voice now with a slight edge, then thrust her tongue in my –

It was as if holidays, Christmas, the Fourth of July, birthdays, Easter, all crashed into one moment. Sweetness and fireworks. I heard a *thump!* as a lamp, on my bed table, fell to the floor. Disturbed by the bed's shaking.

I felt a wetness.

"Mr. Persnickety Neatnik," that's me. But this time, I did not let it stop me in my work. Until, at last, sweet exhaustion took me.

Until morning, and wakefulness, and once again *thumping*. This time a knock on my outer door, then a crash as the police burst through it. Burst into my bedroom to find me screaming, gore-clotted sheets bunched and tangled about me.

But then, beneath me, they saw that even that was not the worst: For, locked in my arms, I continued to embrace the rotting, century-old corpse of a woman.

Dybbuk Hunting
by Shyla Colt

Rochelle clutched the Star of David tight in one hand as the car glided through the slick streets of Cincinnati toward their appointment. A flash of light illuminated the sky followed by a rumble that sounded like a roar.

"You're tense." Efron's steady baritone grounded her.

"Yes."

"Are you sure you're ready for this?" She glanced over to see her husband's stern frown. His peyots fell down on either side of his face, glossy and dark; the chestnut colored curls stood out beneath the black yammakah as they drove under street lights.

"I have to be."

"Hmmm." His silence spoke louder than words.

Efron wasn't like most men. Soft spoken, studious, and godly, the Rabbi never would've appeared on her radar. Until she'd had a nasty run in with a dybbuk, the dislocated soul of a dead person. The battle for her soul had opened something inside her. Thinned the veil, turning her into a conduit who saw, communicated, and vanquished the unruly dead.

Efron saw it as a calling, and together they'd formed a two-person team to take care of the things most Rabbis turned their backs on. Most times the cases were easily explained. Loose floorboards, faulty wiring, mental illness. But occasionally the supernatural were at work. She had a feeling this case would be one of the latter.

"You think I'll falter?" She puffed out her cheeks. Time and time again she'd proved herself, and yet he thought her weak? Heat flashed through her body. Balling her hands into fists she breathed deep, forcing the anger and self-doubt from her body. The dybbuk would only feed on it. Magnify it, and make her slow and clumsy.

"No. You'll do what needs to be done. It's your mental state I'm concerned about. What will this cost you? Every spirit we vanquish costs you. And this particular entity almost took you altogether."

"It also brought us together." Reaching across the distance she squeezed his soft hand. "We both agreed the ugliness in my life had to happen to bring me here with you. How else would we come together? I was a non-denominational believer convinced God had given up on me, and you were a Jewish Rabbi."

The answering pressure on her hand made her smile. "I know this to be true, but a man always worries about his wife."

"I know my love. But the needs of many outweigh the one."

An impolite snort served as his response, and she giggled. Tension broken she centered herself, preparing for the battle ahead. The moment they pulled up in front of the modest, two story, red brick home, dread bottomed out her stomach. Heaviness filled the air, practically casting a shadow that separated the building from the other, festively decorated homes on the block.

"Do you feel that?" she whispered.

"Yes… what do you sense?"

Closing her eyes she tilted her head. Darkness sprang up wrapping around her personal spiritual space. Icy talons of desolation, despair, and rage battered at the wall she kept erect. It pounded against her defenses, with an aggressiveness that stole the breath from her lungs. She opened her eyes.

"Efron, this is bad."

A loud clap of thunder sounded directly above their head, rattling the car. Rain came down in sheets. Frost formed on the windows. Her lungs ached as the air became cold. Water droplets gave way to hail.

"It knows we're here." White clouds formed with Efron's words.

"And it doesn't like it." The hairs on Rochelle's arms and neck stood on end. She peered out the window toward the house. Her breath hitched. There in the window she spotted a pale face. Gone in a span of a blink, the malnourished, spectral set the chill in her bones.

"I just saw it. Anything this powerful has a strong hold on the host it's trying to invade."

They exchanged a look full of heavy knowledge. It might be too late. If the dybbuk's hold proved to be too strong, the attempt to extract it would kill her.

"Let's go."

Nodding she unbuckled her seatbelt, grabbed the satchel at her feet, slipped its strap over her head and opened her door. Clutching the black trench coat tight she bowed her head to keep the stinging balls of ice from her face as Efron joined her and they jogged the short distance to the front door. The porch light flickered, casting shadows. Scanning the area, Rochelle whispered the *Birkhat Ha-Gomeyl*. The Jewish prayer for safety from danger calmed her spirits, and the darkness receded.

The door opened to reveal Joe Baran. His angular face was pale and too slim. Dark circles stood out beneath his gray eyes. The wrinkled white shirt, askew Yammakah and frizzy curls spoke of his hardship.

"Rabbi Milstein, Rochelle, thank you so much for coming." Stepping back he waved them inside. His tongue darted out to moisten cracked lips. "The children are staying with my mother right now, I thought it best."

"You did right, Joe. Thank you for allowing us in your home."

He closed and locked the door behind them. The house had an odd odor she couldn't quite place and the lights were dim, giving her the vague impression of dark furniture, a television against one wall, and a large rug over wood flooring in the living room to their right.

"Please, follow me into the kitchen, I made tea. Excuse my

wife's absence, she's resting."

I'll bet she is. "Of course." Rochelle offered up her best version of a reassuring smile, and followed behind the men. The kitchen held the same abysmal lighting.

"Do you keep the lights low for a reason, Joe?" she asked.

"No, it's been like this for the past week or so. We had an electrician come by, but he couldn't explain it." His voice shook as he busied himself pouring tea from a kettle that sat on the stove top. They took their places around a square table.

"Thank you," Rochelle whispered as she accepted the mug.

Once they were settled Efron spoke. "Can you tell us about what's been going on here?"

"My wife has been prone to bouts of depression her entire life. So, when she began to grow distant and act odd, it wasn't abnormal." He hesitated.

"What changed, Mr. Baran?" Rochelle asked.

"Small things at first, changing. A different manner of speaking, interest in new topics. We're in our late thirties. I thought it was a mid-life crisis. Then she started to know things."

"Know things?" Efron asked.

His gaze darted back and forth between them. "What I dreamed last night, who would call on the phone, things she couldn't have known. Do you know what it's like to have your wife's voice make you feel like bugs are crawling all over your flesh? I tried to ignore it at first. Convince myself I'd put in too many hours, and listened a little too closely to the old stories… Then I heard her speak a language I didn't even recognize." Mr. Baran shuddered. "That's when I knew. She wasn't my Ona anymore."

"Have you noticed anything else?"

Tuning their conversation out, Rochelle turned her body, sensing a presence behind them. The dead eyes that looked back at her from the woman's gaunt, oval shaped face turned her stomach.

"Efron," she whispered, afraid to spook the woman into action.

"Ona, what are you doing downstairs?" Mr. Baran rose.

"Who are these people! I don't want them here!" The shrill screech hit her ears like nails on a chalk board.

"They're here to help you." Mr. Baran held out his hands in an attempt to soothe her ire.

"You can't help her." The warped voice that spoke back was not Ona Baran. Like a cassette tape chewed up and played back the tone was low and slow. "She's ours now." The petite frame hit the ground in a crouch. Scrambling back like a crab it disappeared into the darkness in an inhuman fashion. A blast of energy hit them all in the chest, knocking them to the ground, and toppling the table and chairs.

Groaning, Rochelle clutched her back, rolling to take cover behind the overturned table.

"Rochelle." Efron's voice came from a few feet behind her.

"I'm fine." She gritted her teeth. *You got the drop on me once, you won't get a second chance.*

"Mr. Baran?" Efron asked.

"Yes, I'm okay."

His weary voice tore at her heart strings. Overwhelmed and out of his depth, defeat tinged every syllable he uttered. Low crawling, they lined up one by one, like soldiers on a battlefield.

"Given the circumstances we need to do this now!" Efron stated. "We're in orthodox, it's not the nine point circle the Rabbis recommend, but we'll get the job done. What we need is your permission. Sometimes these things can end badly. My wife's a trained RN. We've brought the basic equipment to revive and stabilize her, but if she's too far gone, once the dybbuk is removed, her body will become an empty shell."

"You're saying there may not be any of Ona left?" His horrified expression saddened her.

"Yes, Mr. Baran. This is a serious possession. Sometimes people just aren't strong enough to fight it."

"Do it, what other choice do I have? Live with that thing in my house, around my children, no." He shook his head. "This is my only option."

"Then we will begin now." Efron glanced at Rochelle, nodding his approval. She began the St. Michael Prayer in English as he guided Mr. Baran in a Jewish prayer in Hebrew.

"O Glorious Prince of the heavenly host, St. Michael, the Angel, defend us in the battle and in the terrible warfare that we are waging against the principalities and powers, against the rulers of this world of darkness, against the evil spirits. Come to the aid of man, whom Almighty God created immortal, made in His own image and likeness, and redeemed at a great price from the tyranny of Satan."

As the words were spoken a terrible sense of calm settled. The house grew silent and heaviness settled on her chest. Rochelle and Efron worked in tandem to empty the satchel. Removing the Torah and the shofar, which she'd mistaken for a ram's horn the first time she saw it, they armed themselves for battle. Unlike the Catholic version of an exorcism, their goal was to heal the broken spirit and restore Ona's soul.

"Can you speak with it, Rochelle?" Efron asked.

"I'll try." Opening her third eye she sought out the being hidden in the dark spaces of the home. An image of sickly woman hunched over, facing away from her in the corner, rose in her head. "Come, we wish to help you."

It turned to her with milky blue eyes, baring its rotted teeth. "No! You only care about the living! No one cares for the lost dead."

"You don't belong here anymore. We will ease your way."

"You lie."

"I tell you the truth!" Her voice boomed in the space between them.

"You have power! She is weak, easy to manipulate." Lust filled its eyes. "I will leave her."

Rochelle narrowed her eyes, tense. The about face didn't feel right.

"And enter into you!" The stench of rotting flesh made her gag, and she pulled out of the connection. Blinking she reoriented herself.

"Rochelle?"

"The dybbuk is a woman. She says she'll leave Ona and come to us." Rochelle frowned. "I think it lies. All it wants is to be alive and cause pain, and misery. I sensed it."

Efron frowned. "We'll do what we must."

The patter of feet on floorboards reached them, and they rose together. Not Ona appeared in the doorframe. Her head tilted slightly as she sniffed the air.

"Come, be healed." Efron gestured her toward him.

"Mr. Boran, get the chair there," Rochelle whispered. He complied.

"Sit." Rochelle gestured toward the wooden seat.

Not Ona remained silent as she sank down and watched them.

"Let's begin." Efron raised the horn to his lips to blow, and shake the spirit loose.

A black cloud burst from Ona, surrounding Rochelle. Its

noxious fumes choked her as it struggled to get inside. Knocked onto her back, she began to chant Psalm 91, choking between words. It felt like taking on water. Her brain screamed in protest as invisible knives twisted their way into the fleshy meat of her brain. Her body convulsed, and sticky, hot liquid ran from her nose onto her lips. A metallic flavor blossomed in her lips – blood.

Suddenly the attack stopped and the crushing weight lifted. Wiping away the sweat that burned her eyes, she focused on the dark shape glued to the spot in front of her.

"Why are you here?" Efron asked.

His voice brought Rochelle home, and she pushed to her feet.

"To get my turn to live!" The lights flickered, and the floor shook. Plates, pictures, and glasses fell onto the floor.

"Your time here is over. You must leave this place." Rochelle forced the words out of trembling lips, impressed with her ability to keep her voice even. A healthy dose of her power made the shadow shrink back.

"You can't force me!"

A piercing tone sounded. Rochelle covered her ears, clamping down her teeth. The blackness once again took on a mass of inky blackness. Rushing Mr. Baran it targeted the weakest point. Tossing him aside like a rag doll it fled through the window, shattering it to pieces. Dazed, and frightened by its power, Rochelle turned to Efron.

"I don't think we've seen the last of her."

"No." Rochelle shook her head.

"Are you okay?" The concern turning his blue eyes to the color of amethyst made her fall in love with him all over again. He'd always seemed too stern and judgmental before she got to know him. Now he could make her melt with one glance.

"I'm fine." She swiped her nose and mouth with her hand, wiping the blood onto her black pants.

"Ona!" Mr. Baran ran toward the body slumped down in the chair.

"Please let me check her vitals, Mr. Baran." Slipping back into Nurse Mode she walked over and took her pulse. "It's steady." Efron appeared beside her with a blood pressure cuff. Strapping it around Ona's arm, she pumped. "Low. But that's normal for someone unconscious. Can you call her name Mr. Baran?"

"Ona." Cupping her face in his hand he gently patted her cheek. "Honey wake up, please."

Her eye lids fluttered open. "J-Joe, what's happened? Why am I in the kitchen chair?" She peered over her husband's shoulder. "Who are this people and what happened to my kitchen?"

"What's the last thing you remember, Mrs. Baran?" Efron asked.

"Sabbath with my family, Rabbi."

"And when was that?"

"The seventeenth."

"T-that was almost a month ago."

Explaining what had happened and that time loss was normal, they recommended she see a doctor before they slipped out into the dreary evening as quietly as they'd arrived. The storm's rage had passed. The house felt normal from the porch.

"Do you think they'll be okay?" Rochelle asked as they watched the mist, not quite rain or fog.

"We blessed their house, and freed her from the dybbuk. The rest is up to them. If she keeps walking around open..."

Rochelle nodded. "I always wish I could do more."

He wrapped an arm around her waist. "You do enough."

Lifting her face up toward him, she sighed when his lips brushed her own. Greedy, she deepened the kiss, darting her tongue between his. She savored his flavor, mint and maleness. Moaning in the back of her throat she pressed her body into his. Nerve endings tingled, and they separated, gasping as if they'd surfaced from the bottom of a pool.

They were alive, and Ona had her soul back. It wasn't quite a victory, but she'd take it. She couldn't win every battle, and the real goal had always been the war. Hands intertwined, they walked into the mist, ready and waiting to defend the innocent from evil.

The Averish House
by Tony Flynn

The Averish House was part of a terrace block on Underbury Lane in the small town of Ashton, and to an outsider walking by, nothing would seem odd about the place, until they waited around long enough to realise that, save for the shadow of an elderly woman sitting on the front porch of The Averish House, the rest of the terrace was totally uninhabited. Underbury Lane was, to all intense and purposes, a ghost estate, save for the two Averish sisters, Penny and Anna, and where they lived, they lived alone, free of any interference from the outside world.

The house had been there for what might have been an eternity and while the younger sister, Anna, would sometimes be seen walking alone through the woods on an autumn evening, only a very few people ever saw the elder. Unlucky people saw her. People who broke the rules saw her. Little Alice Carver saw her, I'm almost certain of that. She was eleven years old that Halloween, and dressed the same as she did every year since she was four years old, as Dorothy from The Wizard of Oz. I cannot tell for certain exactly what happened that night, but when I dream, I have nightmares, and in my nightmares, it goes like this:

#

Alice arrived at the front gate of The Averish House after visiting every other house she possibly could in Ashton. In the front garden stood a scarecrow, with the face of a pumpkin. It was dressed in a Devil's costume, the kind you would by for a kid in a costume shop, and had a flame burning brightly in its head which illuminated its cruelly carved eyes and sharp teeth, like a window into the deepest, darkest pit of hell.

Beyond the scarecrow, just beside the front door of the house, sat a shadow, which Alice looked upon, and yet felt no fear. She felt only hunger, and a desire to say that she had done something which she knew none of her cowardly friends had ever done before:

She had been to The Averish House.

Without a moment's reticence, she opened the gate, which screeched as if in agony as it turned on its rarely used hinges. Walking down the pathway of the front garden seemed to take an eternity, as if the house itself was moving away. Alice passed by the scarecrow, the eyes of the pumpkin seeming to follow her as she did so, and walked towards the shadow on the front porch. As she got closer, the darkness and shadows seemed to creep away, revealing an old woman, sitting ever so still in a wheelchair, her face hidden behind a plastic green and yellow witch's mask.

Alice knew that there were two Averish sisters. Both were old, but one was very, very old. She realised that this one was very, very old.

This was Penny Averish.

Penny did not move when Alice approached her. Alice thought that she must have been asleep, but could not be certain, for no eyes were visible beneath the mask. Just two pools of blackest night.

"Trick or treat," ventured Alice.

Nothing. No sound. No stirring. Penny's head did not move, and her withered old hands stayed firmly in place, clutching on to a dirty, tartan blanket which covered her legs. Impatiently, Alice tried again, louder this time:

"Trick or Treat!"

"Shhh," came a reply, though not from Penny.

Alice turned her head to the front door, where stood, dressed all in black, and holding a red lantern, the younger of the two old sisters: Anna Averish.

Anna Averish was stick thin. An old, black dress clung loosely to the skin-wrapped bones which made up her physique, and her eyes were dark with shadows, as if they hadn't closed in an eternity. Her lips were blue, as if freezing cold, in spite of the evening being very warm. When I was older I saw a picture of a Holocaust survivor from Auschwitz. It made me think of Anna Averish.

For the first time in her life, Alice seemed to be afraid. Afraid enough, at least, to briefly lose all powers of speech, left with no other option than to awkwardly present her Trick or Treat bag, in the hope of some small token.

Anna smiled at the young girl, and opened wider the front door, revealing a hallway lined with bags full of the most delicious candy and chocolates that Alice had ever seen. Her mouth watering, Alice held her bag out further, only to be presented with just three small, golden wrapped pieces of chocolate, which Anna slowly dropped into the young girl's bag, one by one.

Alice looked into the bag, disappointed at the measly share she had been given, and was about to protest and make demands for more, only to look back to the doorway and see nothing. Anna had disappeared. Alice had neither seen nor heard her go anywhere, but like darkness vanishing at the coming of daylight, the hallway was now bare, save for the now unguarded bags of candy.

Thieving was nothing new to Alice. In fact she was quite adept at it. She had stolen lipstick from her older sister; she had stolen money from her mother; she had once even stolen cigarettes from her father but was made so sick that she vowed never to try that one again. For a thief like her, all it took was a perfect set of circumstances, and now here she stood, faced with a bounty the likes of which she was unlikely to ever see again, and no one around to guard it, save an ancient old cripple in a wheelchair, who might as well be, and very probably was, dead.

Even so, the first rule of a successful crime is caution. You mustn't get sloppy. Alice knew this, and was determined that this night would not end badly for her. She slowly and silently approached the old woman, and waved a hand just before her face to check for any signs of life. There was nothing. Alice was almost certain she was safe, but while Penny wore the mask, she could not be sure. She needed to see her face. She needed to know, beyond any doubt, that Penny Averish was asleep. To see her old, tired eyes weighed heavily shut.

Slowly, she brought her hand towards the old woman's mask, but as she did so she felt her heart begin to beat loudly in her chest. Something was wrong. She never used to feel fear like this before a crime. The beating was faster now. Louder and faster, like a drum beat, and for a moment she felt as if her heart was going to shatter in her chest to a million pieces.

Her fingertips grazed the nose of the mask on the old woman's face, and the beating of Alice's heart became so loud that she was afraid that Penny might wake just from the sound of it.

Alice pulled her hand away as if from a fire and, running now on pure adrenaline, grabbed hold of the first bag of candy she could lay her hand upon before running as quickly as she could from The Averish House.

Only after she was clear of Underbury Lane and three streets further did she settle.

#

The rest of the commute home passed more or less without incident, save for a creeping sense of dread that seemed to follow after Alice like a pungent smell, detectible only to the most sensitive of creatures. Birds would fly from their trees as she passed under them. Cats would leap to the other side of walls to avoid her. Dogs would bark and growl. Every animal on the road where she lived seemed to be aware of the crime she had committed. Alice did not feel safe until she had reached her house, and locked and double-bolted the front door behind her.

#

Safe and secure, a calm washed over Alice, coupled with a sense of pride as ill begotten as the stolen goods in her hands. She had gotten away with it. She had not only been to The Averish House, she had seen both sisters, and had actually stolen from them. No one would believe her when she told the story. She resolved to keep at least some of the candy as proof.

#

Alice emptied the contents of the bag onto the kitchen table and riffled through it with glee, like a pirate might a booty of sunken treasure, and with the same giddy excitement ran her hands through the different chocolates and candies which lay before her. She did not know where to start. Everything looked so much more delicious than the usual candy handed out at Halloween by disinterested and cheap neighbours. There was love in these chocolates. Love in the bright, colourful wrapping paper which covered each individual piece. Alice couldn't tell where to start. It was all too wonderful. With undiluted glee, she took one of the chocolates in her hand: a small piece, wrapped in bright gold paper. Slowly and deliberately, she held the candy between the thumb and forefinger of each hand, pulling against the wrapping on either side, relishing the crumpled sound of the plastic as it unfurled, revealing a colour of golden brown beneath, which she stared at for a moment, as if hypnotized, before finally putting it in her mouth.

Her eyes widened. It was like nothing she had ever tasted before. It seemed to at once fill her whole body, but still left her hungry. Wanting more. Demanding more.

She grabbed another chocolate from the table, tearing away the wrapping and stuffing it in her mouth. Again, an unbelievable feeling of happiness, followed by an insatiable hunger. She needed more. She grabbed another handful of chocolate, and didn't even bother to open the wrapping this time. She just stuffed it all into her mouth and spat away the plastic where she could, but ended up swallowing most. It didn't matter. All that mattered was the chocolate. She needed it. It was more vital than air. More vital than blood.

Her heart started to race. She was eating so much so fast. It pounded in her chest, as if begging for mercy, just as it did outside The Averish House. But still she ate. She ate more and more and grabbed a toffee sweet from the table and threw it into her mouth.

That was when she heard the crunch.

She stopped eating. A pain shot through her jaw. She spat the contents of her mouth out onto the table, and amidst a messy glob of half chewed chocolate, she saw something hard. Almost rock-like. She smoothed away the chocolate, cleaning the object as best she could, finally gasping after identifying it as a tooth.

Alice felt around the inside of her mouth with her tongue, identifying a gap, which she confirmed with her hand.

It was her tooth.

A sudden pain gripped her chest, like nothing she had ever felt before in her life. She screamed as the pain forced her backwards away from the table, and took her to her knees, forcing her hands against the floor, where she so desperately wanted to throw up, but couldn't.

Alice looked at her hands, pressed hard against the kitchen floor. They seemed older. Pale and wrinkled. Like a granny's hands.

She brought them closer to her face, staring intently at them before running them through her hair in frustration. She felt the hair on her head become loose, and when she took her hands from her head, she took with them a clump of her own hair. She looked at the mess in her hands, and cried desperately, turning to the back door window, where she could make out a hint of her reflection.

Her eyes were dark. What remained of her hair was grey and clinging pathetically to her otherwise bare scalp. Her skin was wrinkled and dry, like old paper. Her heart beat a thousand beats over, as if aging a hundred years within seconds.

Alice turned from the mirror and screamed in horror when she saw the chocolates, once so lovely, now covered in worms and maggots, which hatched from within the chocolate shells.

A cold grip took hold of Alice's still rapidly beating heart.

Her blood ran cold.

Her bones felt old.

She did not have much time left.

#

A strange buzzing echoed in Alice's ears as she ran down the street. It sounded like crying, but that of a million voices at once: like the sorrowful moans of every person who ever did a bad thing.

She was like a walking bag of bones now as she shuffled down the street, awkwardly moving as fast as she could, fearing that with every step her legs might break beneath her, leaving her alone on the ground with nothing but the cries of long forgotten souls to sing her to sleep. She needed to get back. She needed to make things right. She didn't know how, but it was her only chance. It was this sheer desperation which sustained her as she made her way back to the scene of her crime.

Back to Underbury Lane.

Back to The Averish House.

#

Penny still sat in her wheelchair on the porch before her house. She made not a sound nor a gesture of recognition as Alice moved agonizingly towards her, and threw herself down before her, grabbing the old woman's hands in her own. Alice couldn't speak. Most of her teeth were gone now. The best she could manage was an anguished cry for help.

The old woman didn't move. The only sound of acknowledgement was a deep, hollow laugh, which started softly, and then grew to a deranged cackle and emanated from behind the mask, as if straight from the Devil himself.

Alice could feel Penny's hands in her own. They felt warm. Smooth. Alice looked down and saw her own wretched, old, cursed hands holding tight to the young, revitalised hands of the old woman.

Alice backed away as Penny got to her feet and threw away the blanket which she once held to so tightly. A light caught Alice's eye. It came from the upstairs window of The Averish House. She looked and saw Anna, staring down at her, a silver light glowing from behind her, lighting her up like an angel, though certainly not one from Heaven.

Alice threw her hands up towards Anna in one final desperate plea for mercy. Anna only smiled, and raised a finger before her lips.

"Shhhh."

Alice fell to her knees. The last of her strength had failed her. She looked upon the house, knowing finally that it would be the last thing she would ever see. The old woman walked towards her, graceful now, as if possessed of a body no older than twenty. She leaned down before Alice and then, finally, removed her mask.

All Alice could do was scream. And that scream echoed long into the night...

...and no one was around to hear it.

#

Nobody ever saw Alice Carver again after that night. The grownups all said that she must have run away, but we kids knew better. We didn't know everything, but we knew it was The Averish

House that took her. To this day it stands there, and I know that some kids still dare each other every Halloween to go as far as the gate on Underbury Lane. No one will go any further than that, but those who are brave enough to go even that far all claim to have seen the same thing:

A scarecrow, with a glowing pumpkin head, dressed like Dorothy from The Wizard of Oz, and an empty wheelchair resting on the porch before the house.

I am older now. A father myself. And I tell you this story not to frighten you, but to warn you. There are things in this world that we cannot hope to understand. Powers that we cannot even contemplate. I tell you this story, because you are my children, and you deserve to know what happens to people who meddle with the unknown.

No one ever warned little Alice Carver.

Someone should have.

Her parents should have.

So as your parent, I tell you now, before you take your bags and run off Trick or Treating, stay away from Underbury Lane. Go anywhere else you like. This is a fine town, and you are safe...

But stay away from Underbury Lane.

Stay away from The Averish House.

The Horror on Sycamore Lane
by Victoria Dalpe

It was such a shame.

You could hear that being said all throughout the neighborhood after the incident. It was uttered reverently in beauty parlors and pharmacies, at the park, at the greengrocers. Telephone pole men up in cherry pickers hollered it down to old ladies on sidewalks. The entire town, it seemed, had said it at least once. Head shaking, tongue clucking, it was such a shame.

Barbara, while quiet, had been known all around town as a nice person. A kind woman who was generous around the holidays. She kept her house nice. Her yard was tidy, not flashy, not over-groomed, but tidy. Evenly trimmed grass, perennials mixed in with annuals. The garden a reserved, orderly, rainbow of color.

The dark spot was her husband Bob. Salesman of some sort who traveled a lot. He was not a very social fellow: his jaundiced skin and ruddy nose giving a clue of what his preferred hobby was. He was seldom seen on his days off, save when he trotted down the front path in his ratty old bathrobe, feet often bare, to retrieve the newspaper.

Bob and Barbara had moved to 220 Sycamore Lane as

newlyweds. It was an unassuming street, filled with tidy, middle-income homes. An orderly development of houses where the seeds of the GI Bill had once been planted.

The pavement along Sycamore Lane had some cracks, and the cars were all a little older. But it was still a nice enough place to live. Bob and Barbara had bought their house, 220 Sycamore Lane, with a small deposit provided by Barbara's widowed father, who owned a few dealerships out of state. Bob's parents were elderly, and were dead before they moved into the house.

220 Sycamore was a quaint cape, with yellow siding, and white trim. It had a gray shingled roof and a stubby chimney, also painted white. The postage stamp ¼ acre had a low chain link fence around it. The fence, they had put up as soon as they moved in. It was not the nicest fence, but on Sycamore Lane the neighbors were not the type to clean up after their dogs. And there were enough dogs to discolor and dig up a nice yard.

Barbara, it was said, was terrified of dogs. She had a small scar on her chin. She was good at covering it up with makeup, but at the right angle you could see it. It marred an otherwise pretty face.

Barbara was an average sized woman, curvy, with long auburn hair. She had hazel eyes, almost metallic, the color of oxidized copper. She was fair skinned with a dusting of freckles on her nose that made her look girlish. Outside of the scar, she was a pleasant looking woman with a shy smile and kind eyes.

When they moved into the house on 220 Sycamore, the neighborhood gossiped, as small close-knit streets are apt to. Barbara's widowed father was wealthy, at least by the standards of Sycamore Lane, and it seemed queer that a young rich man's daughter like Barbara would marry someone like Bob. He was considerably older than her, slovenly, and would barely wave if a neighbor called out. His clothes always appeared disheveled, suits rumpled, hair mussed. Even then, when they were newlyweds, his hair was thin, colorless, and not long for this world.

He had what Gloria Danforth of 200 Sycamore Lane called "Dead Eyes." Granted, Gloria Danforth had a spot of dementia, and rumors over why they had a chain link fence put up also included a certain old woman – that looked like Gloria Danforth in a housecoat – who would pick flowers out of their garden at night. But Gloria had always been very vocal about Bob and his dead eyes. There was no soul in them, she would say, he stared right through you like a ghost.

Barbara became pregnant a few years after they moved into the little yellow house. By that point she had a few friends on the street, mostly just other women who waved and would occasionally chitchat on the outside of the fence while she gardened. And at the library, where she volunteered, once a week. With no mother or mother-in-law, the neighborhood women worried for her. Alone most of the time while her husband travelled, keeping a house all by herself, taking care of a new baby all alone.

One such woman, Mrs. Olivia Grady, was as close as anyone ever was to Barbara. She had even been inside their home, her and her husband Jason, for a periodic meal or tea. Olivia had a small brood of children herself and was a stout, kind-eyed woman with a bigger heart than sense. She worried over Barbara, helping her fix up a little nursery, and prepare the diapers and bottles. Olivia was not allowed over while Bob was in town though. It was through Olivia that the rumors of abuse came about.

It was true, most could attest, that Barbara would occasionally have bruises, mainly around her wrists and neck, as if someone had grabbed her there, or choked her there. And it was obvious that she would coat herself in makeup, greasepaint layers like old time movie stars, to hide the marks. But bruises were funny, very hard to cover with makeup, they always seemed to show through.

It was a different time though, back then, and the sanctity of marriage was one of the few things respected to an almost religious level by the residents of Sycamore Lane. And if a brutish husband knocked his wife around once a month, what business was it of anyone's? Even Olivia Grady would agree to that. It was a terribly sad thing, she'd say later, when the police came to her home for a statement, but what could you do? He was her husband.

When the baby came, Bob was away, on one of his many, many business trips. Olivia Grady had been kind enough to drive Barbara to the hospital late in the night. She labored alone, no one even knowing what number to call to find Bob at, and she did not provide one either. In the hospital gown, beneath the fluorescent lights, it was obvious that the dog attack suffered by Barbara all those years before had been much much more severe than anyone realized. Scarred furrows raked down her chin and neck, marring the delicate bone and skin of her clavicle. Her thighs were ravaged with deep grooves. Olivia Grady could only imagine the beast must have straddled her chest, biting at her throat, its hind legs clawing her thighs to find purchase.

Barbara was the model patient, grunting and sweating, never swearing, barely speaking, and a scant few hours later, a tiny wet baby slid out. As Olivia Grady tells it, she gasped, looking from doctor to nurse, aghast. Barbara was exhausted, head leaned away, waiting for the sound of squeals and cries. Olivia could only stare, hand over her mouth.

The baby was covered with hair. A dark downy fur from tip to tail. There was no actual tail, just a regular baby bottom at least. And outside of the hair, the baby appeared ruddy, rubbery, and normal. And after its passages were cleared it sobbed and roared with the angry vehemence of only the healthiest newborn.

The fur though was a scandal, even after the doctor assured both mother and mother's nosy friend that it was normal. The hairy body, called Lanugo, would shed on its own. But Olivia had been a mother three times over already, and had been there for her sister, and for her sister-in-law's births, and had never seen a baby as hairy as this one.

The baby was a girl, which Barbara named Isolde. Isolde was the talk of the street. What a strange name. Why not Sue, or Pamela or any number of normal names? And so hairy. New mother and baby received a lot of visits from the neighbors when she came home. Arms laden with gifts and casseroles, but all secretly wanting to spy the oddly named furry baby and see inside the home.

But, true to the doctor's words, in a manner of weeks after coming home, the baby was as smooth and soft as a normal baby, no fur to be seen. And Bob had returned, so no one else, besides Olivia Grady, dared come up to their door anymore.

With a newborn in the house, Bob's behavior became more curious to the residents of Sycamore. His absences were longer, leaving a young wife and new babe all alone for weeks at a time. And when he was there, he never helped fix up the house, or even mowed the lawn. Even on weekends when he was home, he would stay buttoned up in that little house, the shades drawn. The only clue he was home at all was his big green Ford in the driveway. Or his threadbare bathrobe spied at seven a.m. for the paper.

People gossiped at the grocer as Barbara filled her basket with bottles of Rye whiskey. Steak and whiskey overwhelmed her cart week in and week out. And the talk of Bob the alcoholic, Bob the abusive layabout of a husband, continued with even more fervor.

Barbara seemed happy though, as a new mother, and although she had the puffiness under her eyes, and the visible bruises at her wrists, she smiled and showed off her baby. Isolde had turned into a lovely, chubby child. Her hair was redder than her mother's and her eyes a pale sea glass green. But there was no mistaking the relation; they were the spitting image of one another. Very little of Bob could be seen in the child, which the neighborhood unanimously agreed was a good thing.

Isolde was a charmer too, cooing and waving, smiling toothlessly at all the fawning and attention. Barbara was seen more around town when Isolde was little, proudly pushing her pram, bringing the baby to story hours at the library where she volunteered. She would even bring the baby to the local nursing home to cheer up the seniors there. Isolde was a spark of light everywhere she went.

Bob, if it was possible, had become all the more cloistered up in their home as Isolde grew. By the time Isolde was preschool age, no one even saw him emerge for the paper any longer. Only the green car sometimes there, sometimes not, told the neighborhood he even lived there any longer.

Isolde got older, and eventually started school. She was a shockingly beautiful child, the kind that takes your breath away, like a perfect china doll had been breathed into life. Her red hair fell heavy and wavy down her back, her strangely pale green eyes wreathed with thick dark lashes. She was shy though, painfully so, her reticence to speak in class worrying teachers that she was unable to speak at all. The bubbly infant had turned into a very serious little girl.

Mother and daughter were seen less frequently, and often whispering to one another. That was how Isolde communicated mostly, whispering to her mother, and her mother relaying. Barbara seemed perfectly fine with this arrangement, which caused the rumor mill on Sycamore Lane to explode into a fury of gossiping hordes. The child was simple, the child had been strangled by Bob and had damaged vocal chords, the child was crazy, Barbara was crazy and made the child afraid of outsiders... the list went on and on, growing more fantastical with every phone call and every tea cup it passed by.

Although shy and practically non-verbal, Isolde was a good student, and though she had no close friends – the few attempts to schedule play dates with Olivia Grady went decidedly unwell apparently – she was not disliked. Martha Plomp of 150 Sycamore Lane asked her young daughter, who was in the same class as Isolde, and her child just shrugged. "She's spooky. But okay I guess," was her reply.

Spooky.

Time passed on Sycamore Lane, and the green Ford was now more in the driveway than not. Doris Heath, the aged head librarian, reported that Barbara had told her that Bob had lost his job.

Less and less was Barbara seen out now, and Isolde, a young lady now more than a child, would run errands, to the store and such.

Buying the whiskey and meat that the family seemed to consume exclusively. What got the butcher talking, and the cashiers, were the bruises, so like the ones her mother had. At the wrist, at the neck. As if someone had grabbed her, or tied her down. Not every time she was there, not even every other. Infrequently.

Barbara had volunteered at the library, until one day a letter arrived there – a resignation letter – saying her family needed her too much but thanked them for all the wonderful times. Doris Heath was worried; she would later talk to Olivia Grady about it. The handwriting was sloppier than Barbara's normal script, and Doris even wondered if it was Barbara's at all.

Isolde continued to attend school, now tall and willowy, her hair a shock of copper, heavy and coiling down her back. Her eyes still that same strange green. She was beautiful, intimidatingly so, and although her nickname around school was still 'Spooky' the young boys had started to take notice.

Derek Grady, one of Olivia's own children, asked her to the homecoming dance. He told police later that she seemed surprised to be asked, and blushed. She said yes and it was the talk of the entire school. Perhaps Spooky was actually just shy with a crazy mom and a drunk for a dad. Maybe Sycamore Lane just needed to leave a quiet girl from a rough home alone. Olivia was even supportive of the arrangement, knowing Barbara as she did: or as well as anyone did. She was a nice person. A good girl; surely her daughter would be the same.

When the night of the dance arrived, Derek nervously hurried up the walk, passing the chain link fence that screeched with disuse. He could hear neighborhood dogs barking, causing a terrible racket down the way. This was not too surprising since those damned dogs, Old Man Walker's of 68 Sycamore Lane to be precise, would pick an arbitrary few days to bark and bark and bark. And as soon as it would start, it would stop. It was a strange thing that happened as long as Derek had been alive.

He got to the door and was just about to ring the bell, sweat soaked, knees knocking. He feared Bob would open the door, and he would have to make small talk with the intimidating, rheumy-eyed man. As his finger poised above the buzzer a dreadful racket exploded from within. A scream, genderless in its fear, tore through the house, rattling the glass panes. Derek panicked, unsure if he should run, frozen in place by indecision. Something slammed against the door, the wood splintering. He fell backwards down the few cement steps. Another scream, angry and bestial, shook the door frame.

Derek crab-walked away and down the pathway, calling for help. Before he reached the chain link fence, the front door exploded out, the shotgun blast splintering the wood and sending it raining down. Derek dropped onto his belly in the lawn. Timidly he lifted his head an inch and could see movement through the hole. Bob, wearing a soiled undershirt, shotgun raised, his shirt torn.

While Bob's back was to him, the boy stood and ran to the rusty gate, fiddling with the latch. He nearly had it when Bob slammed against the door. His fleshy back was forced through the shattered wood, ridden down by something dark and massive. His first thought was bear, his second jaguar. Neither made sense, but his brain had frozen as he stood on the lawn, corsage wilting in its plastic cube, while a dark mass of fury ripped Bob apart, savaging his throat and chest. When Derek screamed, the thing froze, its head raised, its eyes a glassy strange green.

Its black lips pulled back, revealing pink, bloodstained teeth, lethally long, and a growl reverberated. He fled. Vaulting the fence, dropping the forgotten corsage, he ran screaming down the sidewalk, police sirens already wailing in the background.

When the police arrived, the scene at the house was baffling. Derek sat in one of the cars with his mother, the ubiquitous scratchy wool blanket over his shoulders and soiled tux. Bob's body lay sprawled outside on the front steps, his throat absent, a dark hole in its place. His yellowed eyes stared out, filmed over, dead.

Inside the house provided even less answers. The walls were scratched up, furniture broken. In the basement they found Barbara, huddled up, nude, bound at the wrist and throat to the concrete wall with a rusty chain. Her chest torn open, her torso traced with scars new and old. The blood surrounded her like a lily pad. Her heart was missing.

Isolde was nowhere to be found. Her room untouched, a pink dress laid out on the bed, pink shoes below on the floor, waiting.

Sycamore Lane had reached a fevered pitch, its gossip mills running at full capacity. Were they sex fiends? Or perhaps they kept exotic pets inhumanely in their basement? A ferocious wild cat that had finally escaped? And where was Isolde?

They had seemed like a nice family, people would whisper. Barbara was so loved down at the library, Doris would say. Olivia would click her tongue and remember taking Barbara to the hospital the night she gave birth. I guess you never really know anyone, she would say.

Derek Grady would often close his eyes, from that night on, and find those strange sea glass eyes staring back at him. He did not admit to anyone who those eyes reminded him of. Needless to say, he never slept much.

It was all such a shame.

HoodRatz
by John F. Allen

Haughville, IN 1979

Chills crept along Charlene's spine.

She slowly opened her eyes and peeked out from beneath her sheets. Shafts of moonlight squeezed through the holes in her blinds. The humid night air clung to her skin and caused a layer of sweat to form. The air from the opened window carried the odor of grass and sewage that burned her nostrils with its pungency.

The room sat in silence as casted shadows formed grotesque shapes across her bed. Glowing red numbers from her alarm clock were the only other source of light in the room, 3:16 AM.

Scritch, scritch…

A faint scratching sound came from across the room and under her bed. *My imagination had gotten the best of me,* she thought.

Scritch, scritch…

There it is again!

Something was watching her.

Charlene scanned the room for the source of her torment. She shrank towards the center of the bed. She trembled with fear, as bright red eyes burned in the shadows like stars in a clear midnight sky.

"What the hell is in here?"

The scarlet orbs stared at her without blinking. The hair on Charlene's hackles raised as tendrils of terror tore through her psyche. She pulled the sheet over her head and curled into a ball. Loud squeaking sounds blended with the scratching and grew louder with each second that passed.

Tiny tugs on the sheet sent a wave of frightful chills down her spine. Her breaths came in short bursts and she squeezed her eyes shut. She hoped that at any minute she would wake from this nightmare. The noises grew louder as the weight of several oblong shapes squirmed over her body in frantic motions. The prodding of tiny clawed feet sent ripples of panic through her mind.

"Get away from me," Charlene screamed.

She kicked and screamed at the sheets in an attempt to dislodge the intruders.

The room lit up in bright white light.

Startled, she blinked away spots.

A familiar voice spoke into the room. "Charlene, what's wrong?" She took in Kevin, who stood by the light switch with a curious look on his face.

The intruders were gone. She glanced out of the corner of her eyes and tried to play it off. "Nothing, go back to bed."

"It didn't sound like nothing with you screaming like that."

She turned to look at her little brother. "Go back to bed, I said."

He looked at her and stuck out his tongue. She threw her pillow at him as he slammed her door.

Mama might bitch at her in the morning, but she left the light on while she tried to go back to sleep. After an hour of trembling beneath the covers, she slipped away into sleep.

#

It was Friday and Charlene decided to go by the park on her way to pick Kevin up and walk him home from school. Her best friend Adele volunteered to bring her nosy ass along, much to her chagrin. When they reached the park, they saw a group of guys playing basketball on the raggedy court.

She knew she had died and gone to Heaven the first time she laid eyes on him last year. Chocolate skin, lean muscles and a tight fro, he was a ghetto Adonis. He was tall, broad shouldered and had a wide sexy smile. He reminded her of Teddy Pendergrass...so fine!

The waves of energy he exuded enveloped her as she watched him playing b-ball on the playground at Riverside Park. His shirtless torso glistened with sweat as he leapt back and forth with quick reflexes and excellent coordination. Tight red shorts hugged his sculpted ass like they were painted on. Long muscular legs ended in white knee socks and black Chuck Taylors.

All the girls she knew wanted to be with him, but so far he hadn't claimed any of them. *Why would it be any different for me?* she thought.

All Charlene knew is that she thought he was cute. She was still a virgin, unlike the other girls she knew, but if she were gonna give up her Kit Kat to anyone, she wanted it to be him. She just wasn't sure she was ready yet.

Charlene often liked to spend the summer checking out the hot guys playing basketball at the park. Ever since she graduated last year, she spent most of her free time – what little she had – away from home. She spent so much time looking after her little brother Kevin that she sometimes felt like she'd been the one who gave birth to him. At ten, he was far from a baby, but he was too young to really take care of himself. Momma felt that he was impressionable and feared that the streets would claim him, much like they did their father shortly after Kevin's birth.

"Girl, are you listenin' to me?" Adele snapped Charlene out of her fantasy.

"Yeah, sure," Charlene stammered.

"Liar! You all up in La La Land daydreamin' about Tyrese. I don't even see why you wastin' your time on him. He ain't nothin' but trouble."

I'm sure he is, Charlene thought. *Just the kinda trouble I want to get into.*

"How would you know?"

"You know he's the leader of that gang called The HoodRatz. They say that Marcy Evans was last seen with him before she disappeared last year," Adele said.

"Please, that heifa was strung out and ran away from her ho ass mama and drunk ass father. She's probably in Chicago somewhere suckin' dicks and getting high."

"Naw, I don't think so. My cousin Erica and her were friends and she said that Marcy planned to leave, but she was headed down to Kentucky to go to college."

"Just because she went off and left doesn't mean that Tyrese was the reason," Charlene said.

"Well it don't matter much anyway because he ain't studdin' you anyhow."

As Charlene decided she'd had enough of listening to Adele talkin' out the side of her neck, she glanced back at the court and caught Tyrese looking at her. His deep set, espresso eyes bore into her. A shudder traveled down her spine and sent tendrils of electricity through her body. Hot air gushed over her like an oven. Tiny pinpricks nipped at her nerve endings.

His gaze held her, gave her roots and drowned out everything and everyone else. The basketball had been passed and was headed straight for his head, but in one deft motion, he caught it in one hand.

It was damnedest thing Charlene had ever seen.

He tossed the ball back to the other players and walked towards her. She could smell almonds and brown sugar, as though the scent materialized from nowhere. A sly grin spread across his face as he kept moving in her direction. Although she had been captured by his eyes, she couldn't help but notice the swagger in his stride. His thick manhood bounced with every step like a snake in thrall of a charmer.

"Yo Tyrese, you gonna play ball or what?" a large, bearish looking guy barked.

Tyrese turned his head and cut the other man a narrow-eyed glance.

"I better get back to the game, I'll catch you later," he said with a grin.

Gooseflesh covered Charlene's entire body. She didn't care what Adele said, she had already been seeing him secretly for months and tonight might be the night that he made her his woman.

#

The evening started out like any other. Charlene had fixed dinner while her mother slept. She'd fed her little brother, helped him with his homework, and went to her room to listen to the radio in solitude. Her mother worked the graveyard shift at Wishard Hospital, sometimes taking extra shifts just to make ends meet. She hated that her mother was hardly home, and often times she was saddled with the responsibility of caring for Kevin.

Charlene yearned for more out of life than being single, saddled with two kids and barely surviving at a dead-end job. Her father had left them soon after Kevin was born and none of them had heard anything from him since. There had been plenty of ignorant ass Negroes sniffin' around her mama over the years, but none of them wanted to stick around and help raise some other dude's kids.

She had always known that she wanted more out of life. Charlene always dreamed of the glamorous life like the white folks on Dynasty.

Her thoughts immediately turned to Tyrese. Tall, handsome, and he got money. She knew that slinging rock was very different than drilling for oil, but this was still the hood...you did what you had to do to survive!

It was about six o'clock when she heard her mother stirring around in the kitchen. Usually she didn't get up until around ten. Charlene wasn't sleepy yet and it was Friday night, so she decided to take the opportunity find out why her mother was up so early. Charlene stood in the doorway and watched as her mother set the coffee maker to brew before she dug around in the refrigerator to put together some food to take to work.

She wore a torn housecoat, and her large afro sprawled atop

her head resembled a used Brillo pad. Charlene loved and admired her mother, despite the fact that she didn't envy her lot in life. She knew that she was a strong woman to deal with the hand she had been dealt and continue to keep her faith.

"Are you just gonna stand there and stare at me, or are you gonna say somethin'?"

Charlene smiled. She swore that this woman had eyes in the back of her head. "Hey, Mama."

Her mother continued to move about the kitchen with a purpose borne of habit. Once she had set all the food she needed on the counter, she paused to turn towards Charlene. Black circles masked her eyes as red veins threatened to replace the whites. Her haggard expression and slumped posture aside, she was still an attractive woman, another thing that Charlene admired about her.

"What do you want?" her mother asked.

"I heard you up and wanted to see what was going on," she said.

"I'm going in early to pick up a few extra hours before I start my double shift. Kevin is going to spend the night over the neighbor boy's house tonight."

"Oh…" Charlene said.

She gave her a stern look and pursed her lips. "You thinkin' about going out to see that boy, ain't you?"

Charlene's mouth opened slightly, but she was unable to

speak. Her mind raced to counter her mother's question.

"You don't have to say a word. I already know."

Charlene let an uneasy smile spread across her face. "What exactly do you know, Mama?"

"I know you went by the park on your way home from school and talked to that fool, even though I told you to stay away from him."

The weight of her mother's words lingered in the air as she hung her head low.

This woman is always up in my business, she thought. *Then again, it was probably Adele's ass that told her.*

"I don't work a shitty ass job to send you to school and save up money for you to take night classes after you graduate for you to be following up after some knucklehead-ass drug dealer. You gonna fool around and end up knocked up and he ain't gonna be nowhere around to help your ass."

"Like mother, like daughter," Charlene said, a split second before her mother's hand lashed out and struck her across the face.

The stinging of her cheeks registered in her mind. Anger welled up inside of her as she glanced in her mother's direction.

"You best watch your mouth, little girl! I tell you what, you want to go chasin' that no good Negro, then go right ahead, but don't think I'll be bending over backwards to help you deal with the mess you make of your life."

Charlene stood in silence and gritted her teeth. "Yes ma'am."

She turned to continue getting her food ready for work.

Charlene went back to her room and knew without a doubt that she had to get the hell out of there. She waited an hour after she heard her mother leave and called Tyrese.

#

Charlene had been sneaking out every weekend when her mother worked double shifts to meet with Tyrese. Sometimes they walked around The Circle downtown and held hands. Other times, they would spend hours in his ride smoking weed, drinking Colt 45, making out, or, on a good night, all three. He had been patient and never forced himself on her. He had stopped when she asked, but he was also very possessive of her. He wanted to know where she was and who she was with at all times.

She didn't like his attitude in that regard, but because he had been so patient and because he was so fine, she put up with it. He never laid his hands on her, but she saw him beat the shit outta some guy who catcalled her downtown once. It was exciting that a man would fight over her, but scary that she had to beg him not to kill the guy.

Tyrese decided he wanted them to stay in that night. They smoked a couple joints and drank malt liquor until she felt herself become giddy. Smoke and liquid courage dropped her inhibitions.

"So, what are we going to do tonight?" she asked. A sly smile spread across her face and she giggled.

Tyrese flashed an impish grin. "I've got something to show you."

He led her to his bedroom and shut the door behind them. She sat on the bed and kicked off her boots. The room was large and dark accept for an orange lava lamp.

"Let me turn on a brighter light," Charlene said, as she reached for a lamp on the nightstand.

Tyrese quickly reached out and grabbed her wrist. "No, I like it like this."

"Let go of me, you're hurting me," Charlene said.

Charlene didn't imagine her first time going down like this. She wanted Tyrese to be gentle and understanding. She thought she was ready, but being manhandled was not sexy.

"Shut the hell up! How long did you think I was gonna keep giving you free weed and beer, without getting something in return? I own these streets and tonight I own your ass!"

She struggled as he grabbed her other wrist and pushed her down on the bed. His breath smelled of weed and malt liquor, and he forced his mouth over hers. Charlene squirmed and kicked. Her breaths were shallow. She tried to scream, but couldn't, because he viciously gnawed at her mouth.

In her high, she was disoriented and weak. She wanted to fight back harder, but couldn't. His weight pinned her down and she could feel his hardness against her. She had wanted him to fuck her, but not like this. All of her lust for him died in that moment, only to be replaced by revulsion and terror.

"Tyrese," a gravelly voice said.

Its echo dripped with terror and stopped him in his tracks.

Both of them turned to see a young woman – not much older than Charlene – standing naked in the corner of the room. Her skin was sienna brown and her hair was a large afro.

"Who the fuck are you?" Tyrese demanded. He spun away from Charlene to face the other woman.

Her eyes glowed crimson and a cursory grin revealed large central incisors.

She chuckled.

"Don't act like you don't know me," she said. She stepped forward and further into the dim light from the lava lamp.

"Marcy," he stammered.

"Live and in living color."

"But you're…"

"Dead? Is that the word you're looking for?" she said, with a dark grin.

Charlene's high began to fade as she began to realize what she was seeing. She sat in stunned silence, unable to move or speak.

Tyrese took a step back and reached into his back pocket. He clicked the switchblade into place and dropped into a fighting stance with his arms out in front of him.

"Stay back, bitch, or I'll cut you."

Marcy closed her eyes and emitted a loud and bellowing laugh. "Fool, I don't think so."

Tyrese lunged at her with the knife, and in a blur, Marcy grabbed his wrist and twisted it. He screamed in agony. An odd lump formed in his forearm and bone pierced the skin.

Charlene shrank against the headboard and cried. She had folded her knees to her chest and wrapped her arms around them. Marcy looked in her direction.

"What do you think I should do to him, sister? Should I tear him limb from limb, or..." Marcy grabbed his testicles with her free hand and squeezed them. Tyrese attempted to scream, but it came out as whiny groan.

"...should I rip off his balls and force him to eat them?"

Charlene watched in wide-eyed horror. The faint sounds of scratching caught her ears.

Scritch, scritch...

It was the same sound she had heard in her dream last night.

Scritch, scritch...

Like soldiers marching in cadence, an army of large, elongated ovoid shapes appeared from the recesses of the room. Glowing red eyes burned in the darkness and stared at Marcy.

"Perhaps we should make him suffer? A quick death is much too kind," Marcy said.

She released Tyrese's arm and he slid into a crumpled mass on the floor.

Tyrese turned towards Charlene. "Help me," he squeaked.

She averted her eyes and buried her face into her knees. A cold shiver of fear crept along her spine and made her body a sheet of gooseflesh.

"Don't hide, you'll miss the best part," Marcy chimed.

Charlene kept her face hidden until her head was snapped back. Marcy had closed the distance between them and stared at her with eyes like fiery red orbs. "Look," she spat.

The ovoid shapes skittered around Tyrese and surrounded him. Wicked crimson stares bore into him as long tails curled around their forms. The energy in the room amped up as Marcy looked towards them.

They converged on him in a synchronized swarm. Tyrese screamed and writhed as the horde of rodents savagely gnawed at his flesh. Charlene wanted to turn away, but fear of Marcy and the surreal scene itself kept her eyes frozen in place.

A mass of rats covered his body so that only his hands could be seen. He attempted to grasp the vermin and fling them away, but for each one he dislodged, three more appeared. His bloodcurdling scream slowly turned into muted mewling and pleas for God to help him.

Hot tears stung Charlene's eyes, while his long arms came to rest on the floor and were engulfed within the squirming mass of rats. She trembled in terror and her entire body was covered in a sheet of sweat. In minutes that seemed to stretch out for hours, the rodents slowly slid away from their meal. Only the wet skeletal frame of Tyrese remained.

Marcy let go of Charlene's hair and walked towards the corpse sprawled akimbo on the floor. She kneeled. Her gaze traveled from head to toe. A grin spread across her brown face and further revealed her elongated front teeth.

"A fitting conclusion wouldn't you agree?"

Charlene looked at Marcy with wide-eyed terror.

"You have absolutely nothing to fear from me, sister. We were both seduced by this asshole's charm and victims of his wickedness," Marcy said.

"What happened to you?" Charlene managed.

Marcy smiled and stood to her full height. She kicked the skeleton in front of her, made her way to the bed, and sat down next to Charlene.

She glanced in the direction of Tyrese's corpse. "That mutha fucka kidnapped me, viciously raped me and then left me for dead on the outskirts of town. I was found by an old lady from Haiti named

Mama Marinette. She pulled me back from the brink of death and infused me with the power to no longer be a victim."

Tiny pinpricks of hot needles pierced the flesh of Charlene's body. A wave of hot energy washed over her and threatened to suffocate her in its intensity. Marcy's eyes grew larger and glowed brighter. A fine sheen of brownish-gray fur sprouted from her soft brown skin.

"You see, Mama Marinette is what the followers of voodoo call a loa – a spirit god. She is very powerful and she is very protective of her pack. We are kindred souls, you and I. Once you've become one of us and tasted the power of our queen, you'll never be a victim of a man's abuse ever again."

Charlene allowed herself to look up at Marcy. She was caught in the radiant glow of her eyes and found she could not move her body. A blur of movement, and Marcy began gnawing at Charlene's neck. Her consciousness slipped away and the room faded to black.

Intelligenterer People
by Johannes Pinter

Bobo strenuously puts his 166 kilos on the chair at the front of the classroom. As far from the bullshitters as humanly possible, just like he always has, and sets his backpack under the bench to the right. It takes him a few minutes to collect his breath again after the arduous climb up the stairs to the second floor.

He looks around. There are probably not as many eraser throwers and bullies as there were when he went to school, he thinks. Quite the contrary. Every one of the seventeen people who came here, to room A264 in the Eastern Real high school, seem okay. Proper. Geeky, his brother would've said. Bobo feels connected to them.

A guy in a white shirt and slipover comes over to check Bobo's ID.

When the clock on the front wall shows 7 PM, the guy shuts the door to the room and starts handing out pencils and A4 booklets which he places face down in front of each participant. His red-haired female colleague stands in front of the group.

"Hello and welcome to Mensa's extra admission test," she says. "It's great that so many people want to join, so we booked this bonus testing. My name is Malin. Michael here hands out the test that you will start answering in a few minutes. No person shall turn the booklets until I say so."

Bobo feels butterflies of expectation in his stomach. It's a pleasant feeling. Like when he went on the magic carpet ride at the Funhouse as a little kid, scary but safe. Today he would not manage the flying carpet – he would certainly not even get up the stairs. Nowadays the feeling comes more rarely, basically only when he enters a new expansion in WoW.

"You will have 20 minutes to answer the 45 tasks," Malin continues. "They are all graphic, progressive matrices. In each task you will select the logical continuation of a pattern of symbols. For each task, there are five possible answers of which you will select one."

Bobo knows exactly what she's talking about. He has taken a number of similar IQ tests on the Internet, including one on Mensa's own website. He has not left anything to chance. The information he hasn't understood he Googled, and found forums where people proposed solutions on how to think during a certain type of task. The key is to not just see the graphic images, but to find the logic behind them.

An example: if you have nine images, each image has a vertical line with different numbers of small white circles to the left of the line and the small black triangle to the right of the line, then simply add downward. The number of circles and triangles in the top and middle picture gives the number of circles and triangles in the bottom. The images almost always belong together in a descending order, rarely to the right as you might think of due to our habit of reading plain text. One simply must try to see the logic behind the images. As in the movie The Matrix, where people and houses and stuff really are made up of descending strings of digits.

"You cannot ask us about anything regarding the tasks. The ones you cannot answer you just skip," Malin says. "Write your name on the paper. When you are finished, you will leave the sample to Michael or me. In about a month, you will know how the test went."

A month? Bobo feels a sting of disappointment. He thought it would go faster. He wants the result tomorrow. No. He would've liked the result *today*. He wouldn't have gone home to the apartment, but straight to mom and dad's. Slammed the test result on the table. Showed them. Shown him what he's really made of!

Dad has always been at him about friends. And girls. And jobs. Comparing Bobo's ineptitude with his brother's successes. "Wow, another golf trophy, congratulations!" Or "good, another sales bonus, congratulations!" Or "Lelle really found a nice girl in Josephine, congratulations!"

As if it was easy. As if one could choose between being successful and social or not. It's not easy when it goes blank. When Bobo sits at home in his small apartment in Aspudden, in front of the computer, playing and chatting, then everything goes so smooth. Like running water. Like running zeros and ones. In real life, however, it always goes blank when he hangs out and is expected to talk about interesting things. When fat Bobo should accomplish anything, the result has always been zero and nothing. Although he's always known that he is smart and has intelligence like few others, there has not been enough. Dad has always demanded proof, black and white, of ability and success. A certificate that Bobo is intelligent enough for Mensa, that he belongs to the one percent of the country's most intelligent people, would convince the old man. Yes, that would do the job! It's now or never. Bobo can't wait to start the test!

Malin raises a stopwatch.

"Then we can start the test. You can turn your papers ... now!" she says as she starts the stopwatch.

Bobo quickly flips the booklet over, the pen already in his hand.

He begins to skim through all the tasks, so that he is mentally in sync with the quantity. Forty-five tasks in 20 minutes; that gives about 26 seconds per task. Say that he instead needs a half minute apiece for the 15 most difficult tasks. Then he has almost 22 seconds per task for the easier ones. It should work. Possibly he might need a few minutes to skim through all the answers again when he's done, to check that he hasn't made any mistakes. But it's doubtful whether a minute of skimming through 45 tasks will provide anything. Nah, it's better to make sure he doesn't make mistakes to begin with.

Bobo starts from the top. Easily fixing the initial 14 by a wide margin. On the fifteenth he gets stuck. There's something about intended squares filled with different amounts of smaller black squares that are not logical either down or to the right. He consumes nearly 30 seconds before he remembers that he must go on as not to blow his time budget altogether. He will have to return to this one later.

He manages five, six, seven more before another tricky one slows him down. A quick glance at his watch shows that he still is pretty good on schedule. He gives it 20 seconds before moving on. He'll leave the tricky ones for last and will, at worst, take a wild shot at them when everything else is finished. But it is a bit worrying that he now has two that he failed at on the first attempt. How many errors can he have and still qualify?

Bobo moves on. Makes ten at a brisk pace. Now he's made 33 tasks in 11 minutes. Nine minutes left for the last 12 tasks, plus the two tricky ones. He smiles to himself, feeling the butterflies again. Not unlike the feeling he has when his guild is about to defeat a particularly tricky boss in WoW. He will make this!

Then he encounters some difficult ones that take more than half a minute each to solve. But each solution seems solid and logical and holds when he tests them a second time.

After 17 minutes, he has worked his way through the whole booklet, and prepares to go back to solve the three tasks that were too difficult the first time. He raises his eyes to see if anyone else in the room has finished – and freezes.

Everyone behind him is lying flat on their faces, hanging over their benches. It looks a little scary. Strange. Like in a movie. What are they doing? Sleeping? Have they fainted? All of them? And at the same time? Bobo has been so involved in solving his tasks that he's neither heard or noticed how everyone for some reason has collectively lost consciousness.

He looks to Malin up front, to ask her what happened. Then he feels a sting to the neck. Before he can make a sound, the muscles in his body become as loose as overcooked spaghetti. A hand softly receives his forehead as he faints, his head dropping to the bench.

#

When Bobo awakens, he's tied to a chair. The room is dim, so it takes a while before he gets a grip on the surroundings. His head is trussed to his shoulders by some kind of metal stand. Like the one people get when they've hurt their neck. He discovers that he has a big wet spot in his crotch. He must have peed himself when he fainted. He drank a lot of Coke some time before the test, so it makes sense that it leaked when the body's muscles relaxed.

He glances around the room that seems to be an old boiler room. Once in second grade, when he and a friend played secret agents and spied on the janitor, they slipped into the elementary school basement and ended up in the boiler room. It looked almost exactly like this, except that the room had a different shape of course, but it could mean that he is still in the Eastern Real high school.

He sees that there are three other people to the left of him with the same head postures. They seem to be still sleeping.

In front of the guy on the chair remotest (a Turkish guy who Bobo recognizes from the test) stand two men dressed in white coats and surgical masks. Beside them is a small metal table on wheels. Suddenly a whining sound starts, and a moment later the shorter man begins to cut into the Turkish guy's head with a small operation drill. A haze of blood stands around the crown.

Bobo jerks at the shocking sight.

"WHAT ARE YOU DOING?" he yells, as he tries to get up.

The men immediately stop sawing. Looking at each other in surprise.

"He should be asleep, right?" says the taller of them.

"Look at his body size. I don't think the first injection was enough," says the shorter, holding the saw.

"Give him another one then!" grunts the tall man.

Bobo starts to wobble on the chair, understanding the seriousness of the situation. He doesn't want anyone to drill him in the head! He manages to get on his feet. But his calves are tied to the chair legs and his hands to the armrests, so he remains in a very uncomfortable position.

The white-robed men rush towards him, trying to hold him while the shorter one collects a syringe. Then Bobo goes mental! He always hated needles. Mommy had to hold him by force when he was vaccinated. So he begins to move toward a door at the far end of the room. He wobbles forward, rocks back and forth violently, bumping the shorter man so that he loses the syringe. It shatters against the concrete floor.

"Lasse," the longer shouts, "fetch a new one!"

"There isn't one here. The other box is left in the car."

Bobo rises like a big bear, lumbering toward the door with the two men tearing at his trunk-like torso. He pulls the ropes that hold him tight. With a bang, one of the armrests breaks. With one arm free, he pushes the short man to the floor. Bobo has never been a fighter, never had reason to solve problems in any other way than with his brain. But when it comes to physical situations, like pushing a car with a broken down engine, his size and weight come in handy. Just like now.

With a crack, the other armrest snaps. Full of self-preservation, he grabs hold of the taller man and pushes him hard against the wall. The impact makes the man pass out.

Bobo rips off his headrest. Bends down, panting and groaning as he tries to remove the ropes around his legs.

Then the door opens. Bobo looks up. A man. With a hammer.

Black.

#

The next time Bobo wakes up he's in pain. He screams in a shrill falsetto, while his brain tries to locate where he is. From a soft black hole to angry red pain in a fraction of a second. Like a Bugatti Veyron that speeds from 0 to 100 in an incredible 2.5 seconds.

Bobo winks away the tears of pain. Stares into the surprised look of a man in a white mask sprinkled with red dots. It is the short man with the drill again, Lasse.

Terrified Bobo stares at him, feeling that his head is back in the fixating metal stand.

"Gunnar ..." says Lasse.

The taller man, Gunnar, enters Bobo's view. He carries a scalpel and a shiny metal bowl. His clothes are also contaminated by red.

"Again?" questions Gunnar. "How much did you give him?"

"Double the dose."

"You should have tripled it."

Bobo looks at them. Who are they? What the hell do they do with people's heads?

"What are you doing with people's heads?" asks Bobo. He doesn't like the sight of blood, especially not his own. Right now he feels drops of it running across his temple, along the cheek and down the neck.

The door opens. Into the dark boiler room, a hunched old man with a cane enters, supported by a neatly dressed woman. Behind them is a younger man in a shirt and tie with a file tucked tightly under his arm. The old man has a dark blazer over a white shirt without a tie. The gray dry hair is tidily combed back.

"Again?" The old man stops when he sees Bobo.

"Yes. He woke up when Lasse started working on him."

"What about the others?"

Gunnar shows the contents of the large metal vessel. Bobo tries in vain to see what's in it.

"Basically ready," says Gunnar.

"Basically?" echoes the old man. "Either you are ready, or you're not."

Gunnar lowers his eyes like a reprimanded school boy. "Not ready. Have to collect a part of that guy. Well, then it's the fatty of course."

Bobo understands that it's him Gunnar is referring to. He starts tugging his arms in an attempt to break free, to get out of here. But he is now tied to a modern metal chair that won't give way as easy. He stops immediately.

"What do you want from me? Why are you doing this?" he sobs.

The neat woman turns angrily to the doctors, pointing at Bobo.

"Well give him another shot then! We cannot have him –"

"Jenny, please," the old man interrupts, putting his hand reassuringly on her arm. "He's been such a fighter, managing to struggle his way up to the surface, not only once but two times. Maybe he deserves to know. I appreciate a curious man; it's only those asking questions that have the answers."

The woman takes a step back. The old man walks up to Bobo, taking his tied hands with his claw-like fingers.

"Bobo? My name is Jay. Nice to meet you," says the old man.

"It was Mr. Alastair who started Mensa in Sweden," the tie man proudly fills in.

"Thank you, Henry," the old man says. He considers Bobo's head. "Oh my!"

He produces a handkerchief from the breast pocket of his blazer, and wipes Bobo's left temple with it. A red stain blossoms on the handkerchief.

Bobo swallows hard, pushing aside an impulse to faint. He looks at the old man.

"What are you doing with me? Why would you cut me in the head? "

"Bobo ... Have you heard of *Sophos Aponoimosyni?*"

Bob tries to shake his head.

"It's a science that was started by Mensa in the U.S," the old man continues. "After having successfully tested and developed it over a couple of years in the sixties, we began to practice it in a number of selected Mensa associations around the world. Sweden was one of them."

"Science? Do you mean your intelligence tests?"

The old man patiently makes his best to clarify.

"No. Not the tests. I'm talking about something that we would never let the public know anything about."

The old man comes closer, more engaged, looking steadily into Bobo's eyes. Bobo notices that the old man smells of pipe tobacco and yogurt. Vanilla yogurt is quite tasty, he thinks.

"Intelligence has never been possible to point at, could not be measured with a ruler or weighed on scales. It is one of the most basic and primitive and mysterious secrets of the nature of man," says the old man. "And at the same time, it is our most important, most powerful and strongest shiny tool, that separates us from the animals. It is from the primitive corners of the world, where intelligence is facing the toughest battles against the brutish primal forces, where our science has been inspired and gotten nutrition," he says, hands raised, marking especially important words and phrases.

Bobo briefly glances at the others in the room. They listen attentively to the old man's talk.

"Have you heard of the Irokes Indians and the Tribes of the Six Nations? Or the Congolese Patriots in the UPC guerrilla?" the old man asks.

Bobo tries to gather his thoughts. Somewhere he recognizes the names and expressions, but he is too divided to be able to think really clear right now. The old man wipes the blood off Bobo's cheek once more.

"The similarity between them," continues the old man, "except that in some aspects they were very primitive cultures, was that they saw the possibility, and the extension of the profits, to absorb an enemy's strength and courage."

"Voodoo tricks?"

"No, no. By *anthropophagi*," replies the old man.

Despite his condition, Bobo knows what *that* means. He grimaces when he realizes what the man is talking about. Man-eating. Cannibalism.

"By eating the flesh of their enemies, they could benefit from its strength. By eating the enemy's heart, they could assimilate its courage. What we found, after years of research, was that one also could benefit from another person's intelligence."

The old man waves at the taller doctor.

"Gunnar."

The doctor holds up the metal bowl in front of Bobo. It is filled to a third with gray porridge like human brain.

Bobo leans forward as much as the fixing head position allows, and vomits so hard it splashes on the old man's sailor shoes.

Sailor shoes? Who wears sailor shoes in November?

The others in the room instinctively step back. But the old man stands still.

"*Sophos Aponoimosyni* is Greek for Wisdom of Intelligence," says the old man. "The board management in each selected country shall each year consume the seekers' intelligence. To, as we say, secure the level of the brain trust."

Bobo coughs and spits, trying to get rid of the mucus that smears his palate. He shakes his head, and a few drops of blood drip onto his green-gray sweater.

"People can't just disappear. People will miss us. Miss *me*."

Then, the tie man steps forth, opening the file he carries under his arm.

"Unfortunately I have to disagree with you on that. Do you know how big a percentage of the people seeking entry into Mensa are living alone? People who haven't been able to find anyone to share their life with? People that don't have anyone to go home to, or anyone that will miss them after taking the test?"

Bobo sighs. "Many," he whispers.

The tie man nods.

"When it's time for a smart boost we collect all of our inquiries that are living alone for a special test occasion," he says. "Afterwards, it takes days before someone is missing. By then, the traces back to the test cooled long ago."

Bobo's misty brain tries to digest the information.

"You get intelligenterer?" he asks.

"Intelligenterer?" the old man grins. "Yes, something like that."

He gives the tie man a sign to back off. Allows the neat woman to take his arm and leaves the room. The shorter doctor gets a new syringe filled all the way up. Bobo looks at the sharp needle. He will never get used to syringes. Then he thinks of something.

"Wait," Bobo says. "How much?"

The old man stops.

"How much what?"

"How much did I score on the test?"

The old man looks at the tie man, who opens his file again. Browsing. Finds the right side that he shows to the old man.

"You had three issues remaining, but it is within the margin of error. You made it, welcome to Mensa. Congratulations," the old man says and leaves.

Bobo smiles. Imagine that! To slap that in the face of Dad. To finally be able to show him, in black and white, what he's really capable of.

Then he feels a sting in his neck.

Poetry Among The Ruins
by Frank Roger

Doyle was happy when he arrived in Beresford Heights. The road was in a bad state of repair and even for an experienced mountain biker the ride had been difficult.

Beresford Heights was after all a ghost town, must have been for a considerable time. No one ever came here anymore, apart from Doyle. The road was closed off for all regular traffic.

He came here because he found inspiration in the town, stripped of its population for God knew how long. He hadn't bothered to research the place's history. That was not what interested him. The ideas for many of the best poems he had produced in recent times had been sparked off by walks down the desolate streets and squares of Beresford Heights. He had discovered the place by accident on one of his frequent mountain bike rides, revelled in its tragic beauty, made some pictures and yielded to its apocalyptic charms.

As soon as he had recovered from the ride, he started his "city tour." He took the route that would lead him to the town centre with the partly collapsed church. Arriving at the market square with its once majestic buildings always felt like a homecoming: after walking the streets lined with buildings slowly crumbling to dust, the view of the town's no doubt most picturesque part was simply breathtaking.

Even though he had visited this place many times before, he was once again awe-struck and stood still, taking in the sight of the town hall, the church and other magnificent architecture – still impressive despite or perhaps because of its poor condition.

He wondered how life must have been here, back in the days when Beresford Heights was still inhabited. He closed his eyes, tried to conjure up images of the place bristling with activity. Who had lived here? What kind of community had it been? Did they have their own poets too? Had they ever realised their town would one day inspire visiting poets, long after they had left for greener pastures?

He opened his eyes again, the bleak desolation of the ruins replacing his fantasy images. The spires and dome of the church, partly collapsed but still catching the sun's light. Weeds and small shrubs growing between cracks in the pavement, reclaiming territory once lost to man. The eroded gargoyles jutting from the façade of what probably was the town hall.

Wait a second… Doyle peered closer at the gargoyles. He had seen them before on his previous visits, but either they were different now, or he mistook them for similar structures elsewhere in town. He reached for his camera and took a few pictures. Would the earlier ones still be there? He didn't take that many pictures and changed the memory stick only when it was full.

He quickly checked. Yes, there they were, pictures of the very same façade, taken on a previous occasion. The gargoyles were barely recognisable as such, whereas now they were in better shape, even if still partly eroded away. Yet this made no sense. Their condition could not have improved. What was this supposed to mean? Was this something exceptional, or were there other cases of ruined architecture somehow "repairing" itself?

He did a tour of the square, but could find no further evidence. He recalled having taken some pictures inside the church, and decided to go back there and compare. Only part of the structure could still be visited – the dome's collapse had brought down vast quantities of debris, closing off half of the interior.

Thanks to the enormous hole in the roof, sufficient light came in to have a good view. He looked at his pictures and found to his amazement that the outcroppings on the walls were bigger now than they had been before. Were these perhaps rudimentary decorations that "grew" or "reappeared" from the walls? Were these buildings possessed by some kind of life, a cancerous fever that produced this inexplicable effect?

This is ridiculous, he thought, there is no such kind of life. Stones and brickwork are inanimate. Deserted buildings may sag and collapse, but they don't consciously assume different shapes. They are subject to erosion, but there's nothing that can reverse the process, apart from human hands which were absent here.

Yet it was clear from the evidence in his camera and from his current observations that this place was being transformed, more precisely undoing the damage caused by erosion. Perhaps this process could be defined as "life", in the widest sense of the word.

What if a new kind of life had developed here, a strain running parallel with organic life and hitherto undiscovered? Maybe this "life" only occurred where there was no organic life, or where organic life had vanished a long time ago. Or just suppose the life force of the original population still hovered here, and was now turned into this bizarre kind of pseudo-life?

Doyle shook his head. I shouldn't get carried away like this, he thought. There's no point in coming up with all sorts of crackpot theories. I'm not a scientist, I lack the knowledge to produce a sound explanation for this phenomenon. And basically that's not what I'm after. I came here to find inspiration. Well, isn't this magical discovery inspiring? Shouldn't I simply marvel at it, try to take in as much of it as I can, and draw creative power from it? The results might be awesome.

So let's proceed that way, he decided. I'll explore this place and revel in its mysterious splendour. And when I've seen enough, I'll go back and inform others of what I've found. They'll just have to deal with it as they see fit.

He did a quick tour of the still accessible part of the church, staring at every irregular piece of brickwork, wondering if its shape was due to the collapse or to the phenomenon he had just discovered.

As he passed by the stairs leading to the crypt, he hesitated.

He remembered the entranceway from his previous visits, but had considered it too dangerous to go down. If the already damaged roof or walls yielded while he was in there, he would be trapped, beyond any help. Yet now he felt a strange urge to explore the crypt. He realised he would have to take extreme care, and return as soon as he no longer felt safe.

To his relief nothing happened as he slowly descended the flight of stairs. The crypt turned out to have suffered only minor damage. Shafts of light pierced through cracks and crevasses, offering him a limited view while creating a chiaroscuro effect of stunning beauty.

Slowly he advanced, allowing his eyes a few moments to adjust to the murk. Although the roof and the walls were still largely intact, everything seemed strangely bent and warped, as if tectonic forces were tearing this place apart. Could it be the phenomenon was more active down here, did it perhaps originate from under the surface of the earth and slowly work its way up? Had the church collapsed because its foundations were shaken by this disjointing force?

What unfathomable process is going on here? And is it a form of life, radically different from anything known to science so far, or just a force of nature still waiting to be discovered by man? Was he imagining things, or were the floor, walls and roof actually moving, even if barely perceptibly so? And could he see it so well thanks to the few rays of sunlight coming through, or did these ancient stones produce their own pale light? Did fluorescence mean life? Or was his overly receptive mind playing tricks on him, was he seeing what he desperately wanted to see?

It doesn't matter whether I'm witnessing an unusual kind of life or not, he reminded himself. I should merely expose myself to it, allow this eerie but fascinating force to suffuse my being, to titillate my creativity. It might lead to inspiration of an unprecedented level, to poetry of a mesmerising quality.

He slowly made his way around the crypt, soaking up the atmosphere until he could almost feel the force throbbing in his veins. There was definitely a presence here, indefinable yet almost tangible. Were the faint ripples that ran through the structure caused by the flickering and shifting beams of light, or was this place actually trembling ever so slightly? Was this evidence of the powers he believed to be at work here? He squinted, trying to determine the true nature of his surroundings. Did the light, however faint, brighten and darken with a sort of pulsating quality? No, he probably just grew tired and his vision was blurring in this murky environment. He should try to remain level-headed and not jump to conclusions.

He did his final tour of inspection, then rested a while, leaning against a wall and panting. He wished he could stay here longer, but realised it was better to leave before nightfall. He wouldn't like to ride back in the darkness, what with the road in bad condition and unlit. That would be way too dangerous.

But what an incredible experience this has been, he thought, as he turned around and retraced his steps, tearing himself loose from the strangely soothing surroundings of the crypt. Emotionally involving, enriching beyond imagination, but also physically exhausting.

It was only when he walked up the stairs that he realised how tired he was. Maybe he hadn't rested enough after his bike ride, or maybe his exploration of the city and especially the church and its crypt had sapped his reserve more than he had assumed.

When he finally came out into the open, he noticed that the sky was darkening already. I must have spent more time in there than I imagined, he thought. But I can't go back right away. I just have to sit and rest for a while. A heavy bike ride awaited him after this eventful day, but he would have to postpone it until he had gathered the necessary strength for it.

He sat down on a socle that must have supported a pillar or a statue in bygone days, and felt how fatigue gave way to drowsiness. Too bad there's no hotel here anymore where I could check into, he thought. Or at least a building offering shelter for the night. But of course spending the night here was out of the question. As soon as he had recovered his strength, he would jump on his bike and get back home.

But right now he needed to take a short nap. Totally drained of energy, he yielded to sleep.

#

"I'm afraid we found no trace of Doyle," the rescue team's leader said. "Fortunately the man had told a few friends where he had gone to, so when he was missing for more than a day, we knew where to look.

"We are sure that he went to the deserted town of Beresford Heights indeed, as we found his mountain bike and his camera, in two different locations. There is no evidence indicating an accident or violence. His bike was parked against a wall, without any damage whatsoever. His camera showed pictures of the town, and of the interior of buildings, which was apparently of great interest to him.

"We were led to believe he was strongly attracted to the ghost town of Beresford Heights, where he was a regular visitor. The rumours that Doyle decided to stay in the town he liked so much appear unfounded. My team searched the entire place, and found no evidence of Doyle's presence anywhere. We have no idea what happened to him. His current whereabouts are a complete mystery.

"There's little more I can say. The town is in ruins, with most of its structures partly collapsed or about to collapse. There's no way someone could live there.

"There's one final thought I'd like to offer for what it's worth. We were struck by a statue of a resting or thinking man on the central square. It was the only thing in town that wasn't damaged or time-worn, as if it had been put there recently. It formed a marked and inexplicable contrast with the rest of the ravaged city."

Voodoo 101

by Eden Royce

You will be tested
Many before you have passed.
Can you do it, cher?

You've studied the spells
But this time, it's a closed book.
You foolish chile. Think.

Moon fat in the sky
Fill the bowl – a wooden one
Time is ticking down

Chant over that bowl
Blood from the heart of a bat
Discard all the rest

Teacher is watching.
Tie the Devil's shoestrings tight
He got a long run

It's hot in this room

Powdered brick and graveyard dirt

In gritty lines on your face

Nine minutes to go

Grinding it all into paste

No one else matters.

Teacher approaches

You look up, hopeful you've passed

Hold up your bowl

She touches the ash

With a trembling brown finger

The sign of the cross

Mixes with your sweat

Seeps into your weary flesh

Your will is now hers

She smiles tenderly.

You live for that smile only

It is night and day

You have passed the test

"Go now, my zonbi," she says.

"There is much to do."

Watcher
by Leigh Jenkins

Every day he watched.

Not that it was creepy, his watching the Presbyterian church – at least, that's what he told his doctor. Ed visited Dr. Johns once a month, as ordered by the state, and no more.

The rest of the days he watched. Sure, on Wednesday he visited the men's group home, where the nice man and woman from the Presbyterian church came and read from their big book. And every other Saturday his sister came down from Hillsboro and took him to lunch at the café, where he could order fried chicken.

But the rest of the time he watched, sitting silently at his window on the second story, looking down onto the parking lot of the church, the front glass door just out of sight behind a tree. Big glass windows lined the white concrete slabs that contained the preschool. To the left of the doors was the sanctuary. Having been built much earlier than the preschool, the sanctuary was wood-paneled, inside and out. Fewer windows on that side, but a large pyramid atop the building for the roof. A few trees littered the outside, but it was mostly a parking lot, with a decrepit old backboard that had long lost its hoop standing guard along the edge.

There was a playground as well, a bit down the hill from the preschool, but Ed rarely looked to the playground, as it was constantly filled with the wives of doctors and lawyers, all sitting along a bench their husbands' hard-earned-money paid for. Occasionally a child would run up to a mother and stretch out a grubby hand to be rewarded with a cookie or bottle of juice. Satisfied, the child would then run off like a wild thing, shrieking. Ed always hated the time between one and three when the playground was most crowded. It made the watching that much harder.

Shelly, the young woman who Ed's sister was currently paying to stay with him, did not seem to mind the watching. Barbara, the older woman who was there before, seemed to hate it and would try to pull him away from the window, sending him into one of his fits. He had ended up at the emergency room more than once that way, until his sister had finally brought in Shelly, who only seemed happy that Ed was occupied.

Certainly, though, she would be upset if she knew that he woke from his bed after only an hour of sleep to return to his window every night. Shuffling to his chair, pulling back the pink frilly curtain, and peering through the dark night. The Presbyterian church had only one street light, although the youth minister, always the last person out, would often leave a light or two on inside by accident. She was young, and by far Ed's favorite of the church employees, her late night comings and goings impossible to predict. The others at the church, save the pastor, had strict schedules, other demands on their day. And the pastor never graced the door of the church past eight. It was only the young youth minister, her black hair always tied at the base of her neck, who could be seen at all hours.

Ed's favorite times were the lock-ins. At one of the Wednesday night suppers he managed to stutter out to the nice man from the Presbyterian church that sometimes, and without warning, there were kids at the church with the youth minister, coming in and out of the church all night, never seeming to sleep. The man had laughed and said those were called lock-ins; during them, all the teens stayed at the church and attempted to not sleep. His reassuring voice made Ed feel better, and he now looked forward to lock-ins, as they gave him no end of things to watch.

It was a warm night, perfect for a lock-in, when Ed witnessed what he should not have.

A dark black car that Ed did not recognize pulled into the parking lot. Two large men, one with gloves and a red ball cap pulled low over his face, the other wearing a ski mask, climbed out and walked around to the back of the car. Ed saw then that it was old, the paint on the trunk they were now opening a different color from the rest of the car. Below it Ed could just make out the license plate. PY187.

Anxiously, Ed started to tap on the windowsill.

The man with the ball cap pulled out a crowbar and, bypassing the large glass doors, went to the first window into the preschool. He pulled the large gleaming piece of metal back and then drove into the window. His first swing missed, hitting one of the window supports instead. His friend laughed at him.

Both hands began to tap the windowsill, Ed shifting back and forth in his chair. PY187.

The second swing connected though, and the window shattered. Ed realized then that both men were wearing thick gloves as they began to pull large chunks of glass out of the window before making a hole big enough for them to climb through.

There was a keening sound, though Ed did not realize it was coming from him. PY187.

Soon both men slithered through the window, the one in the ski mask cutting his arm on a final piece of glass that had not been removed. He jerked back but made it through the window, and soon a light was turned on.

The keening noise grew louder and Ed's hands were shaking as he banged on the windowsill, the rattling growing unspeakably loud.

Soon the hall light came on. He had woken Shelly. Ed's eyes grew wide, knowing that she would never again let him watch at night. "Sleep is sleep," she would say. Knocking aside his chair, Ed dove into bed and pulled his covers up over his head, shaking. PY187.

The door to his room opened and the light from the hallway poured in.

"Damn old house," Shelly muttered before closing the door and heading back to her room. Ed waited until the light had been turned off and her door shut before standing and going to the window again.

There were more lights on, this time the one in the preschool office. Ed could see the shadows moving around and he sat on his hands to keep from tapping them. He must not make noise and bring Shelly back to interrupt the watching.

Soon the light from the preschool disappeared and Ed held his breath, waiting for the men to come through the shattered window. Soon they were back at the window, tossing a large bag out the hole, and the first one began to climb through, slowly this time.

"PY187," Ed muttered as he waited. "PY187."

Ed felt the scream more than he heard it.

The youth director didn't always drive to the church. She lived just down the street and the neighborhood seemed safe, so she often walked between work and home, doing her best to stay fit.

The first man was halfway through the window and jerked back in, cutting his other arm on the same piece of glass. Ed saw the shadow of the man with the baseball cap leave the window and suddenly there were three shadows running through the preschool, their forms slipping in and out of view as the two men chased the youth director through the connecting doors of the preschool rooms.

Ed began to sway back and forth but remained sitting on his

hands, his lips moving quickly as he muttered "PY187" over and over, watching the shadows dance.

She tried to run toward the doors, the large glass doors at the front, but there were two of them and only one of her and she could never make it. There was a back door, a door the two men wouldn't know about, and she tried for that, but they were faster than her, and now there was no escape.

Minutes passed as Ed continued to whisper, his swaying slowing to a gentle pace. Finally, the big man reappeared, moving through the window as gently as possible this time. He turned his back and leaned through the window as his partner pushed the youth minister through, her body limp, the crowbar still inside of her skull. This sight sent Ed rocking again, his muttering growing louder, but not loud enough for Shelly to hear.

"PY187, PY187, PY187."

Soon the youth minister's feet were through as well and the first man placed her on the ground as the second man began to crawl out. While waiting for his friend, the big man pulled off his baseball cap and wiped the sweet from his brown hair, before replacing his cap and neatly pulling his crowbar from the youth minster's face.

The siren scared Ed as much as the two men. Startled, they looked at one another as Ed jerked forward in his seat, trying to look up and down the street for the police car. Quickly they moved, both reaching out for the bag instead of the girl, and lifting it easily as they ran to the car. How forgetful they had become of her, tossing the bag into the back seat and leaping into the car, the one without the cuts on his arms driving. The siren was growing louder now as the two men pulled away, turning to go through the neighborhood behind the church rather than onto the street towards the siren.

But it wasn't for them. The siren moved swiftly past the Presbyterian church and the youth minister's body, going off into some other world. Ed continued to sit, watching over the youth minister and muttering.

That was how Shelly found him the next morning, shaking back and forth, as she delivered his English muffin to him.

"PY187!" Ed said with conviction, now that Shelly was awake and could not force him back to sleep. He pointed out the window. "PY187!"

Shelly smiled and nodded, placing his food down next to his chair.

"It certainly was a loud night last night," she said conversationally, walking towards the closet to pull out Ed's clothes for the day.

"PY187," Ed replied.

"Um-hum," she responded. "I think the blue slacks today."

Ed sighed and turned back towards the window. The pastor had arrived now, seeing first the window then the youth minister. He seemed shocked, reeling away from the body but soon had his cell phone out, shouting down the line. Ed tapped along the window.

"PY187," he muttered as Shelly puttered around behind him. She had just laid out his shirt and was preparing to chide him when the sirens pulled in.

"Oh not again," Shelly said with a roll of her eyes. "Those sirens kept me up last night as well."

She moved to Ed's window, looking down at the Presbyterian Church in curiosity now.

"What in the devil?"

"PY187," Ed answered.

The two then watched together as the ambulance came, no sirens this time, and collected the youth minister. By this time, the preschoolers had begun to arrive and the head of the preschool had to stand by the entrance of the church, turning each car away for the day, apologizing, and explaining what had happened in hushed tones.

Ed watched the long stream of cars, peaceful during the morning, and both he and Shelly jumped when a loud pounding came from the front door.

Shelly flew down the stairs and Ed followed at a slower pace, stopping at the top of the stairs to watch in his own house.

"I'm sorry," Shelly was saying to the police officer in the doorway. "I live here with Ed Swanson, he has several disabilities. We were both asleep last night. I know he was in his bed as I checked on him just after midnight."

"Are you sure neither you nor Mr. Swanson saw anything at all?" the police officer repeated, a slight desperation in his voice.

"I'm sorry," Shelly responded. "I am guessing there is little to go on, if you're over here asking good people who were asleep at a decent time last night. I hope you find whatever devils did this, but we certainly cannot help."

Shelly and the policeman exchanged a few more words, a phone number and a promise to be alert. Shelly closed the door, muttering to herself as she went into the kitchen to begin lunch. At the top of the stairs Ed shuffled back into his room and began to watch as the ambulance turned slowly out of the Presbyterian church, the youth minister lying in the back. Ed placed his hand upon the window in farewell.

"PY187."

Angels (When God Closes a Door)
by Jim Becker

Oh my God. What have I done?

The bed sheets rustle beneath the constant whirr of Amanda's ceiling fan. She showers while Harry Connick, Jr. croons from some movie soundtrack. I don't think I'm going to sleep tonight. Maybe never again.

We're eighteen – we're supposed to screw around. But she's the pastor's daughter. And we were meant for so much better than this. God had plans for our lives. Missionaries. Evangelists. Messengers to spread the Gospel and bring hope to the hopeless. And now, this. So much for our calling.

The water stops abruptly. Curtain rings scrape along the rod and I discern an olive figure within the steamy mirror. Oh my God. She's so beautiful.

One time. One time! I used a condom! Unlike tonight. Like it matters. It's not like she can get more pregnant.

Amanda wipes a spot clean and smiles at my reflection. I feel myself getting excited again. No! *It is better for you to lose one part of your body than for your whole body to be thrown into hell.* How am I going to explain this to my parents?

As my angel emerges from the bathroom, I cover my privates.

She drops her towel before climbing under the covers beside me. "Need me to start a cold shower?"

"We need to talk, Amanda."

She props herself up on her elbows. I look into her eyes, down to her lips, further to her breasts. *Anyone who looks at a woman lustfully has already committed adultery with her in his heart.* If I've already sinned with my heart... What's one more time, anyway?

She rolls over and rests her head on my thigh. Wet hair drips between my legs. I shiver, not altogether because of the cool water. I want to run. I want to scream. I want to hide where no one will ever find me. But there is no out now. I should have followed Joseph and run from Potiphar's wife while we were still pure. One night two months ago, and I'm on the road to becoming a father.

I clear my throat, but I have no idea what to say. We already talked and talked until we ran out of words, and that was at dinner time. It's two in the morning.

I excuse myself to the bathroom and close the door. I navigate the minefield of candles and bath supplies, then stand over the toilet. My bladder empties with a cleansing ache, and the hardness mercifully subsides.

This is not what I expected when she called and invited me to her apartment. I'd meet her roommates, she'd show me around the campus, and we'd catch up on how things were going in her first semester – not trimester.

My stomach hurts. I should eat something.

I finish my business and wrap a towel around my waist. I check with Amanda to see if she needs anything from the kitchen. She yawns.

By the time I return from the kitchen with a sandwich and two Diet Cokes, she's asleep. Naked, pure, a precious angel.

I resist the urge to drop the food and spoon with her.

God is faithful. He will not let you be tempted beyond what you can bear. But when you are tempted, he will also provide a way out so that you can stand up under it.

What now? We'll have to get married. And move. I'm sure Pastor McCormick would want us to be near family, but I can't bear the thought of the congregation gossiping about how such a good girl could have gone so wrong and what kind of a fraud I must have been. Jesus will wash me white as snow. But the church? I'll be crucified.

I wander into the living room for something to do. The television might wake someone up and I'm not supposed to be here. Amanda's roommates don't know yet.

I recite Scriptures to comfort my trembling heart. *Cast your anxiety upon him because he cares for you. Do not be anxious about anything, but in everything, by prayer and petition, with thanksgiving, present your requests to God. And the peace of God, which transcends all understanding, will guard your hearts and minds in Christ Jesus.*

The words carry no weight tonight.

I cringe at the aspartame aftertaste of my soda.

Only four months ago, our youth group conducted experiments with Diet Coke and Mentos, spraying two carbonated liters all over the center. Pastor McCormick wasn't happy, but he forgave us. "You kids have to think through potential consequences. What would happen if someone swallowed these and their stomach blew up?" We couldn't stop laughing. The youth room was always full of laughter.

I want to go back in time and plop in my favorite beanbag chair, surrounded by friends. Back to my virginity, when most of life's problems had solutions on stupid posters: Faith isn't faith until it's all you're holding on to. God plus one equals a majority. When God closes a door, he opens a window.

Amanda's bomb destroyed all of my doors. They're not just closed; they don't exist anymore.

I gaze at the sky out the window. The city's glow is too strong to see much for stars, so I turn my attention to the ground. Immediately, I feel woozy. My head spins, but I strangely feel no nausea. Is this what vertigo feels like?

I brace my hands on the sill to steady myself. Though my brain refuses to sleep, maybe my exhausted body will override it. I stagger to the sofa, flop down on my back and close my eyes.

"Dear God," escapes my mouth, a defeated whimper, but not a prayer.

A breeze rustles back issues of Utne Reader on the coffee table. Odd, I don't remember opening the window. Fourteen stories up, shouldn't the panes be permanently shut?

I return to the window, my thoughts getting dizzier with each step. I release the locking mechanism and slide the stubborn pane downward. In my haze, I accidentally nudge out a miniature flower pot.

The flower doesn't spin or come free from the plastic container as it drops out of my line of sight. No noise reaches me when it hits the ground – too small, I suppose. My forehead thunks against the glass and I spot a Rorschach splotch of dirt on the parking lot below. Thankfully, it didn't hit a car.

A brief wobble and I'm prone on the couch. Before I can succumb to slumber, light fills the room. A police spotlight? Did someone see the plant drop? Nobody's hurt, right?

I want to return to the window, but I can't until the light stops shining. I've put Amanda and myself into enough trouble for one lifetime. Paul managed his time in prison well enough, but he was a better apostle than I could ever be. Plus, he didn't sire any illegitimate children.

I crawl to the wall and count to one hundred after the light vanishes. The glass lifts much more easily than it closed.

Peeking out, I check the ground below. No body. Nobody. Thank God.

A sweet wind caresses my face and I am overwhelmed with euphoria. For the briefest of moments, I glimpse the universe. Endless majesty. Infinite glory. I experienced an orgasm less than an hour ago, but that feeling doesn't compare to the weightlessness I feel near this window.

Amanda beckons me to come back to bed. But the window beckons stronger.

I want to fly.

Young men stumble and fall, but those who hope in the Lord will renew their strength. They will soar on wings like eagles.

I force my thoughts and legs away from the window. When the devil tempted Jesus to leap off a temple, Jesus answered him, *"Do not put the Lord your God to the test."*

I roll onto the floor and wedge myself between the sofa and table. It's uncomfortable, but not nearly as distressing to deal with as my visions. If I leaped, when would I die? Would the sheer fear jolt me into a heart attack? Would my corpse bounce? Or would I reach the ground and splatter like a watermelon? I clutch at my chest, feeling my ribs pierce my heart and burst my lungs, leaving a cavity of broken glass and bloody pulp. As my skull shatters and my eyeballs pop, I am free of this mortal body. Free to be with my Lord and Savior.

My back arches from the shuddering. This must be how a seizure feels.

Amanda is suddenly here; her naked body pins me down as she grabs at my flailing arms. For different reasons, neither of us is composed enough to pray. I convulse again and my elbow jerks upward and clubs her across her temple.

She collapses like a beanbag chair on top of me, unconscious. I shake for another minute before my body comes to rest. And then, in my sinful nature, regardless of her drool on my chest, despite my mental and physical condition, I become excited.

No! *It is better for you to lose one part of your body than for your whole body to be thrown into hell.*

I struggle to my feet and rush to the window. I place my member across the sill and firmly grip the top of the pane. With every bit of strength I can muster, I execute the guillotine.

I've never known pain like this. Warmth trickles down my leg, but I dare not open my eyes or the window. I don't even move. If the spotlight returns, so be it. *A man reaps what he sows. The one who sows to please his sinful nature, from that nature will reap destruction.*

Cool air blows across what's left of my crotch. A cursory reach forward lets me know the window is again open.

God will not let you be tempted beyond what you can bear. But when you are tempted, he will also provide a way out. When God closes a door, he opens a window.

I recall Matthew 7. *Enter through the narrow gate. For wide is the gate and broad is the road that leads to destruction, and many enter through it. But small is the gate and narrow the road that leads to life, and only a few find it.*

I found that gate. I'm ready to walk that road. Naked. Pure. An angel.

I lean forward and take my first step of faith.

The Risen Within

by Mark Taylor

There it was.

It was in her eyes.

But it *was* her.

It was where she was sitting.

The heavily polished windows of the department store held the reflection of the bus and its occupants, the drab city blurred behind it, and then the monster.

Anna turned away. She looked at the woman on the seat next to her who was looking past her, out of the window. She returned her gaze as if nothing was wrong. The sweet old woman smiled silently at her much like her own grandmother after she had been taken by the madness of the mind. Anna smiled back then returned her eyes to the thing that sat in her seat on the bus.

It too smiled at her. Its teeth showed in a dull forsaken grin.

The doors at the front of the bus hissed to a close and then a lurch and the bus was moving: The windows, the reflection, gone.

She was overcome with sadness. Maybe she had contracted Gran-Momma's disease early.

She hoped not. She was only twenty-three.

It had not been the first time that she had witnessed such a thing. The first time was a week ago. She had gotten out of the shower and was looking at herself in the bathroom mirror. Her eyes hadn't seemed right. A look of anger flashed within them that was so unbecoming of her that she had taken a second look.

When she stared into her reflection, she had seen hatred.

She left the mirror behind her and returned naked across the second floor of her house to the bedroom where she had left Greg – or was it Grant? – asleep. They had only just met last night.

She hadn't been surprised to see him gone. It hadn't been the first time that had happened either. But still she felt empty.

And after that it had happened twice more before she had gotten on this bus to ride to the coffee shop before work. There were little things in reflections that should not have been there. And it was as if only she saw them. Looks – the demands of her own eyes betraying what she knew: Anger, hatred, a fire...a burning lust. She knew of herself that she could not be those things she saw.

When after she left the bus that morning she found herself standing next to a young man by the name of Simon, and she knew instantly that these things were not of her...

Anna watched Simon as the two of them shared coffee. He

was sitting opposite, staring deeply into the foam cup: shy. She thought it cute. They had barely said hello after bumping hands that held coffee before they seemed to fall into chat and ended up at a table, sitting together. He had a soft face and bright, alive eyes. Anna glanced around the shop, a little out of discomfort herself, with Simon not speaking suddenly. On the rear wall – as they sat by the front window – a feature mirror ran across it. She looked at herself. Her hair flowed, a deep brown, and her lipstick was still in place. She looked at Simon's reflection. He had his eyes closed. He said, "I kinda like you." The sound came from beside her, but the reflection moved in perfect time from what looked like an eternity away.

It made her warm to hear it.

"I like you too." She glanced at him, his eyes still closed, and then returned her gaze to the other him on the other side of the room. He nodded his head gently and opened his eyes. He looked at her while she watched him all the time. His reflection was sad. Was it her? What had she done? She turned to face him.

He was smiling.

"What is it?" he said in reply to her look of sudden anguish.

"No," she said, "why the frown?"

"What frown?" Simon raised his eyebrows and his smile crooked.

He was right. He wasn't frowning. He looked quite...happy...actually. Anna returned his gaze. "Sorry." She shook her head dismissively and looked back into the mirror. He was frowning there. Anna snapped her head over to look at him. He jumped in surprise, but was still quite happy.

"What?" he asked.

Anna brought a new smile and decided not to look at the mirror again. "Nothing." Embarrassed, she looked into her coffee. "I like you," she echoed, looking away. *Damn. Stupid. Just said that. He's going to think you're retarded.* She looked him in the eye and winked. *Damn. Now he thinks I'm easy.* She looked back to the mirror again. At least she was safe from herself over there.

She watched as Simon stood...he opened his lips and beamed a broad slit across his mouth, his fierce teeth showing within the gape. His eyes looked dead as they stared into the side of her head, glazed and milky white. He was an abomination. She turned to him. He was normal and fine. Handsome even.

His smile changed from pleasant to awkward. "I should be going," he said.

Shit. She was scaring him off. She wanted him. After Glen – or was it Gary? – she felt like she needed some sort of vindication. "Can I call you?" she blurted.

His strange look eased. "You can." He took his cell from his pocket. "I can never remember my number." He tapped at a few buttons on the old cell as Anna got her phone from her bag and slid her finger gently across the screen. He gave her his number and the two of them parted. Before he left the coffee shop Anna told him she would call in the next couple of days.

She sat and took a slow sip from her drink. The potent flavour of Columbian beans filled her nose and overpowered her senses. She was happy, warmed by the sensation. Ten minutes later, she put down the empty cup, pulled her bag onto her shoulder and stood.

A glance in the mirror showed her death in her eyes, her skin tight on her flesh, and cracks appearing through which bare flesh glistened. She pretended it wasn't there, turned and left.

"Hi, I don't know if you remember me, but...you do?" Anna glowed. She had left it two days – the perfect length of time according to the internet – and Simon wanted to see her again.

#

Simon was coming over in an hour. Anna sat in the bath, the warm oiled water running over her body. She had sunken into it an hour previous and was lounging in the liquid, eyes closed. As she breathed in, the ambient scent of the water drifted into her, its calming effect reaching out to each part of her body.

She smiled, happy and relaxed, and pulled herself from the water. The tiles on the floor of the bathroom were cold on the bottoms of her feet as the warm water slid from her body onto the ceramic.

Standing in front of the mirror that hung over the sink, she looked coyly away. Something she practiced to look sensual. She thought it worked.

She dried and dressed. She had already prepared the lobster, so she was happily sitting on the couch with a glass of dry red wine when the doorbell rang out.

Simon looked her up and down, his lips widening to a grin. "Good evening," he said.

Anna stepped back and allowed him to pass. A mild aroma of something musky teased her nose. "How are you?" she asked.

"Fine, fine." He held out a bouquet of roses to her, "For you," and a bottle of white wine that was slippery in her hand when she took it, still cold from the refrigerator.

Anna took them as her heart beat faster. "Thank you." She made for the kitchen. "Would you like to come through? It's nearly ready."

Simon followed Anna as she made her way through the house, picking up an empty vase on the way. In the kitchen she slipped it into the sink and turned on the faucet. The water gurgled into the empty vessel. "Wine?" she asked.

"Thank you."

Anna picked up the bottle from the counter and three quarter filled the glass she had ready next to it. When she replaced the bottle and picked up the glass to hand to Simon she noticed that her reflection hadn't. It still held on to the bottle, long jagged nails on the end of bony thin fingers. She couldn't see her face – its face – hidden by the curve of the glass, but she knew it would be smiling. "Here," she said.

Simon cocked his head. "You seem distracted. Is everything okay?"

"Mm," she nodded, "fine. Did you have a good day?"

"Work was a bore," he said sipping the wine, "*is* a bore. This is good." He reached out to take the bottle. "What is it?"

"*No.*" Anna sucked in her breath and spun around, afraid that Simon might see what lurked on the bottle too, but knocked it with her flailing hand and it toppled on the counter, bouncing once as the cool red liquid spilled from it. Then it cracked and shattered when it landed again, the glass and fluid spilling across the surface. "Damn," she sighed.

Her in the reflection of the wine shook her head and then brayed with laughter. Her cold, dead eyes betrayed her thoughts of Anna a fool.

"Never mind." Simon sidled up behind her and put his hand on her waist. "I smell seafood, right?"

Anna nodded. "Yes," she said quietly.

"Then the white will go just as well," he said, releasing his grip and taking the white wine he had brought from the counter and unfurling the wrapping around the cork. "Do you have a corkscrew?"

"The top drawer," she said, pulling off paper towels from a roll and laying them in the pool of red. As she mopped up the reflection, it moved from the viscous surface of the liquid to the hundred shards of glass.

You can't get rid of me, it was saying.

She slid the towels across the surface, the liquid wiped away, and then the glass with a brush and dustpan. It chinked as she dropped the hundred tiny mirrors into the trash.

As she and Simon stood opposite each other, finishing the last of the red in silence, he watched her, looked into her eyes, and she stared at the monster in his glass...staring back at her.

They moved to the dining room and Anna made her guest comfortable, leaving him to open the second bottle of wine with her returning to the kitchen. She took the Thermidor from the oven and plated it, ignoring the monster in the glass door of one of the cabinets.

And the one that watched her from the side of the knife...

She tried to blink them away and took the two plates to the table.

"Lovely," Simon said, inhaling the sweet aroma of the lobster. Anna sat and watched him eat, a smile on her face the whole time. She didn't want to take her eyes from him as he was a more than pleasant sight, and in case she saw something that she didn't want to.

There was a glance – every now and then – when she caught *it* staring at her from the cutlery, the wine glass, but nothing that spoiled the moment for her.

If she could just hold it together, she might be able to impress him.

Maybe this one would stay.

As dinner concluded, Simon was gracious enough to make coffee, leaving Anna sitting at the table absently rubbing her necklace between her fingers.

"No," he was saying through the open door, "I'm not really into sports. I go running twice a week, but that about does me."

"Mm," she agreed.

Simon brought the two cups back in and sat opposite Anna. "So how about you?"

Anna glanced to the side, the monster looking back at her from the drinks cabinet. "No, I don't know," she said absently. She looked Simon straight in the eyes. "Would you like to stay?"

He looked surprised – briefly – before he tried to hide an embarrassed smile. "Um," he said with a waver in his voice.

"Oh," Anna lifted her cup and hid behind it, more embarrassed than he, perhaps. "I'm sorry."

"No," he said, "well, yes, I mean," he corrected hurriedly. He looked down and laughed nervously. When his eyes came back up to meet hers, Anna had returned her cup to the table and was smiling warmly. "I'd love to," he said.

Simon lay on the bed naked with Anna straddled across him, slowly rocking back and forth, her fingers slipped into her hair allowing him the full view of her nude form. He kept making satisfied noises under her, his hands gripping her hips as she rocked.

"Oh, God," he muttered.

Anna took this as a sign that he was getting close.

She looked over to the mirrored closet door. The thing was riding him there as well. It stared hollow sockets back at her, its skin flayed from its flesh, the soiling of its blood staining the man beneath.

It was saying *it is time*.

Simon started to buck under her weight, "Anna," he was saying over and over.

She leaned forward, covering his body with hers, "Just relax," she whispered, "it's coming."

"Yes," he moaned.

Anna rocked harder, her hand sliding down the side of the bed and grasping the single shard of mirror that lay beneath it.

As Simon called out in pleasure, Anna rose up over him, the mirror in her hand, the monster doing the same in the closet door, and the reflection from the weapon bouncing infinitely between the two, she plunged the deep red, crusted shard into Simon's neck.

His impassioned scream of pleasure became his own death knell.

Simon struggled beneath her for a second, his life draining red onto the sheets.

Anna panted as his twitching ceased and his eyes grew dull. She looked into the mirror.

The monster was gone.

Anna got off the corpse and pushed her arms into her gown. She unraveled the sheets from the bed and wrapped Simon in them, pulling him, mummified, from the bed, a dull hollow thud as he hit the floor. She dragged him from the bedroom, struggling with his weight, and pulled him down the stairs behind her.

She got to the bottom of the stairs and let the sheets she gripped so firmly drop, unlocked the basement door and swung it open.

A putrid smell rose from the darkness making her retch.

She pulled the sheet-wrapped corpse to the top of the steps and rolled it in...the darkness enveloping it.

Anna shook her head and closed the door, locking it.

Returning upstairs, Anna dropped the robe from her shoulders and got in the shower. As the warming water rolled down her body, she wondered if Steve – or was it Saul? – would be there when she returned...or if he would sneak out...just like the others.

Cuppa Joe
by Craig Faustus Buck

I wake up feeling logy. I head for the kitchen and grab the mix from the freezer, throw it in the blender and give it a whirl. Then I dump it in Mr. Coffee and turn on the drip.

The brew comes out at a perfect ninety-eight point six degrees but it's the smell that warms me. It feels good to be alive. I swirl the rich liquid in my mug. My morning cuppa Joe. He was my brother-in-law until I switched from cappuccino to decapiccino. He's listed as missing. Has been for two weeks. I'm running out.

My sister and Joe were pretty happy before Joe and I had our little falling out. It happened on my day off. Joe had stayed home from work, feeling fluey, so my sister asked me to look in on him. He was feeling better by the time I got there, so the two of us grabbed our fishing gear and drove out to the lake.

We were bobbing for bass, sharing a thermos of Java, and he was going on and on about how my sister blows her paycheck on hair products when he could be doubling her money in Vegas. The only dumber clod than this bozo is my sister for hooking up with him. So he was yammering on, driving me nuts, when all of a sudden we both got a strike. After a few minutes of struggle, we figured out there was no fish involved. Our hooks were entangled. Joe made some lame joke about our worms fucking and as I gave him a guffaw, just to be polite, a huge bass took the bait. I never dreamed that two men could catch the same fish at the same time, but it happened. Joe started in about how he caught it first and I told him to eat shit because he wasn't about to be eating my bass and one thing led to another and I found myself garroting Joe with his own thirty-pound-test fishing line.

A dripping ring of blood bloomed around his neck when the line broke his skin and I became fixated on the physics of the thing. Would the line break before Joe did? Would thirty pounds be enough tensile strength? Would he die by asphyxiation before the line got deep enough to sever his carotid artery? Would his tendons be cut? My enquiring mind wanted to know.

So many questions, so little time – though in the moment, it seemed like an eternity. Thank God I wore gloves or the monofilament would have sliced my fingers off. Damn if he didn't linger a good five minutes before the light finally drained from his eyes. I thought he'd never stop breathing. Just to be safe, I didn't let up until he turned blue. I was sweating like a pig and the next day my biceps ached like a sonuvabitch.

I felt lucky that he'd brought thirty-pound-test because I doubted my own twelve-pound would have withstood the strain. I'd choked him as hard as I could but it probably still took longer than it should have because I wasn't in the best of shape. Then and there, I resolved to go back to the gym.

I wound up releasing the bass and gutting Joe instead. It was not easy. I wanted to avoid making a mess that some hiker might find, so I drained him into my bucket. Luckily, the bass I'd set free was the only fish we'd caught that day, so the bucket was clean. That's how I wound up tasting his blood. Can you imagine sipping a cuppa Joe that smells like fish? It would have been undrinkable.

I'd never killed a person before. I'd hunted deer but it's a lot easier to drop a buck with a bullet than to strangle your brother-in-law with a garrote. It was an eye-opening experience – for me, not for Joe. Dealing with the body wasn't too bad, either. Not all that different from dressing a deer, except you don't collect a deer's blood.

Most of Joe ended up in the garage in my roadkill freezer, along with two possums and what's left of a luscious fawn. But there was something hypnotic about the blood, so I brought it inside to the kitchen. It separated pretty fast as the red stuff coagulated and the clearish serum rose like cream to the top. But when I tried putting it in the blender, damn if it didn't reconstitute like silky red gravy. So I figured, what the hell? And took a slug.

I expected it to taste like biting the inside of my cheek, but there was something about it being Joe's blood that made it taste foreign. And I mean that in a good way, like exotic cuisine. So I divvied it up into Tupperware and stored it in my kitchen freezer.

My first cuppa Joe was a religious epiphany. The angels were singing in five-part harmony and my previously incomprehensible life finally made sense. Thanks to Joe, the purpose of my existence was revealed to me. I now knew why I was put on this earth: to fulfill my biological imperative, which is killing for sustenance. Man has been doing it since we were Neanderthal. Our species evolved to hunt, and among our prey were rival tribes of homo sapiens. Over the millennia we became civilized to excess and that essential humanity was encased in a cultural shell, a screaming pearl in an impenetrable oyster. Luckily, Joe came along to shuck my oyster, release my essence, reintroduce me to the perfect local sourcing of sustainable food.

But I digress. I've become addicted to my morning pick-me-up. Yet one good exsanguination only goes so far. The average man contains about four-point-seven pints of blood. After spillage and coagulation, I only got three out of Joe. And of that, only a few cups are left. I need to restock.

I've given the matter considerable thought and have come to the conclusion that a woman might be a better choice next time. Don't get me wrong. I love my morning cuppa Joe. But he's just a maintenance drug, like taking a statin. A woman! Now we're talking recreational drugs. Something with a kick, with some sex appeal. Not to mention the joy of dismemberment. No offense to Joe, but his rough, hairy skin made mine crawl. Joe's flesh is to a woman's like sackcloth to silk.

A cup of feminine essence in the morning. The thought makes my breath flutter like first love. I imagine her on my kitchen table with her long blonde hair cascading over the edge like a golden waterfall, her slender body parts strategically placed to approximate what she looked like in life, freckles intact, legs long and lean, breasts frozen forever pert. I wonder if postmortem nipples react to the cold. Only time will tell.

There's definitely something arousing about the thought of drinking a woman's blood. I reach down to feel myself starting to harden beneath the heather cotton of my sweat pants. Joe may have been my first, but he was an opportunity, not a selection. A woman would be a feast of my own choosing. It feels so right, I can already taste her.

My doorbell chimes.

I wipe Joe's blood off my lips and close the kitchen door behind me to hide the blender and coffee pot. Joe must be my little secret. I head to the door and look through the spyhole. It's a woman, standing with her back to me. Her hair is blonde and stringy like cornsilk. I picture my fingers running through it to grab a firm handhold as I let her body fall away from her severed head. The image brings a giddy smile to my lips.

"Who is it?"

She turns and tries to peer through the wrong end of the peep hole. Her eyes are red and teary. "Open the door, jerkoff."

My sister Lurlene. I open up.

"You've been crying," I say.

"You should have been a detective," she says. She's being sarcastic, seeing as how I'm an LAPD Detective II. She sweeps past me and throws herself on my couch. "The cops aren't doing shit. They think Joey probably ran off with some lover. Are they idiots? No woman in her right mind would want that asshole."

"Except you." I hate stating the obvious but it had to be said.

"Fuck you, Ernest."

"I thought you loved him."

"Why are you talking past tense? Do you think he's dead? Did you hear something at the station?" There's real panic in her voice.

"I didn't hear anything. It was just a figure of speech."

"Well for your information, I do love him. What do you know about love, anyway? Nothing, that's what.

We've been replaying this scene in one form or another since Joe went missing into my freezer. Lurlene claims she loves him but acts like she hates him. I can never tell. But her life has been an endless stretch of misery since he disappeared, so maybe she did love him. Would it be an act of kindness to kill her? To lift her out of her depression? She is a woman, after all, which satisfies the primary requirement.

Is it incest to drink your sister's blood? Maybe roast her loin for Sunday supper? There's no sex involved. No danger of inbreeding. In a way it would reunite her with her beloved Joe. It's got a poetic ring to it. A renewal of vows in my bowels.

My stomach rumbles. I realize I'm not feeling a hundred percent. Is that my conscience poking around? Maybe it isn't morally ideal to feed on one's sister. Still, she is a bird in the hand. And even if it is incest, isn't that a petty crime in the shadow of sororicide?

"Love is complicated," she says. "Too complicated for your sorry ass."

My eyes are drawn to her throat. Lurlene's body is trim from teaching Pilates five days a week, but she's got a triple chin. Just like our mom. There's a crease in the fat just above her neck that might as well be one of those dotted lines that show you where to cut. I start to salivate.

A woman is softer than a man. I wonder if that makes her tenderer. Maybe the twelve-pound-test would be strong enough for Lurlene. Though a good sharp knife would take much less effort and probably be just as fun. The only downside would that that her death wouldn't last very long. There was something very satisfying about the lingering part. Maybe I should tie her down and bleed her out slowly. But even if I did it in the basement, one of the neighbors might hear her screams. I guess that's what gags are for.

Is it worse to kill your sister than to kill a stranger? I weigh the pros and cons. A stranger might have a husband or boyfriend who would miss her. My sister, thanks to me, does not. A stranger might have a happy life that would be cut short. My sister is depressed and likely to become more so as the weeks turn to months turn to years with no sign of Joe.

My stomach growls again. This time I feel a little queasy. Is it my cuppa Joe? I've been drinking him for over a week now with no problems. I'll bet it's yesterday's tuna salad.

"I need some water," I say and head into the kitchen.

As soon as I open the door I see the bloody appliances. Shit! I grab the coffee decanter with one hand, the blender jar with the other, and jam my foot on my garbage can pedal just as I hear my sister drag herself off the couch. I lower the glassware carefully into the garbage so nothing breaks. The lid falls closed just as she walks into the room.

"He's been stealing from me for years," she says. "Did I ever tell you that? He thinks I don't know but he's been skimming our vacation savings and blowing it at the poker tables in Gardena."

"Isn't that money community property?" I move to the sink to drink sideways from the tap. When I lower my head for a sip I get dizzy.

"Community property means it belongs to both of us," she says. "When he sneaks it out, knowing I wouldn't allow it, it becomes stolen property. It's in the law."

I stand up straight and use both hands to steady myself against the counter. One hand falls on the handle of my boning knife.

"Can you cite the statute for that?" I say. "Because we didn't learn anything about it at the Academy."

My eyes return to the line across her throat.

"Shut up, Ernie. You're not funny."

I wasn't trying to be, but I keep my mouth shut. I think I can see her pulse beating in her neck like a little drummer urging me on. My toe starts to tap to the beat.

Then I realize she's still talking and I haven't heard. I've zoned out. Not something I usually do. Am I being sucked so far into my blood fantasy that I'm losing touch with reality? It's almost like I'm blacking out. I force myself to tune back into the conversation.

"...last week I found a motel receipt. Not only was he cheating on me but he was spending my money on her!"

"Who?"

"Are you not listening? His secretary-slash-whore!"

"Joe had a secretary?" I'm shocked he could afford one. He told me his business was in the toilet.

"Hey!" She snaps her fingers in front of my face. "Focus on the 'whore' part." Her face seems to melt and her eyes tear up, finally breaching her lower lids. She whispers, "I thought he loved me."

I feel awful for her but I can't tell if it's because I know Joe's not coming back or because Lurlene was betrayed by him. Either way I think she's my sister and deserves better. The little drummer in her throat is throbbing, calling me to rescue her from the quicksand of her despair. My fingers snake around the knife handle like a python around a stripper.

"I thought he loved me!" she shrieks, then erupts into sobs. I'm getting a migraine from her agony. I've got to make it stop. I slide the knife off the counter and hide it behind my back.

Lurlene forces back her tears and grabs a paper towel to blow her nose.

"He's dead," she says. "I know it."

"You don't know for sure."

"Yes I do." She starts crying again.

My hand tightens on the knife.

"I've been feeding him cyanide," she wails.

I feel a surge of reflux as my stomach acid torches my esophagus.

Lurlene steps on the pedal of the garbage can to toss her phlegmy paper towel. The lid flips open and her eyes widen at the sight of all the blood. She turns to me in shock.

"Whose blood is that?"

I have to end this before comprehension breaks her heart. I lunge toward her, knife extended. But my stomach clenches like a choke chain. I manage only one step before the pain slams me to the floor. The knife skitters away. I can't breathe.

"Ernie, what's wrong?"

A scream of agony struggles to explode from every pore in my body, but my muscles are locked tight and I can't get it out. If this is death by cyanide, it's taking for-fucking-ever. I sure could use a cuppa Joe right now.

Nine Lives
by Dawn Napier

It hadn't rained for weeks, and the air was dusty and dry. David walked home from summer school with his backpack slung over one shoulder, breathed the heavy air, and wished for rain. The forecast had mentioned scattered thundershowers, but apparently they had scattered elsewhere. David felt like his breath was being squeezed out of him.

There was a dead cat on the side of the road. Its fur was rusty orange, the same color as the dead grass all around. Here and there were oases of green, liberally tended by spinning sprinklers, but David's home was not one of them. Dad said it wasn't worth the high water bill just to have a pretty lawn. "You'd just have to mow it more anyway," he'd said, punching David's arm. David was too embarrassed to admit how much he hated the dead, orange grass and would mow every day if it meant green grass all summer. It looked so dead, like the end of the world.

David wandered over to the dead cat, morbidly curious in spite of himself. He was fifteen, too old to be interested in dead cats and frogs and mud. Maybe he was just really bored. He was grounded for the summer because of his last report card, and he had to attend summer classes to make it up. He was in no hurry to go back home, where there was nothing to do but read the same books and play the same video games over and over again.

The cat was sprawled out on its side with its eyes and jaws open. It looked angry, as though it knew that it was not supposed to end like this. Cats were fierce and dignified; it was beneath a cat to breathe its last lying in the dirt on the side of the road.

Its fur was matted and stiff and streaked with blood. David slowly, gently touched one of its paws. It was like touching a fur-covered piece of wood. It was like touching nothing.

David hitched up his backpack and hurried home. If he was late, Dad would kick his ass.

The sky clouded over that night, and the next day it began to rain.

#

David walked home in the downpour and savored every sodden step. It had been so hot for so long that there were still clouds of steam puffing up from the road. He held his umbrella over his shoulder, covering his backpack, but he left his face exposed so that he could enjoy the coolness of the fresh summer rain.

The dead cat was still there, and David's good mood sank a little. It was completely drenched, its orange fur darkened. "Well, at least you can't feel it," he said to the cat, wandering over. "You wouldn't enjoy a shower as much as me."

The cat lifted its head and looked at him.

"Jesus!" David stumbled back, dropping his umbrella. The cold rain beat down on his head and shoulders and expensive designer backpack. The cat did nothing, only studied the boy with the casual expression of one who has seen it all before. It licked its lips, washing away a drop of dried blood.

David grabbed his umbrella and walked quickly away from the cat. Too confused to run, he walked backwards to the end of the block, never blinking nor taking his eyes off the cat. When he turned the corner and the cat fell out of sight, he started to run. His heart thudded in his throat.

At home, Dad noticed his pale face and heavy breathing and frowned at him over his e-reader. "You should have texted me," he said. "I would have come to get you if you didn't want to walk in the rain."

"Sorry," David panted, tracking footprints and dripping water across the carpet and up the stairs to his room. "I'll remember next time. I thought you'd still be working."

"Nope, today's my early day. Tomorrow I'm staying late." David's father returned to his e-reader. Probably it hadn't been the rain at all, the man thought. David had stayed after class to flirt with some girl and then had to run to be home on time. As long as the kid stayed within the letter of the law, he wasn't going to worry about it.

Worrying was a mother's job.

David did his algebra homework and read ahead in his history book until dinnertime. Normally he hated schoolwork and fought tooth and nail to avoid it. But today he welcomed the monotony. The real world was suddenly too exciting today, and boring old numbers that fit a recognizable pattern were like soothing music. Death and destruction that had happened hundreds of years ago was about as exciting as David wanted to get right now.

Mom knocked on his door to signal the arrival of dinner, and David took his history book downstairs with him. Mom normally objected when he brought a book to the table, but when she saw it was a school book she let it go.

"Got a test tomorrow?" Dad asked around a mouthful of pizza.

"Day after tomorrow," David said – which was the truth. But he didn't give a damn about the test. He just didn't want to socialize. The cat had lifted its head and looked at him. It was dead, had been dead for days. Its mouth hanging open and caked with dried blood. And it had lifted its head. It had looked at him. David had looked into the dead cat's eyes, and it had seen him.

Oh God, stop thinking about it now. He would go crazy if he kept thinking about it over and over like this.

David hunkered down in his chair, picked up a slice of pizza, and concentrated on Napoleon. He was very close to understanding what the fuss was about Waterloo.

#

In his dreams, David stood over the dead cat again, and the rain was warm. The cat raised its head and looked at him, and David blinked hard. When he opened his eyes again, the cat was again lying properly dead. Then it looked up at him again. And again. And again.

"Please make it stop!" David cried out.

Then he realized he was shouting into his darkened bedroom. His air purifier hummed comfortably near his bed, and above him the ceiling fan twirled gently.

David rolled onto his side and curled up like a baby. He didn't think he'd ever fall back to sleep, nor did he want to. But a few minutes later, exhaustion conquered fear, and David slept dreamlessly.

#

He awoke with the sun dancing in his eyes. Mom must have opened his blinds to wake him up faster. His alarm clock buzzed, and David slapped it and knocked it to the floor.

David looked around his sunny, summer-lit bedroom and decided that he must have imagined the whole thing. It was all that made sense. Mom was always saying that those scary comics would warp his mind; maybe that wasn't all paranoid-parent bullshit. He'd let his imagination get away from him, and he'd had some sort of brain-fart. That was all it was.

Feeling better, David rolled out of bed and ran downstairs in search of breakfast.

David looked for the cat on his way to school, but he couldn't find it. He thought for sure he'd seen it in the gutter near the mailbox shaped like a fire truck, but now it was gone. Good riddance. Maybe the rain had washed it away, or maybe the people who lived there had cleaned it up. Nobody wanted a dead animal next to their house, especially people whimsical enough to have a fire truck for a mailbox. Any way it had happened, the cat was gone. David could forget all about that weird brain fart and move on with his life.

As if in agreement, David's day at school went swimmingly. Both his algebra and history teachers praised him for speaking up in class, and Alyssa Benson first asked him for help with her math work, then smiled at him when he explained the FOIL method to her. David walked home that day in high spirits. Being grounded for the entire summer wouldn't be so bad if every day was filled with well-mannered teachers and pretty girls.

When he got home, Mom was already there. She sat in the middle of the living room floor with something furry in her lap. "Hi David!" she said. "Look what I found sitting on the porch this afternoon."

It was the dead cat. It lay curled in Mom's lap, its eyes half-closed in a comfortable drowse.

David dropped his backpack. The cat's ears twitched at the sound, but otherwise it did not react.

"Goodness, what's wrong?" Mom asked. "You look sick all of a sudden."

David shook his head and picked up his backpack. "Sorry. Stomach cramp or something. Um, cute cat. Does it have a name?"

Mom shook her head and stroked the top of its head. "I'm going to ask around first and make sure it doesn't belong to anyone. But I think I might go with Grady."

David couldn't think of anything to say to that, so he just nodded and went upstairs to do his homework. Boring old algebra had never seemed so appealing.

At the back of his mind, though, the cat still lingered and clawed at his thoughts. Coincidence. It had to be. The dead cat had been washed away by the heavy rain. This cat was also orange, but that meant nothing. There were hundreds of orange cats out there. Probably millions. None of this meant anything. David wasn't losing his mind, and he wasn't being haunted by an undead zombie cat. Shit like that was for the movies.

"Dinner!" Dad called up the stairs.

David very reluctantly put his books away. Coincidence or

not, it was a freaky occurrence, and he was in no hurry to look at the cat again. But he had to. He had to get a good long look at the cat so he could confirm it was not the dead cat he'd seen on the road.

Dinner was leftover pizza and spaghetti, and David ate quickly. "Oh, look who's come to join us," Mom said. The cat was slinking around the doorway, sniffing here and there. It saw David, and their eyes met. Then it crept slowly over and looked up at him.

David stared down at the cat, looking for a ragged ear or a white spot or something, anything to distinguish it from the dead one. The cat sat and regarded David with a calm, interested expression in its golden eyes. It blinked slowly. When its eyes opened, they were full of writhing maggots. Blood oozed from the dead cat's jaws.

David dropped his fork on the plate with a clatter. The cat startled and blinked, and its eyes were clear and gold again. The cat yawned, stretched, and sauntered off with its tail in the air like a flag.

I am losing my mind, David thought, staring after it.

#

Nobody claimed the cat, and Mom named it Grady as planned. It settled into its new existence with ease, eating and drinking and shitting in the litter box like any other cat. David watched it whenever he had the misfortune to be in the same room with it, but there was nothing really to watch. The cat spent most of its time curled up in Mom's lap or on a sunny windowsill. By all accounts, it was just another cat. Mom adored it, and even Dad – a lifelong dog person – commented more than once that it was nice to have a pet in the house. If either of them noticed that David wouldn't touch it no matter how close it came to him, neither mentioned it.

Summer school drew to a close, and David looked forward to a few weeks of freedom before tenth grade began. Both his algebra and history teachers praised him personally for his remarkable improvement in both subjects. With his high scores and "adjusted attitude," his house arrest was almost over, and his best friend Jake was finally coming back from his dad's house in Florida. It was like a heavy thunderstorm was finally lifting.

Two days after summer school let out for the last time, Mom and Dad called David into the kitchen for a family meeting. David's heart plummeted to his shoes, and his sat down at the table with a boulder in his stomach. This was how Jake's parents had announced their divorce.

"We didn't plan this," Dad began, "but we're still happy about it, and we hope you'll be happy too."

"I'm pregnant!" Mom cried.

David felt faint, either from shock or relief he wasn't sure. Mom was pregnant. They were having another baby. That little brother or sister they'd promised and never delivered on was finally coming – almost sixteen years later. But they weren't splitting up, and

David would stay in the same house with the same room and the same bed he'd always had. Good – that was good. David felt a little dizzy. He started to smile.

Then the cat strolled into the room.

Mom and Dad were watching him, waiting for a reaction. David couldn't speak. He couldn't take his eyes off the cat, the strange unnatural cat that had been dead and now wasn't anymore. The cat yawned, exposing pale gums and a tongue that was almost white in color. No – its tongue wasn't white. It was covered in maggots. One dropped to the floor and squirmed there on the hardwood floor. Neither Mom nor Dad seemed to notice. They were still watching David's pale, confused face.

The cat stared at David. Then slowly, deliberately, the cat licked its chops.

Then it strolled out again.

"I'm sorry, Mom," David blurted. "I'm just in shock. That's great, it's really great. I'm happy that you guys are happy." Then he got up and hugged them both. Mom squeezed him fiercely, and he could feel her relief. Dad clapped him on the back.

#

Two days later, David was once again walking with his backpack over his shoulder. The pack squirmed a little, but there was no feline cry of protest. The cat was completely passive. More evidence, David thought, that it wasn't really a cat. No cat alive just lay there and let someone put it in a bag and zip it up.

The Deep Lake forest preserve was almost five miles away, but David was angry and frightened, and the stress lent strength to his legs. He barely felt the ache of unfamiliar exercise, and he was there in what felt like no time at all. He crossed the parking lot and found the hiking trail that passed over the Deep Lake River.

The backpack squirmed a bit more as David approached the bridge. "Back in the old days, in Puritan times, they killed cats all the time," David said casually. "Cats were supposed to be the devil's servants or something, and they were thought to be totally evil. They burned cats, they hung them, and they drowned them."

David stood on the bridge and looked down into the swift, dark water. He took his backpack off his shoulder and held it in both hands. The beast inside growled.

"Water is supposed to stop evil," he said softly. "Vampires can't cross it, and neither can demons. I don't know exactly what you are, but here's hoping this works. You're not going to hurt Mom's baby."

David let go, and as it fell he saw the backpack writhe and thrash in a fury of movement. Just before it hit the water, he thought he saw a single paw poke through an opening, clutching at the air as if for purchase.

Then the thrashing bundle disappeared into the dark water. With all the rain they'd been having, the current was swift and powerful. Take it away, David thought at the river, take it away, to the Mississippi, to the ocean. To hell.

Then he headed home. Mom was going to kick his ass and probably ground him again for losing a fifty-dollar backpack.

#

Six months later, Mom gave birth to a healthy eight-pound baby girl. She named the baby Sydney, and Dad went nuts snapping picture after picture. After an hour of holding his sister and smiling painfully, David felt like he was going to have a cramp in his jaw and permanent spots before his eyes from the flash. But they were happy, and it made David's heart feel good to see him smiling so much. Even Mom looked good, tired as she was.

That night, David woke up from an uncomfortable dream that he couldn't quite remember. He opened his eyes, but the room was completely dark. Something smelled bad, like gone-over meat. There was a cold weight on his chest, and it was hard to breathe. David inhaled and almost choked on the maggoty stench.

The cat was purring.

Blood of the Chosen
by Tom Olbert

"You can't leave me alone with this freakin' psycho!" the man screamed from the back seat of the squad car, his face and body half-covered in blood. The wild-eyed man handcuffed beside him stared out through the rain-streaked window, his eyes shining in the parking lot lights like a rabid dog's on a dark night.

"Shut up!" Pete Duggan shouted, kicking the driver's side door closed. "Backup'll be here any second!" He gasped with exertion, his deputy's arm around his neck, his blood half-covering his uniform. "Stay with me, Sullivan," he panted under his labored breath. "They'll fix ya up in ER." The pouring rain was drenching him as he tried to haul Sullivan's 190-pound frame to the hospital entrance, trying his damnedest to hold the blood-reddened handkerchief over the gunshot wound in the large man's side. He glanced over at Sullivan's burly face. His eyes were clouded, the rain water streaming down his cheeks shining in the lamplights. Sullivan's head was bobbing up and down as he slipped in an out of consciousness, his voice babbling like an infant's. "Hang on, dammit! Get me some help out here!" he shouted at the top of his lungs.

The ER techs showed up, running out into the rainy night and getting Sullivan onto a gurney. "You're gonna be fine, Sullivan. You hear me? Just stay with it!"

"We got it, Sheriff," one of the doctors muttered as they wheeled Sullivan in.

"You hit, Sheriff? Sheriff?!"

"What?" He barely heard them, his head spinning. "No. No, this ain't my blood. It's Sullivan's." He mopped the rain water out of his eyes as he stepped through the entrance into the lobby. Medics in green scrubs all around him. Patients with blood and bandages. "You give my deputy priority, you understand?" The doctors and nurses just glanced at him absently as they filled out their precious paperwork. The buzzing of announcements over the PA and beepers going off. He hated hospitals.

He was out of breath, his head buzzing like a swarm of angry bees as he sat down in the first empty seat he could find in the waiting area. People sitting next to him moved further away. He glanced over the cheesy Halloween decorations taped to the walls. Stupid-looking wide-eyed jack-o'-lanterns, ghosts and witches. Candy-stripers were handing out candy corn and caramel popcorn to the little kids. He'd forgotten it was almost Halloween. He remembered Sullivan's two little kids, Ron and Emma. How much they loved trick-or-treating. He winced, clenching his fists at the thought of facing Sullivan's wife, Carol.

"Duggan!" The Chief's voice startled him back to full awareness. He stood, rubbing his eyes and looked up. Chief Landry was walking towards him, looking half-scared and half-angry, Behind Landry, Deputies were bringing in the two men Duggan had left handcuffed in the squad car. The bloodied, wounded man with the blonde crew cut was being helped in by ER techs. And, behind him, the freak who'd shot Sullivan was being led in. Duggan's blood boiled, his hand reflexively reaching for his gun. How he'd restrained himself from blowing the freak's head off back in that chamber of horrors he'd just left, God only knew. "Duggan!" The Chief was right in front of him, his eyes red and clouded, his face half red, like he'd just been pulled out of bed. "Are you okay?"

"I...I think so, Chief. Not wounded, anyway."

"Then, do you mind telling me what the hell happened?"

Duggan took a deep breath and tried to gather his thoughts. "Well, we...Sullivan and me...We were mindin' the store. Jean Morris called in." He sighed, visualizing that fat, half-crazed old biddy who lived in that rotted old dump back in the woods with her two no-account kids and those mangy, stinking dogs of hers. She was always calling in with some crazy complaint or other. He could just hear her hoarse, scratchy swearing over the phone. "Claimed she'd heard screams coming from that other house back there, just past her property. You know...the old abandoned one. The one where those cult murders are supposed to have happened, back in the '60s."

"Yeah. And?" The Chief's eyes flared.

"Well, we didn't take it seriously, at first. But, we figured we'd better check it out anyway, just in case Jean got trigger happy with her shotgun again, or her dogs got out of control. Well…" A cold chill rattled him to his bones. "Chief…"

"Sit down and pull yourself together, Duggan!" the Chief said, pushing him down into the chair and sitting beside him. "What the hell happened?"

"Well, that freak over there…" he looked at the madman with the long black hair and beard who'd shot Sullivan. They were treating his injuries. Him and the other guy. "The one with the beard. He shot Sullivan. The other guy, the soldier type…Well, we found him down in the cellar…chained and manacled. Some kind of sick, ritual stuff. I think the freak would have killed him, too, if Sullivan and I hadn't…"

"Whoa," the Chief interrupted. "What do you mean 'too'? Who else did he kill?"

A memory of what he'd seen in that cellar flashed though his mind, and his guts boiled. He was afraid he'd vomit right there at Chief Landry's feet. Sullivan wiped the sweat and rainwater from his face, his hand going over his mouth. "Chief…Those missing college girls? I think we found 'em."

The Chief's mouth dropped. He just sat there and stared at Duggan for a minute. "I think you'd better get your thoughts clear and make out a full report, Duggan. The FBI's gonna want in on this."

#

Duggan was in the chapel when the Chief found him. Duggan wasn't a religious man by nature. But, he'd never had a man shot down beside him before. Not even in the army. He'd figured a sheriff's job in a quiet little part of New England would be a nice, safe place to work toward retirement. He rubbed a tear out of his eye as Landry sat down beside him. Duggan looked up. "Any word on Sullivan, Chief?"

"Not yet." The Chief looked down and sighed. There was a distant roll of thunder. "It doesn't look good, from what little I can get."

"Uh...has Carol...?"

"She was visiting her mother in Massachusetts when word got through. She's on her way. I think her brother's driving her in."

Duggan sighed, trying to picture the look on Carol's face. "Have they ID'd the shooter?"

"Yeah." The Chief flipped through his notebook. "Robert Pendleton. No priors. He's a professor of antiquities at the university upstate. The one where those five co-eds disappeared. He's not talking. No apparent motive."

"And, the witness?"

The Chief flipped a page. "Joe Barrett. Recently discharged from the U.S. army. Back from the gulf a few months now." He smacked his lips and shook his head. "Long list of priors, that one.

Pretty violent stuff, mostly against women."

That worried Duggan plenty. Not much of a witness. The thought of that freak Pendleton walking free set his blood on fire. If only he'd killed the swine when he'd had the chance! Would he have to spend the rest of his life feeling guilty for not having done so? He looked up as the door swung open. A thin young man with reddish hair walked in, a white lab coat hanging from his round shoulders, a stethoscope hanging from his neck. The worried look on the doctor's face sent a cold knife sliding into Duggan's gut. "Sullivan...?" The name caught in his throat.

"I'm afraid he might not make it, Sheriff." Duggan's blood ran cold, his heart dropping into his shoes. "He needs a transfusion desperately, and we have no A-Negative blood in the bank. The thing is...we've located a potential donor, but...I wanted to run it by the two of you first, since there may be legal issues."

"What the hell are you talking about?" the Chief demanded.

"Well, it's...one of the two men you just brought in. A Mr. Barrett."

The Chief stood up. "Is he refusing to donate?"

"Well, no, but uh..." The doctor cleared his throat. "In view of the circumstances, I wasn't sure we should do anything that might be brought up in court later. You see...as you know, Mr. Barrett was injured when he was brought in. His injures were superficial but you see...not all the blood on him was his. In fact...very little of it was."

#

Pendleton choked, his face twisted in pain as Duggan pressed his night stick against his throat. The lights dimmed, the power flickering for a moment in a lightning burst. "I want to talk to my lawyer!" Pendleton managed as Duggan eased up the pressure a bit.

Duggan grabbed the creep by the shirt collar and pulled him upright on the exam table. The handcuffs shackling Pendleton to the table clinked. Pendleton winced. "Do I look like I'm in the mood to give a damn?" Duggan warned under his breath, pulling Pendleton's face into his. "My deputy could die because of you, you twisted pig! You think anybody's gonna give a damn if I do you right here, right now? Huh?" He shook him. The light was dim in the exam room that was now doubling as an interrogation cell. But, Duggan could see well enough to know the creep was scared. "I want answers, Professor. Why'd you kill those girls? Why'd you try to kill Joe Barrett?" Pendleton's eyes shifted around in the dim light. Duggan pressed the stick under the creep's jaw and raised his dark eyes to his. "I won't ask again."

"I didn't kill them," the man sputtered out, drooling from the corner of his mouth.

Duggan sneered and nodded. "Right. Who did?"

Pendleton smiled, a sick look in his eyes. "Who do you think killed them, Sheriff? Haven't your colleagues filled you in yet on Mr. Barrett's...colorful past? Hmmm?" The smile grew broad and ugly. Duggan felt queasy.

"You're saying you saw Barrett kill them? All five victims?"

"Oh, yes. I watched with rapt, fascinated attention." He chuckled. Duggan slapped him hard, back-handed. Pendleton glared at him, wiping the blood on the back of his hand. "Surely, forensic evidence has already proved I killed no one, Sheriff. You just wanted to hear me say it, didn't you?" That god-awful, evil smile crept back.

Duggan paused a bit, studying those cold eyes. Barrett's sort, he'd seen before. But, Pendleton...this freak was something new. "Do you deny kidnapping those five victims from your university, Professor?"

Pendleton sighed, lying back on the exam table, his uncuffed arm behind his head. "I brought them to that house. A house I very carefully selected. You know of its history, I assume? It's something of a local legend."

Duggan rested his stick on the edge of the table. "Some kind of Satanic cult is supposed to have killed people in that house, back in the 1960s. Some kind of ritual murders. Human sacrifice to the devil, or something."

Pendleton laughed. "Crude, if roughly accurate, Sheriff. Not really a Satanic cult, exactly. Rather, a kind of demon worship that pre-dates the Christian concept of the 'devil' by several thousand years. The cult to which you refer offered human sacrifices to a demon-god of ancient Sumeria. But, the founders of that so-called cult were pathetically amateurish and uneducated. They didn't know what they were doing. Their rudimentary knowledge of the few incomplete translations available led them to a few childish attempts at summoning. It failed miserably, of course. The condition of the burned, twisted bodies of several of the cultists continues to baffle science to this day, does it not?" He looked directly into Duggan's eyes and smiled. "But, in destroying themselves, they did succeed in partially opening what is commonly referred to as a hell gate; a portal into the netherworld beyond this dull plain of existence. That's why I chose that house as my altar. As the threshold of a true summoning!" He sat up, his eyes brimming with dark fire.

Duggan flinched, his hand going to his gun. "How does Barrett figure into all this?"

"Ahh…" Pendleton smiled and lay back again. "That is where my translation of the ancient tablets of the Sumerian priests turned up something no other scholar has correctly interpreted. The almost forgotten demon-god Azgaaroth…" Thunder cracked. Duggan shuddered to his core, the lights flickering. "He did not eat virgins or the pure of heart, Sheriff." He chuckled like a madman. "No…he was an embodiment of evil that fed on evil. Pure, unadulterated evil. You see, those five young women were not the sacrifices. They were but fuel for the fire of Barrett's evil." He trembled with laughter, his eyes shining. "Evil raged in Barrett's blood...the blood is the life, the source, the vehicle of passion, good and evil. Man has known that since the dawn of time. As Barrett tortured and killed those women I procured for him...the evil coursed through his blood like an all-consuming virus, growing stronger and stronger..." His face was twisting into a trembling mask of maniacal rage. Duggan's hand tightened on his gun. "Barrett was to have been the blood sacrifice. If only you hadn't interfered." His teeth clenched, his fingers tightening on the bed frame.

"If we hadn't interfered, then what?!" Duggan demanded.

"Then, you idiot..." Pendleton growled through clenched teeth as he leaned towards Duggan. "Then, at the stroke of midnight on this, what the Druids called All Hallows Eve...when the veil between worlds runs thin...I would have taken Barrett's blood...his blood...so richly charged with evil...into my own veins. That gun with which I shot your deputy was originally intended for myself, you see. Only by bringing myself to death's very door at the precise moment of the Solstice, the chosen one's blood coursing through my veins..." His eyes were totally glazed over with madness now. He was frothing at the mouth. Duggan took a step back. "Only thus could I become the vessel of Azgaaroth." He looked to the thundering sky beyond the ceiling. "Only thus could I become One with the Dark Lord and become his incarnation on Earth!"

Another crash of thunder, and everything went pitch black.

The hairs stood up on the back of Duggan's neck, his knees turning to putty as Pendleton's scream went through him like a skewer, deep to the marrow of the bone. The lights came on again moments later, though dim and smoky. Duggan's breathing was shallow, his eyes frozen to the sight before him. Pendleton's pale form hung limp from the exam table by his handcuffs, his dead eyes staring blankly at nothing, blood dribbling from his open mouth onto the floor.

Duggan was strangling, choking with fear as he ran from the exam room into the lobby. "Duggan..." Chief Landry said, running over to him. "What is it?"

"He's..." Duggan could barely breathe as he pointed into the corridor behind him. "He's dead."

"You idiot!" the Chief growled under his breath, his eyes flashing as he glanced around. "I just told you to rough him up a little. Don't you know better than...?"

"Chief...I swear I didn't..." He glanced at the clock over the reception desk. One minute to midnight. Something clicked. Once he could think again, ice water rushed through his veins and touched his heart. "Chief...Sullivan. Did they give him the transfusion?"

"Yeah. He's in surgery now. I guess they're pumping Barrett's blood into him this minute. They said he almost died, but..."

Duggan grabbed the other man by the lapels, blood pounding through his head. "Chief...for God's sake, stop them!"

"Get your hands off me! What the hell's gotten into you?" A

flash of lightning, and the lights went out again.

"Where's that emergency generator?" someone shouted.

Duggan ran through the darkened lobby, toward the operating room, his mind a black wave of numbing fear. "Duggan!" the Chief yelled after him. "Where the hell are you going? Come back here!!"

"Sir, you can't go back there!" some woman shouted. "Security! Stop that man!"

It was pitch black when he reached the operating theatre. He lit his lighter, finding his way through the operating room door. No one. No one at all. He broke out in a cold sweat, his heart pounding, blood drumming through his ears. His feet found something on the floor, here and there. Like sacks or mounds of laundry. Soft and yielding. As he stumbled along, he felt at times he was walking through something like garbage. He felt something soft and wet oozing under his shoes. He held the light high, afraid to look down. His breath grew more rapid.

"Hey, Duggan." He nearly jumped out of his skin at the sound of Sullivan's voice. He turned, his light flickering across Sullivan's face, deathly pale and faintly smiling as he stood directly beside him. "Come to visit me?"

"Sullivan," he choked out, barely able to fill his lungs with enough air to speak. "Is that....you?"

"Who else could it be, ol' buddy?" He grinned, a cold

chuckling deep in his throat that crawled with icy fingers up Duggan's spine. Duggan's mouth dropped, the lighter shaking in his hand as Sullivan's eyes brimmed over with blood that streamed down his cheeks. Serpentine tentacles and monstrous claws tore their way out from inside his body.

Duggan screamed. He dropped the lighter and ran, tripping over the horrid obstacles in his path, the soles of his shoes slipping over what was on the floor. The lights flashed on and off wildly as he crashed through the doors. That hideous laughter. Guards and orderlies screaming in terror, shielding their eyes at what was coming through the door behind him. Duggan didn't want to look. But, something pulled his eyes backward toward the thing coming after him. His eyes froze in the flashing light, a scream catching in his throat. It was a nightmare. He screamed again and again in his mind. It couldn't be real. Like a crawling, slithering swarm of nameless vermin flowing into a single wave, a single mass, congealing to form some unimaginable tentacled monstrosity with countless clicking mandibles, an immense, sucking maw opening into multiple lashing, fanged serpentine mouths, like the writhing heads of a hydra.

People were torn apart in front of him, their screams echoing in his ears as they died. He drew his revolver and emptied it into the writhing maw of hell he saw before him. The muzzle flashes sparked into the darkness until the hammer fell dull and uselessly. The laughter grew louder. He ran, screams all around him. He covered his ears against the sound of tearing flesh and shattering bone. He crashed through the doors of the chapel and fell to his knees before the crucifix, his hands clasped, his head bowed.

"Dear God," he whimpered, his eyes tearing. "Dear Son of God, please..."

"Help me!" a woman screamed, somewhere behind him. He turned and saw her, pounding at the window of the chapel door, flashing light behind her. It was Carol Sullivan. "Help me, please!" He bounded to the door and pulled her through. Her blue eyes flashed with wild fear. "My God, Pete, what's going on out there? What's going on?!" She ran to the crucifix and fell to the floor in front of it, crying hysterically.

"Carol...it's okay," he said. It sounded as stupid in his head as he thought it must have sounded to her. He just wanted something to cling to. Someone to take care of. "I...I think we're safe as long as we stay in here."

Her sobs turned slowly to laughter. His blood slowly froze as he realized it wasn't terrified, hysterical laughter. It was the same cruel, delighted laughter he'd heard in the operating room. She turned to him in the flickering light, her eyes brimming with blood. "Surprise," she said as the crucifix bled and shattered. He screamed as something inhuman grew, tearing its way out of her dead body.

The Child Inside

by Tony Wayne Brown

The baby's cherubic face is plastered against the outside of one of Flight 1689's windows, looking at me with moon-size eyes! Never before realizing how much it looked like me, I close my eyelids tightly, grind the heels of my hands into them, and reopen them to find that, of course, the child is not there. Something is crusted all over my hands and flakes of it fall on my eyeballs, causing me to blink like a fluttering moth. Finally tears wash whatever it is away and I turn my palms up and see that they are covered with dried blood.

My God! My wrists are slit! Luckily the wounds are not deep. With a shudder I look forward to see who could have perpetrated such a cowardly act. The other five passengers, all of whom were fast asleep prior to my unconsciousness, are in the same positions as before, but now with not even a miniscule motion of respiration, and with their heads tilted downward unnaturally. Each one has a small airline blanket covering their upper bodies, though I do *not* have one near me.

Odd, indeed.

Bobby and Rich, the brothers of mine who dislike each other as much as I despise them, are sitting on opposite sides of the aisle, one in a seat just ahead of mine, the other all the way forward, slumped like the rest. The two low-life rats got the bulk of my father's estate in the court ruling that I had demanded must be made last night, no matter the hour, and here am I this morning, forced to share this commuter turboprop with those scumbags.

My sister Mary, who got most of the rest of his ill-gotten wealth by pretending to take care of the old man, is seated in the row just opposite. Absolute silence reigns in the plane; the only exception is the reassuring roar of the engines. The silence is a pleasant change from the cackling that was going on before, I must admit, but there is an eerie nature about it. Something is wrong here far beyond the unexplainable cuts on my wrists.

Despite my trepidation, I rise and lean over the seat ahead of me. With a start I see that my oldest brother is pale-white and lifeless. His neck has been slit and a river of dried blood covers the front of his starkly white designer shirt. It will certainly never be purely white again. What a shame.

A more careful examination of my sister across the aisle reveals that she has suffered the same awful ending. She will never benefit now from kowtowing to our father and using her womanly ways to beguile him into depriving me, his oldest child, of my rightful inheritance.

My youngest brother, on the right ahead of me, is ashen white also. Surely that means that *I* now will be driving my father's new

Cadillac instead of him, assuming, of course, that the people in the Motor Vehicle License Division who have been conspiring to deny me the right to drive can be forced to mend their ways.

The task of revealing their plot against me shall have to wait, though. A monster has been at work here. I immediately think of that damn cherubic child, but surely...

I check the other two passengers, and the story is the same. Oddly, they all look at peace, almost as if they know that only their transference to another place could allow true happiness to come to me. The only passengers on this small jet other than my brothers and sister – the couple in their mid-thirties who had kept broadcasting to the world about their fantastic sex escapades even after I'd politely requested twice that they keep their carnal lust to themselves – are leaned over, touching heads as lovers do. Still they keep at it despite their mortal wounds. I can't help wondering if they would trade the chatter about their great sex life for life itself, given the chance. Often, as I well know, there are no second chances.

Still wobbly from the loss of blood, I cannot help smiling as I think of how my brothers and sister will not enjoy a single day of the life of ease they surely had anticipated having after plotting to convince our father that I was a paranoid schizophrenic psychopath who would squander whatever portion of his estate he might have left me. I must push the ironic humor of it all aside, though, to find the child and determine that it is alive, and not responsible for this massacre.

It strikes me that I am likely to soon succumb to a similar wound. I feel a great weakness and – knowing what I'm likely to find – probe my neck gently with my fingers, only to discover that it has not suffered the same ghastly fate as the others who lie scattered around me like sweet-smelling scythed hay. It must be the surface cuts across my wrists that have made me pale and lightheaded.

Why is my wound so much slighter than the others? Did the child grow tired of its amusement? I fight the thought. Of course that smiling face could not have done such a thing. As awareness returns more fully, my thoughts are full of the child. While it cannot be outside the airplane, I see it nowhere inside it either.

The plane's engines are still humming and it is flying level as though nothing is wrong, thank God, so the pilots must have been blissfully safe from this massacre, but the baby is nowhere to be found. It cannot be on the outside...it just *cannot*. The only two places I haven't looked are the small bathroom and the pilots' cabin. I quiver as I approach the restroom, though I know the baby must be in it and that a tiny child could not have any responsibility for such horror.

What a strange thing! Several airline blankets are covering a lump on the floor just beyond the restroom door, in the snack area. One of the blankets has a bloody imprint of a half-missing pinkie finger such as the one my younger brother bit off my right hand in a fight long ago. My missing blanket!

Could the culprit really be the child within after all?

I cease breathing for a moment as I tug ever so slightly at the blanket and a lifeless hand flops out. It does not belong to a child, however, so I must proceed. Carefully I lift the other blankets one by one, revealing the uniformed body of the captain of the plane atop the body of a woman with a short blue skirt whom I recognize as the bubbly blonde waitress who had been so nauseatingly filled with joy over her upcoming marriage to the co-pilot of this very craft.

A rounded crater is in their skulls, and I realize they've both been struck by that same steel coffeepot she had been using when she'd poured hot coffee on my new outfit I bought last week so I could go out on the town after what I'd thought would be my extensive inheritance. I silently forgive her stupidity for spilling that vile liquid on me, wishing that I had accepted her sincere apology over her moronic actions. How insignificant such a minor transgression seems now.

If only...

It seems that the pilot, who had been regaling us with his tale of being able to retire early after this very flight because he'd inherited a vast estate in Bolivia, had been kneeling when he'd been surprised from behind while examining his co-worker. I close my eyes and give a short, ardent prayer that whatever evil thing committed this nightmare against this lucky man suffers an eternity in the lowest reaches of Hell, no matter who it might be.

Slowly I turn the bathroom door handle and ease it open, only to find a stark contrast to the mayhem I've seen. The restroom is pristine, not having been used at all during the flight, it seems. There is no sign of the child in there, though, but it couldn't disappear from a plane in mid-flight...surely not! I go back over each seat, searching...searching under them all...in every little crack, yet it still is not to be seen.

There is only one logical conclusion. The co-pilot must have discovered the child and taken it into the cabin, not suspecting what now seems likely. What else could he have done, having found such carnage in the bowels of this aircraft and probably presuming me dead? Moving to the front of the cabin with utmost fear, I travel at a pace that the slowest of turtles would race past. I cannot bear to even look at the cabin door, knowing that if it is unlocked the child has to be the one who performed this awful deed, as crazy as that sounds. I, after all, was passed out and on the threshold of traveling to a better place myself.

Finally looking at the door just in front of me now, I snort in shock. It is not even fully shut and the smudge of red on the handle portends what I am likely to find beyond it. Trembling without the possibility of cessation, I must, nonetheless, continue. Again I hesitate, anticipating the horror I will surely find. The child is a monster. That cherubic face has somehow caused all this evil, and I am its progenitor. I have sensed for many years, I reluctantly confess, that such a scene might occur. The aura of madness that has emanated from it ever since it came into being has been constantly palpable. The madness of it all will surely drive me insane, also, for I know what must be done if that proves to be the case. Easing the door open a crack, I see that the seat to the right is empty.

A sigh of regret escapes me as my head rotates to the left. A bloody pilot's cap is draped over the plane's throttle in the center and a thin ribbon of dried blood runs from left to right on the floor coming from the direction of the co-pilot's chair. An instrument panel light indicates that the automatic pilot is engaged. I open the door a tad further, my heart pounding with incredible force that shall surely puncture the surface of my heaving chest even as I strive mightily to not make a noise that will betray my approach. The sound of the "Tubular Bells" theme from *The Exorcist* is exploding from above me...behind me...all around me. I tremble as I recall hearing that repetitive tune over and over and over and over again when I had watched the movie ten times in two days back in 1973 – the same year that the child of horror came into my world. How many hundreds of times after that had I played the album of Mike Oldfield's haunting tune? It rains down now, showering me from every direction and within my skull, even coming from outside the hull of the plane!

Ever more slowly I twist my head around the door and see my evil progeny sitting alone in the co-pilot's seat...no, the co-pilot *is* there, but a river of dried blood is down his side, puddled on the floor, and the child is sitting on his lap. How can the man not hear this cacophony of echoing, resounding music pounding, pounding, *pounding*? And it's obvious that a terrible struggle has taken place there, for he is hatless and part of his jacket is ripped. His head is touching his chest, and it seems only his safety harness keeps him from falling over. How can he not know that the "innocent" child in front of him is a monstrous thing that has performed truly despicable work this day? Yet the man stares ahead at the night sky, though at an odd angle, and without any motion at all.

I fully enter the cabin, determined to end the killing spree. I must do what has to be done, what God surely wants to be done – what he *commands* me to do. From my vest pocket I take the crimson-covered sliver of granite that I have kept for such an occasion since I first sensed the child's true nature, reach around the chair, and swiftly, *deeply*, draw the rock's razor-sharp edge across the co-pilot's pale-white neck. He makes not the slightest sound as the eternally-cherubic child now looking at me from outside the cockpit window smiles, and I smile back, knowing we are now safe against the evil that lurked within the bowels of Flight 1689.

Watching the Eater
by Shaun Avery

The guy on the screen before me was eating and eating and eating.

They kept putting stuff in front of him and he kept shoveling it down.

It felt like some kind of weird dream, only I knew I was awake right now. Awake and bored and alone, as usual, so I'd slumped into the main room and switched on the TV.

And there he was.

The Eater.

There were two people standing next to him, one at either side, a man and a woman, and they were the ones feeding him, handing him burgers and hot dogs, a seemingly endless supply of food, and although he looked happy enough I still kind of felt sorry for the guy, even then. That said, he had two companions there with him whilst I sat on my own, so who was *I* to pity anybody?

That wasn't exactly a good thought to return to bed on. But time was pressing and I had work in the morning, so I switched off the TV.

Then stood there in the silence.

Something I was used to.

Still unable to sleep, I watched the show the next few nights. I was starting to feel like The Eater was my only friend.

Until the day in the work canteen, later that week.

"It's amazing," Jimmy said. "You wouldn't believe the amount this guy puts away."

"You mean they just keep giving him food?" Sandra said.

"That's right."

"And he eats it, no matter what they give him?"

"Yep. No matter what."

Jimmy had the habit of doing that, repeating your own words back at you. Thing is, though, he always sounded smarter saying it than you did.

I looked across at them – four of my colleagues around a table, Jimmy and Sandra, Peter and Melissa – from the table where I, of course, sat alone. I listened, too – not exactly eavesdropping, more wanting to be a part of things but not possessing the words to do so.

Yet.

"So what's so fun about watching that?" Melissa wanted to know.

Jimmy looked at her. "Are you kidding?"

"No," she replied. "I really want to know."

Peter cut in here, saying, "If you saw the guy, you'd know why it's funny."

"Well," Sandra said, "I might give it a try, then."

She looked at Jimmy as she said this, and even from over here I could tell that the words were spoken mainly for him, to impress him.

Jimmy seemed to miss this fact, though, saying, "You'd better be quick. You already missed the first episode last night."

Then something strange happened.

Something very strange indeed.

I entered the conversation.

Those words probably sound simple to you. But if you'd sat in the corner so many times, wanting to be one with the group but never daring to make a move, you'd know what a pretty big deal it was.

They looked across at me.

As if seeing me for the first time.

Jimmy asked me, "What did you say?" before floundering for a few seconds, clearly unable to remember my name.

Sandra came to his rescue. "Tim, right?"

"Actually," I replied, "it's Tom."

"Oh yeah, Tom." Peter nodded. "So, what did you say, Tom?"

"Last night wasn't the first episode," I repeated. "I've been watching it since Monday."

"Monday?" Jimmy said, sounding surprised. "You mean I've missed three whole days of him eating stuff?"

"Well," I shrugged, sort of uncomfortable and yet thrilled at the same time, "yeah."

Jimmy grinned and said, "Tommy, my boy, you'd best pull up a chair and tell me what I've missed."

And with a huge grin on my face, I did just that.

As the weeks progressed, we learnt a little bit more about the people behind the show.

"I'm Bud," the male half of the hand-feeding duo said. "And you can call my good lady friend –"

She was probably supposed to say her piece straight away. But she was busy placing a bucket full of chicken wings in The Eater's meaty fingers, and so missed her cue. It wasn't until he had begun to work them into his constantly crunching mouth that she looked to the camera, mounted on its faithful stand, and said, "Sarah. That's me. And our friend with the healthy appetite is . . ."

"The Eater," Bud cut in, earning himself a look from Sarah that struck me as dark. "What?" he asked her. "That's the name of the show, that's the only name our good buddy needs."

Bud patted The Eater's cheek.

My mobile phone vibrated.

Bud ran a hand down The Eater's chins.

I read the text message.

"He's the star of the show," Bud said.

My text said, *you watching?*

"Aren't you, buddy?"

It was from Jimmy.

The Eater said, "Food."

I texted back: *sure am.*

Back on the screen, the chicken wings had long since gone, the only trace of their existence the bucket, which The Eater had pulped in his hands to get at the food contained within, and the grease from them, which stained his face. There was just no stopping the guy, though, and he was already on to his eight pizza of the night, Bud bemoaning the fact that the slices were too small.

Sarah cut him off mid-rant, saying, "We're almost done here tonight. But be sure to tune in tomorrow, for a very special episode!"

I received another text then.

Wonder what she means by that?

Then Jimmy made a suggestion.

"I wonder where they get all the money for the food," Melissa said.

I use the words "Melissa said." But it was hard for me to think of the woman sitting across from me as actually *being* Melissa. I was so used to seeing her in work clothes that her current jeans-and-trainers combo made her look like someone else entirely.

Sandra came back into the room, carrying bowls full of nibbles. "I see what you mean, Jimmy," she said. "I wondered why anyone would want to watch this, but it's kind of addictive once you start."

She laid the bowls down on the table before me and said, "Crisp, Tom?"

"Yeah," Jimmy said, readying the TV. "Tuck in."

In case you hadn't guessed, I had been invited round to spend some after-hours time with the guys. So we were all sitting in Sandra's front room, waiting for the eating to start.

I took a nibble and, well, nibbled it.

Whilst Peter brought in the drinks.

He handed them around and we drank and we talked and everyone was having a good time.

But then Jimmy reached in his pocket.

Pulled out a small, clear bag.

Let us all see what was in it.

"Jimmy," Sandra said, giggling slightly. "You're naughty."

Unlike Melissa's casual attire, Sandra was wearing a dress, and it was pretty obvious that she was using her clothing – and what lay beneath it – to try to make Jimmy notice her.

Apparently oblivious to this, he asked, "Anyone else get the munchies off this stuff?"

Jimmy addressed this question to all of us, not just Sandra, and I saw her pout at this.

"I don't," Peter said. Looking at his body, which was stick thin, you could believe it.

"Some do, though," Melissa added.

Jimmy turned his gaze on her. "Do you?"

"Ah now," she said. "I don't do that stuff." She winked at him. "I'm a good girl."

Sandra's pout increased significantly at this.

But I could tell that it wasn't the girls Jimmy was interested in right now.

Looking at me, he said, "Think that's how The Eater got started?"

"I don't know," I told him. "Why do you ask?"

"Just wondering," he said, "if we could ever make our own version of the show."

Still looking at me as he said it.

His gaze kind of intense.

But then Sandra said, "You going to open that bag or not?" and the moment was broken.

"Yeah," Peter told him. "Get sharing."

"And make it quick," Melissa insisted. "The show's about to start."

"Right, right." Jimmy seemed to snap out of it then, his intensity fading, and he hopped over to the TV to switch it on.

But just before the show began, I caught him looking over at me again.

"Now," Bud was saying onscreen, "our good friend The Eater has chowed his way through some fine delicacies these past few weeks."

The Eater burped his appreciation of this fact.

"About 700 bags of chips, a vast array of kebabs – doner, chicken *and* shish varieties, food followers – greasy chicken wings and breast and every type of pizza on the menu . . ."

"And a few that aren't," Sarah put in, sounding proud. "Ones we had to create ourselves."

"He has also," Bud continued, "drunk quite a large amount of soft drinks. Though TV regulations prohibit us from naming names –"

"Lousy regulations," Sarah commented, forcing The Eater's mouth open with a surgical clamp.

"However," and here Bud's voice turned serious, "certain viewers have been complaining that our food choices are not good – not *healthy* – for our friend."

Hearing this, we all looked around at each other.

"*I* didn't complain," Peter protested.

"Shut up, dummy," Jimmy told him. "Think we're the only people that watch this show?"

"We've been accused of poisoning our friend," Sarah went on, "by giving him cheap, mass-produced food."

"How come they never let him speak?" Melissa wondered.

"Maybe he's not good at public speaking," Sandra replied.

Her frustration at Jimmy now seemingly gone, she was focused on the TV.

"He's not *there* to speak," the object of her earlier desire said. "He's there to eat. That's all."

And was it the contents of his little bag making me paranoid, or did he look at *me* as he said that?

"Just to show that this is complete rubbish," Bud said, "tonight we'll be giving The Eater a meal fit for a king."

Off-screen, Sarah rustled a bag, and I swear I saw The Eater drool.

And I don't know what it was, maybe the smoke in the air and in my lungs, maybe just the euphoria of finally having friends, but my eyes seemed to meet The Eater's own, and I don't mean just through the TV but as if we were in the same room, as if there was no screen between us, no barrier at all, and then he was sucking me in, eating my spirit and soul as if I was the food he had been eating those past few weeks, and then I was inside him but I was also *him*, the man himself, two halves of the same soul, and that soul was pained, in torment.

I felt what he felt.

Saw what he saw.

"Caviar!" Bud announced. "A nightmare to get when you can't spell the word, let alone know what it is. But I came through!"

Sarah brought the bag across to The Eater.

To me.

Her face twisting into something demonic, her hands becoming claws as they pushed the food towards The Eater's waiting mouth.

I was out again now – I was back in Sandra's front room, back in myself. But I still felt what I had felt inside The Eater. And for the first time ever, I felt bad about watching this.

Sarah said, "Plus, of course, champagne – the finest our budget could afford!"

Then she poured some into The Eater's mouth.

My friends all laughed at this.

But I could only feign a smile.

A few days later Jimmy stopped by my desk and said, "No need to thank me."

I looked up at him.

"What?"

"For what I just did for you . . . no need to thank me."

I decided to go along with it. "What did you just do?"

"I booked us all tickets, man."

He grinned.

"The Eater's coming to town."

#

Back at Sandra's, Jimmy had implied that we weren't the only people who watched the show. When I saw how packed the stadium was, I realised that he was right.

I should have been thrilled to be amongst this many people – not just the colleagues who had become my friends, but thousands of others, too, all of us united here by our love of watching a man eat and eat and eat. Wasn't this what I had dreamt of, sitting alone in my house for so long?

Yep.

It was.

My problem?

I had stopped watching The Eater.

Something had changed for me, watching it at Sandra's house. I'm not saying I believed I had *really* bonded with him during that strange little vision, but I had seen a part of him that no one else seemed to see, certainly. I felt sorry for him.

So why was I here?

Good question.

A roar went through the stadium as Bud and Sarah stepped onto the grass down below. A place where football games were normally played, now it would be party to a live eating show.

The feeders were wearing headset microphones, and Bud said into his, "welcome to the show!"

"The *interactive* show!" Sarah added.

That word made me uncomfortable, and I turned to Jimmy and said, "What does she mean?"

He grinned, and I realised I was starting to dislike that expression on him.

"You'll see," he said.

Then all chance of conversation was cut off as The Eater emerged.

He was unable to support his own weight, so they carried him out on the tines of a forklift truck.

The crowd booed *and* cheered him.

Then people began to walk down the stairs that separated the rows of the audience, and I saw they were carrying vast arrays of food.

And I finally understood where the "interactive" part of the show came from.

The Eater's face was displayed on a huge screen before us all, and I watched as Bud nudged him and said, "Get that mouth open wider, fatso."

"Unless you want us to use the surgical clamp again," Sarah added.

I gasped.

Whilst everyone around me laughed.

Without the TV screen between us, it was like we were seeing a different side of the feeders.

Jimmy, though, was staring at Bud with something close to awe.

Mouthing the words he had just said.

The audience were buying food from sellers, and they were all poised with items in hand, ready to start throwing them.

At The Eater.

Whose face, up there on the screen, no longer seemed wet with just the usual sweat and grease.

Jimmy handed me a sloppy sandwich.

"One I made earlier," he said. "For you."

He did not smile.

"What am I meant to do with this?" I asked.

"Your choice."

He shrugged.

"Throw it. Or eat it. Up to you."

I looked up at the screen.

This time, The Eater seemed to be staring into *my* soul.

Jimmy was, too.

I looked down at the sandwich in my hand.

Then stood . . .

Along with everybody else . . .

And I made my choice.

The House on the Corner
of Brim and Stone
by Marcia Colette

A red Dodge Intrepid pulled up behind Yvette Mills's car. She lowered her sunglasses enough to see Carolynn Dearborn, real estate agent extraordinaire, sitting behind the steering wheel, face red with anger and talking to someone on her cell phone. After turning off the engine, she hung up and got out. Whatever slipped up her skirt, Yvette hoped she wasn't caught up in the aftermath.

When Yvette opened the door, summer heat gushed inside her car. She swallowed and took in a deep breath through her nose and out her mouth. Just like that, her body adjusted and Savannah, Georgia's choking humidity lost its effect on her.

Black locks bounced a few inches past Carolynn's shoulder. She adjusted her glasses and held her hand out to Yvette as she hurried onto the sidewalk in front of the three-bedroom Colonial home. They stood about the same height and size, but Carolynn had a way of always looking her best whenever they touched base. Today, she wore a red business suit with black heels and a white shirt underneath.

"I'm sorry I'm late," she said in a nasally voice. "Traffic was awful trying to get here because there was an accident on the thruway."

Yvette checked her watch. "I wouldn't call six minutes disastrous."

"I wish all of my clients were as patient as you." Carolynn pulled out a packet of papers and began reading. "This home has three bedrooms, two baths, and a Jacuzzi out back. But the best feature is the redone basement that can be used as an in-law suite. Didn't you say your mother was moving in with you?"

Rather than answer her question, Yvette glanced around the neighborhood and noted the spacing of the surrounding homes. "It's a nice area. But it's a little crowded too. I mean – more than what I was hoping for."

Anyone else taking in the neighborhood would probably say it was gorgeous with the overhanging trees and enough room between the houses to park a couple of cars. But there was something about the standoffish neighbors that bothered her. One of them watched from a distance before shaking his head and plunking his garbage on the curb.

With a charming smile, Carolynn began writing something on her packet of papers. "So we're looking for a place with neighbors spaced farther apart. But since we're here, we might as well take a look at the place. You never know."

Yvette glanced at the second floor. Something from inside brushed the curtains. Though she didn't see who it was, she hoped the owners weren't home during the showing. That would be seriously awkward.

"Yeah sure," she said, unable to take her eyes off the second-floor window.

Carolynn dug inside her purse and pulled out a small piece of paper. Using it, she fumbled with the key compartment lock long enough to retrieve the keys and unlock the door. Glowing hardwood floors greeted them along with bright light radiating from the numerous windows. Carolynn stepped inside the foyer.

"Now this is a two-story Colonial," she said, arms spread wide. "The floors and the paint have just been redone. There's new carpeting in the living room and all the bedrooms have been redone too." She pulled another sheet of papers from her satchel and glanced over it. "Now I know you said you wanted all of the bedrooms on the second floor, which is what we have. But, the only one with a walk-in closet is the master. Let's go take a look at the living room, since that's where the built-in bookshelves are that you had hoped for. "

Yvette said nothing. A chill throughout the house made her rub her arms. But there was something else. A presence. But that was silly. Even though she thought it, she didn't believe it. Yvette had her share of strange phenomena in her line her of work. Hence, the reason why she wanted more space between her house and the next door neighbor's.

The smell of smoke was so thick that it touched more than just her nose. The scent came out of nowhere. Yvette glanced around the living room as though she was checking things out, but she wasn't. She was looking for a fire that wasn't there.

Another chill ran across her shoulder. She shivered. This was one weird house. The central air vents were high on the walls, so it wasn't like the air came from there. Another breeze ran across her throat. She jumped back.

"Are you okay?" Carolynn asked, reaching as though to steady her.

Yvette gulped. "You said the price was twenty thousand below market price. Is there something I should know about? Water damage, noisy neighbors, creatures in the attic, etc...? This isn't a foreclosure, is it?"

Carolynn stepped through the archway and into the separate dining room. "It's not a foreclosure. I promise. All I know is that it came up on the market three days ago and so far, eighteen people have been through the house, but nobody's made an offer. Here's the kitchen. As you can see, all the appliances have been updated."

Nobody bought it? That was weird. What in this house would turn people off? It was gorgeous and the price was definitely right. Heck, the place was practically a steal.

An unintelligible whisper came from behind. Yvette whirled around and stared, but nothing was there. A second whisper turned her around again. Other than Carolynn walking around the room and talking about the views from the windows that included a garden, the room was empty of anyone else.

The next breath came close to Yvette's ear. Rather than flinch, she held her ground despite the bone-chilling-type cold that crawled all the way into the marrow. A burnt almond stench invaded her nostrils, nearly curling the hairs. *What the fuck was that?*

Carolynn continued down the hall with her heels clicking on the hardwood floor. "This hall leads to the laundry room and the huge deck."

"Excuse me," Yvette interrupted. "But is there a bathroom I can use?"

"Sure." She pointed to one just as they were about to pass it.

Yvette stepped inside and closed the door. Light from the flooring in the hall seeped under the door, making it hard for any normal person to see.

Yvette wasn't normal.

Her mind had cleared and her senses opened up to her surroundings. Standing in front of the mirror, hands on either side of the sink, she lowered her head between her shoulders and mumbled a prayer. When the pressure dropped in the small room, she looked up.

A dark figure standing behind her stared back at her from the mirror. She hit the "on" switch on the wall and smiled, meeting the ghost's eyes.

The man looked to be in his mid-fifties and had a long shaggy beard around his thick lips. Worn overalls clutched the middle of his protruding belly. He wore a ragged shirt with a solid-colored patch on the elbow, and a pair of black boots covered in mud. He reminded her of the typical gold prospector back in the 1950s. The ghost carried a large pickaxe across one shoulder and a perpetual scowl etched on his dirty face. When he tilted his head forward as if in greeting, a gaping hole on the top of his head with bits and pieces of chipped bone and brains stood out. The dried blood straining his overalls and shirt made sense now.

A name came to mind.

"Roger Boatwright," Yvette said, not amused. "You're the reason why these people are selling their home so cheap? Even worse, you're keeping others away."

He tilted his head, his face etched with confusion. "Ain't even afraid of me," he said, with a thick southern accent. "Whenever I did that to the others, they ran outta here like a deer during hunting season."

She sighed and crossed her arms. "Ghosts can talk like anyone, assuming they have a sensitive enough ear to listen. Mediums or channelers have that gift. I'm neither."

"Then what are you?"

"You might say I'm a really good observer."

"It's my land, you know," Roger said as though he were up to standing his ground from the first visitor to the nineteenth. "I've laid claim to it."

"What happened?" Yvette asked.

"Don't know. Something hit me. An explosion, I reckon. How's it that you can see me? That you're not afraid? One tip of my head sends 'em running. Two women busted their asses when their heels slid across these fancy floors, trying to get out of here so fast." He laughed.

"I'm an angel sent by God to walk among the living. I have a sixth sense that lets me know when otherworldly things are around. You're a ghost, so that sets my senses off, both sixth and otherwise."

"An angel?" He waved his hand. "You're shittin' me."

"No, I'm not."

He dropped the pickaxe and reached for her hand. When his fingers went through hers, he pulled back and stared at his palms. "Lord God Almighty." Letting his hands rest at his sides, he tilted his head again and appeared confounded. "Wow. A colored angel. I guess y'all go to Heaven too. Good thing our folks taught you some Christianity rather than all that hoopin' and hollerin' y'all are used to. Tell me something though. Why has God done this to me? I was only tryin' to protect my land. Then came Jafferty and the others. They've been trying to take what's mine for ages. So they took me to court. When they didn't get their way, Jafferty promised he'd blow me off the property. I guess he succeeded."

Yvette hardly listened past the "C" word. Yes, she was African

American. But, having been a white woman who had spent nearly 200 years switching from body to body, even she had become sensitive to racial slurs. That was her human half encroaching on her angelic half. It was one of the side effects of being a land-walker angel.

She closed her eyes and breathed in through her nose and out through her mouth, calming her antagonized nerves. "I can't answer your question because it's *His* plan. Just because I'm an angel doesn't make me privy to what's going on in God's mind."

He waved a finger at her. "Look here, missy, I'm a good, church-going fella. I reads my Bible every day and take communion like I'm supposed to. Why has He forsaken me? Why aren't I in Heaven? Hell, why aren't you?"

Yvette half-smiled. "I told you, it's not up to me to decide who goes and who doesn't. But like you said before, this is your land and you won't let it go. If you won't let it go, then why would God take you away from something that you love more than the paradise that He promises? Obviously, your heart is here. Tied to earthly things. Not tied to what matters."

"Then all I have to do is let go, right? Denounce this land and He'll take me up in the clouds."

She closed her eyes and sighed. "Not exactly. This is only a guess, but I'd say you have to learn forgiveness, too. Jafferty killed you. There's no mistake about where he's going. But you've held a grudge for..." She had to stop and really think about that one. Other than a name, Yvette couldn't read ghosts as well as one would think. "…a while, I suppose."

"What year is this?" Roger asked.

Most ghosts had lousy memories. Their sense of time and space would never change, so it didn't make sense for them to keep track. That was why ghosts only haunted the areas with which they had familiarity. They walked the same paths, repeated the same gestures. That was all they knew.

"It's 2013," she said. "You've been here a long time."

"Then how do I leave? How do I go to Heaven like you did?"

She sighed. They had already discussed this, so she didn't want to rehash it again. He'd forget before she could get to view the finished basement. Even worse, he'd pester her until she gave him some sort of answer.

A knock came at the door.

"Is everything okay in there?" Carolynn asked.

"Fine," Yvette shouted. "Just a slight stomachache. It might be some bad sushi I had before I came. I'll be out in a minute."

Roger dove for her hand again. And *again*, his slipped through.

A cold spot settled on her skin. Emotions ruled a ghost's interaction. That meant the longer Yvette stayed, the easier it would be for him to interact with her.

"Don't go," Roger pleaded. "You're an angel sent from God to help me. These weird people stole my land. They don't know nothin' about God. They go to church on Sundays, but then they come home to lie, cheat, and steal. They call themselves Catholics, but I call them heathens."

"He who is without sin, let him cast the first stone." Truth be told, Yvette didn't know the bible from front to back or memorize any scriptures except those that stuck to her brain after hearing them repeatedly. Since most Christians knew that one, hearing it come from an angel might have a greater impact. "These people are not your concern. But you'd get along a lot better if you stopped trying to harass them out of their home."

"You goddamn, useless nigger. I'm not going to let–"

"The year is 2013 and this is *not* your home anymore." She glared at him, trying her best to keep her voice low. "Don't make me exorcise you from this house. If I have to force your behind out, then you're going straight to hell. So my advice to you is to get yourself right with God first. That'll at least put you on the right path to Heaven. Now I've given all the guidance I can. You have to decide what you want to do with it." Dismissing him, she waved her hand through his solid-like form and said, "Be gone with you."

Like that, he floated upward through the ceiling.

Yvette had the ability to push ghosts out of her vicinity, which was easier than exorcising them from a house. An exorcism took too much energy and needed the backing of an archangel. For both their sakes, she simply invoked her corporeal "right" of passage on this spiritual plane. Unfortunately, there were still those who had enough darkness to push a young angel such as herself off this plane, too.

Yvette turned back to the mirror and gazed at her five-foot-five, 130-pound frame. She wouldn't have been walking the Earth had it not been for Mr. Cummings. He strangled her back in 1806 because she had befriended a colored man on her pa's plantation in Georgia. He called her a "nigger-loving bitch-whore" so she slapped him. Mr. Cummings had it coming to him. Ever since she was old enough to visit the country store on her own, his snake eyes always watched her in such a shameful manner. That weasel had prowled the aisles, looking at her whilst she picked up flour sacks and perused the newly stocked bundles of material for a new dress.

Her names changed with each rebirth. Today, she was Yvette Mills, Angel of God, here to monitor the paranormal world. Since she walked the Earth like everyone else, they would be judged by the same standards. Sadly, it also meant she was just as prone to sin, too.

Another knock.

Sighing, Yvette clicked off the light and opened the door. "Sorry it took me so long. You – uh – might not want to go in there."

Concern marred Carolynn's face. "Are you okay? Do you want to continue the tour?"

She nodded, wondering if there were any other ghosts haunting this house. "Yeah. I'll be fine. Just little nausea I guess."

Yvette had seen everything she wanted to see and decided against this house the minute she saw the claustrophobic neighborhood and smelled the smoke.

"So what do you think?" Carolynn asked as they rounded the second floor banister.

"It's okay," she replied. "But it's not what I'm looking for. I don't need a Jacuzzi or a swimming pool, and certainly not on a back deck for the neighbors on either side to see. I'd have to put up a privacy fence, which isn't in my budget." It was a weak argument at best. Still, she'd have to keep a close eye on the house, if Roger kept running people off.

Carolynn smiled. "Well, that's okay. Since this place met some of the other criteria, I assumed it was worth a shot. No matter. We'll find you that perfect house if it's the last thing we do." She gestured her to go first down the stairs.

Everything seemed to move in slow motion. The smell of burnt almonds, a cold breeze against the back of her neck. Just as her toe was about to land on the first step, something shoved her heel out from underneath her. Yvette jutted her arms out in front of her catching only air. She pitched forward and hit the steps hard, tumbling and watching the white banister, hardwood stairs, and Carolynn's terrified face pass by.

When her body came to rest at the bottom, the dizziness had yet to settle. Gulps of fresh air helped her ease down the nausea that volleyed in her stomach. Everything hurt, especially the knee that twisted on its own. Or she should say, the one that someone had helped twist for her when they tripped her down the staircase. A sore shoulder that felt like someone tried to rip it out of the socket didn't help.

"Don't move," Carolynn said as she dropped by her side. "I'm callin' an ambulance. Everything will be okay, hon, just stay still."

"No. I can't..." Yvette lifted her head just enough to stare at the ghostly presence sauntering down the steps.

Was this the end? Was God recalling her? He let her stay for decades and this is how he wanted her to transition to a new body? What did she do? What happened to dying of old age?

Roger Boatwright chuckled to himself, both thumbs hooked into his overall's pockets. Over Carolynn's shoulders, and invisible to her, he stared at her with a smirk splaying his wrinkled face. "Hee-hee-hee-hee-hee. You thought you had the best of me, you colored bitch! Thought you could cast me away. Well, I sure showed you. Just like I showed that pompous bellied bastard when he got a priest in here to bless the house. No one's throwing me off my property, you hear? No one! This here piece of land is mine."

"Wrong." Yvette extended her hand to him, fingers spread wide. "Roger Sommersby Boatwright, I cast you out. As a child of God and His anointed judge, by all that is holy. I banish you from this place, never to return. Convicted by your own words, let Proverbs

24:20 be my guide."

Roger's face drooped. Then without warning, he let his head fall backward and shrieked so loud that it splintered the swaying chandelier above the foyer.

Carolynn, oblivious to the withering ghost that stood behind her, dropped her cell phone and ducked as glass shards sprayed everywhere. She threw her frightened body on top of Yvette's to protect her from the explosive energy that blew through the house. God would put a jewel or two in her crown for that – Yvette was sure of it.

As Roger's solid body turned to nothing more than a translucent smoke screen, she felt his presence being swept away with him.

"Tell the Van Gorkums," Yvette breathed, painfully trying to get to her feet, "that their house is clean. They'll understand." The room swam around her, her energy exhausted beyond recovery.

"But you're hurt," Carolynn said, taking her by the arm and helping her off the floor. "You need to go to the hospital or something."

The more Yvette moved, the more that statement rang true. "Just get me out of here," she wheezed. "I need to catch my breath."

Yvette feared doctors because visiting them usually resulted in more pain than she could bear. An angel's sensitivity was off the chart and drugs rarely worked on her. This was what she got for exorcising a ghost without channeling the power of an archangel.

When they made it to the door, Yvette stopped and gulped. Nervousness gnawed at the pit of her stomach.

Dozens of demonic ghosts and wraiths stepped out onto the street, all of them staring back at her. There was a reason why the neighbors weren't so friendly. They were all scared to death. This place was a gateway to hell.

Sighing, Yvette turned to Carolynn and said, "I've changed my mind about the house."

The real estate agent looked at her confused. "But I thought you said–"

"I'll take it…now that I've got my work cut out for me."

Moonsbreath
by J. H. Fleming

I didn't go straight to the witch's house when I arrived in the town. After months of searching, I'd finally found what I was looking for. There was no need to rush. So I rented a room at the inn, The Silver Knight, and unpacked my few belongings. When I'd set out on my journey I left the majority of my possessions at home, instructing my closest neighbor to sell everything if I wasn't back in a year. No need for that now, since I'd reached my journey's end.

The sun was beginning to lower in the sky, its fading rays casting everything in a bright orange glow. The anticipation was almost too much, so I left my room and found a seat downstairs in the common room. A few of the younger men eyed me distrustfully, but an old man on his own doesn't present a danger, so I was left alone.

I listened to every bit of conversation I could, hoping to learn more of the witch. The last town had sworn by her powers, so I hoped she was as good as they said she was. Yet though I was attentive to the barest whisper, I could catch no trace of her. They seemed to talk of everything *but* her.

I finished my meal in silence, still listening, but I already knew I would get no help here. My source had told me she lived in the woods just off the path that led north out of town, so I hurried there when I'd finished at the inn. The sun was lower now, resting just at the edge of the rooftops, and a cool breeze brushed past me on my way. After all this time, my wish would finally be granted. I'd come close to giving up several times. Who could say that what I wanted was even possible? But I clung to my hope, for it was all I had left.

I reached the end of the houses and entered the forest, keeping a close eye out for the path that would lead to the witch's cottage. It was darker and colder beneath the canopy of leaves, the sunlight blocked by thousands of branches. I'd been raised in a similar forest, hundreds of miles away. My cottage sat dark and empty now beneath their sheltering arms, but not for much longer.

A narrower path branched off from the main one and disappeared into the forest on the right. I followed it with renewed eagerness, knowing I was moments away from gaining my heart's desire. After another couple minutes the trees opened up and there the cottage sat against a large hill. I took a deep breath and knocked on the door.

There was the sound of movement inside, then the door cracked open. The witch's face appeared in the opening, her eyes narrowed and suspicious. She was even older than I was, her face a network of craggy lines, her hair gray and scraggly, framing a round face. "What do you want?" she asked. Her voice was rough and deep, like that of someone who'd spent a lifetime yelling orders.

"I was told you'd be able to help me," I said. "I'm looking for a spell."

She frowned but opened the door and motioned me inside. It was small, but cozy. Plants and bottles and books covered every available surface, and a blazing fire roared on the far side of the room. There was only one other door in the room, probably leading to a bedroom.

"Sorry for dropping in on you like this."

She waved as though to say she was used to it. I took a seat on the couch and nervously cleared my throat. She sat in a chair facing me, leaned back, and crossed her arms.

"So. What brings a man like you all the way out here?"

"Please, I've searched for years, and I'm told you have the answer I'm looking for."

She blinked once, waiting for me to continue, so I said, "I want to bring someone back. Someone dead."

Her eyes widened and she opened her mouth, but I interrupted her. "Just this once, I want to see her again. I'm old, and it may not be too long before I join her. But I don't know what will happen then, so this may be my only chance, you see? I'll pay whatever you want."

She was shaking her head before I was through. "No good will come of it. Let the dead stay dead and move on with your life. You've survived this long already."

"Only because of the hope that drove me. If I could see her just once more I think I could finally be at peace."

"You're out of your mind," she said, standing and moving to the door.

I stood too, desperate. I'd waited this long; this couldn't be the final answer. "I'll give you whatever you want. Just name your price."

"You think you're the only one who's lost someone? Death is a part of life and there's nothing you can do to change it. I suggest you get used to it."

She stood in the open doorway, waiting for me to leave. But I couldn't accept it.

"You're right, I'm not the only person to have lost someone. And for that reason you should understand the need that drives me. The fear that this may be the final chance I have to see her. I'll take whatever consequences come with it."

I stood firm, daring her silently to try to turn me away. I would camp outside her door until she gave me what I wanted. What seemed like an eternity later she sighed and shut the door.

"You're a damn fool," she said. "Only trouble will come of this, and you'll regret you ever met me before the end. Sit back down. We've business to discuss."

#

The answer was simple in the end, and not at all what I

expected. A song, passed down through the generations, that pulled the souls of the dead back into our world. Moonsbreath, she called it. I'd learned to play the flute years ago, so I picked up the melody and practiced a few times, cutting off before the end so it wouldn't take effect yet. When she was satisfied with my rendition she sent me on my way, my coin purse reduced by more than half. I almost ran back to the inn, the pale street lamps guiding my way since the sun had sunk well below the horizon. I stumbled up to my room, latched the door, and began to pace. Should I play it now? I had intended to go home before using the witch's spell, but I didn't think I could wait that long.

I brought the flute to my lips and played the song in its entirety, focusing only on her as I did so, then listened to the last notes fade into the walls. Then I waited.

The minutes passed by slowly and still nothing happened. I wondered if I'd played it wrong, or if it just took a while for it to work. Or worse, if the witch had lied to me. I didn't know what would happen if I played the song again, so I continued to wait, but the stillness soon became unbearable. It couldn't possibly take this long.

The witch would just have to fix it, or give me my money back. I was down the stairs a moment later and halfway through the common room when I realized there was no sound: no talking, no laughter, no tink of forks against plates. All around me the patrons sat frozen in place, not a single eye blinking, nor a chest rising and falling. A few had even stopped in the middle of an action: walking, eating, reaching into a cabinet, sweeping. I peered into a few faces, moved my hand in front of their eyes, but none reacted. Before I could try to make sense of if I heard the screaming.

It was coming from outside the inn, a high-pitched keen of terror. I wrenched the front door open and looked up and down the street. At the far northern end a woman was running, stumbling over her own feet, looking behind her at every other step. In the dim light I couldn't tell what pursued her, but I could guess. The witch had mentioned them, the Gate Keepers, the guardians between the realms of the living and the dead. They would pursue her relentlessly until they had taken her back where she belonged.

"Over here!" I yelled, waving to get her attention. She moved closer until I could finally make out her features, and my breath caught in my throat at the sight. I'd known it was her, but knowing and seeing are two different things. Every feature was just as I remembered, from the curl of her long blonde hair to the bright blue shade of her eyes. I was just about to reach out and touch her when she pressed past me into the inn. Dark shapes moved at the end of the street and I quickly shut the door and latched it.

She sat at a table breathing heavily, her left arm caked in blood. Her eyes wandered over the room, noting all the frozen people, and I could see the questions building in her eyes. More than anything I wanted to take her hands in my own, smooth her hair away from her face, and press her close to me. But all she saw when she looked at me was an old man. I meant no more to her than any of the frozen people did.

"Let's find something for your wound," I said, unable to say anything else.

"What happened here?" she asked, her voice a familiar shock through my body. Even after all these years she held power over me, and she had no idea.

I found a towel behind the front counter and pressed it against her wound, a deep gash near her elbow. She flinched just a little, then sat still.

"Do you know where you are?" I asked. "What attacked you?"

She pressed her lips together and shook her head. "I was walking in the woods when those monsters attacked me. I've never seen anything like them before."

"What were they like?"

"Dark," she answered. "Cold. More like shadows than living beings."

The bleeding had stopped, so I wiped the rest of the blood off her arm and threw the towel in the wash basket under the counter.

"My name's Ezrielle," she said as I came back to the table.

"Micah," I answered instinctively, though that wasn't my name.

She smiled. "That's the name my husband and I have picked for our first son, if we have one. Poor Noah. He must be worried sick."

Something pressed against the door then, the knob turning repeatedly.

"They're here," I said, standing.

"Those monsters? Why did they follow me?"

"Come on," I said, grabbing her hand and pulling her through the back room. Glass broke as the Gate Keepers sought an entrance.

"What's going on?" she asked as I pulled open the back door. "You never said what happened to all those people. Are they connected?"

"Maybe," I answered. "We need to get to the witch's house. She'll know what to do."

"Witch?" she said, stopping in place. "I won't have anything to do with a devil worshipper."

"She's not like that," I promised. "She'll help us. She may know how to stop those things."

She considered a moment, then a Gate Keeper appeared around the corner of the building. It was like a living shadow, its body nothing more than pockets of darkness. It reached for her, but we were already running. More stumbled down the alley separating the buildings as the ones inside began to emerge from the back door. It was impossible to tell how many there were, with more appearing every second.

As we were about to clear the town and disappear into the forest a Gate Keeper reached out and grabbed Ezrielle's hair. She screamed as her hand was pulled from my grasp. I punched what I assumed was its face, my fist connecting with something solid but malleable. It stumbled back for only a moment and I pulled her to me, freeing her from its grasp. Then we were running again, plunging into the deeper darkness of the forest. They were everywhere, appearing behind every tree trunk until I couldn't tell what was wood and what was shadow.

"Faster!" I yelled, weaving through the trunks to avoid reaching fingers. In the distance I thought I could see a flickering light so I pulled her faster, my lungs straining for air. She was flagging behind me, every breath a struggle. It was only a bit further–

She fell to the ground, nearly pulling me down with her. A Gate Keeper emerged from the darkness, its fingers pulling at her hair. She screamed and I rammed into it, knocking us both to the ground. We scrabbled a moment, limbs twisted and caught, but I finally managed to free myself and pull Ezrielle to her feet. We burst through the trees into the clearing that sheltered the witch's house. I pounded on the door repeatedly.

"Open up!" I yelled. I could hear her shuffling around on the other side, taking her time. Finally she opened the door, her wizened face peering out at us.

"You again," she said, not sounding the least bit happy. "Haven't I done enough for you?"

"It's not for me!" I said. "Do it for her. I'll pay you whatever you ask."

"Damn right you will," she answered, pulling the door open for us to pass through. As soon as we were clear she closed the door and latched it. "I'm guessing they're not too far behind?" she asked. I just shook my head. She grunted and muttered some garbled words, closing her eyes briefly until she finished. "I made a barrier. It won't hold them for long, though."

"How do we stop them?" Ezrielle asked. "You deal with black arts and demons. Can't you control them?"

"We don't stop them," the old woman answered, ignoring the rest. "They won't stop until they take you back with them."

"Take me where? Why me?"

The witch shifted her gaze to me. "You mean you haven't told her?"

"I… I couldn't."

"Tell me what?" she demanded.

The witch folded her arms and cackled. "Well, go on then," she told me. "You went through all this trouble. Tell her what you did."

"Please, I just want to fix this. There must be a way–"

"You think you can just say you're sorry and everything will be all right?" the witch asked, her eyes narrowed and flashing. "There's only one way this will end, and there's nothing you can do about it. Now tell her what you did."

I looked at Ezrielle, and seeing her staring at me, scared and confused, completely ignorant of my sin, my heart broke a second time.

"My name's Noah," I said, my voice barely audible. "Fifty years ago my wife Ezrielle died."

"But that's..." she began, shaking her head. "What are you saying? We have the same name?"

"The witch gave me a song. Moonsbreath. It brings back the dead, and I played it. That's why the Gate Keepers are here."

"You think I'm your dead wife?" she asked, incredulous.

"I know you are."

She laughed, but there was no mirth in it. Seeing our serious faces she frowned. "Why would you think that? I'm not dead."

"You have a birthmark on your inner thigh," I said. "Your favorite flowers are violets. You've dreamed of seeing the ocean since you were a girl."

The blood drained from her face, but she was still shaking her head. "It doesn't make sense. If I'm dead, why don't I remember dying? I don't know how you know about me, but all of this is just... wrong. I want to go home."

"I'm sorry," I said, softening my voice. "I just... wanted to see you again." I had no better explanation, no motive that would make everything acceptable. Only my own selfishness. Seeing her confusion, her distrust of me, I realized I'd never have her back the way she was before. She was trapped in time, but my life had moved on, my body had aged. There was no going back.

The witch was glaring at me, no doubt feeling self-righteous. "Are you satisfied?" she asked. "Get everything you wanted?"

"Enough!" I said. "I was wrong. Don't you think I know that?"

"Then fix it," she said. She left us then, disappearing into the bedroom and shutting the door.

Ezrielle was silent, staring blankly at the floor. I approached her slowly, gently laid a hand on her shoulder. She recoiled from me, her eyes filled with something close to hatred.

"I love you," I said, not knowing what else to say. "Always."

I knew her face better than my own, even after all these years, but the eyes that stared at me now didn't belong to the wife I remembered.

"You make me sick," she said. "This was your plan all along, wasn't it? From the very first you wanted them to take me. What did you do to get the information? Who told you about me?"

There was no way to answer her, nothing I could say that would reach through the walls she'd erected around herself. There was only one thing to do, so I forced myself to do it. I walked over to the door, lifted the latch, and pulled it open.

They were waiting at the edge of the barrier, clawing at the air, searching for any weakness. The panicked look returned to her eyes. "No, I won't go with them!"

I'd never refused her before, not when it mattered. But I didn't answer. I walked back and reached for her hand.

She drew back, refusing to let me touch her again.

"I'm sorry," I repeated.

She started crying, looking for another escape, but there was nowhere to go.

I grabbed her hand and dragged her to the door. She screamed, trying to pit her feet against the floor, the furniture. For fifty years I'd longed just to see her one more time, willing to give anything for it.

The barrier broke then and the Gate Keepers surged forward. I pushed her through the doorway and released her. I could still remember the way she'd looked when I'd first seen her, the way she'd fiddled with her hair.

She fell to the ground and immediately tried to crawl back inside. Before she could I shut the door and collapsed against the frame, tears streaming down my face as she began to scream my name.

Fifty-five Shades of Green
by Ross Baxter

Harrison stepped slowly out of the limousine and looked around, completely lost. The driver closed the door behind him and silently pointed him in the direction of the non-descript building ahead. Harrison nodded his thanks and hesitantly walked towards the closed entrance door, noting the lack of windows in the grey-clad structure and a total absence of any distinguishing features. In the darkness he could see little of the unlit surroundings, but the quietness and lack of other visible lights indicated that he was a long way from the city.

Behind him the stretch Lincoln pulled smoothly away, leaving him alone in front of the anomalous building. He paused, looking around to fully regard his surroundings, but nothing gave him any clue of his location or the nature of the construction.

"Can I help you?"

Harrison turned back, startled, towards the door, now open. A figure stood in the doorway, silhouetted by the bright light from within.

"I'm here to see Mr Grant," Harrison replied, quickly regaining his composure.

"And you are?"

"The name's Harrison."

"Good evening Mr Harrison," said the large silhouette, stepping back through the door. "This way please."

Gripping his briefcase tightly, Harrison stepped into a modern reception room, practical and business-like, but with no company name or any logo in evidence. He followed the hulking figure silently through the empty reception and down a carpeted corridor with closed doors on either side. Stopping midway down the passage, the giant knocked gently on an unmarked door before opening it to let Harrison past.

"Mr Harrison," said an older man, rising from his chair behind a sumptuous wooden desk. "Please come in."

Harrison walked towards the desk to meet the proffered hand.

"I'm Mike Grant. I'm the one behind our recent correspondence."

"Three months of correspondence, and an hour's ride in a limo with windows you can't see out of," Harrison correctly curtly. "I hope it's going to be worth it."

"It is a long process," Grant conceded, returning to his chair. "But secrecy is for our mutual benefit. I'm sure you won't be disappointed."

Harrison nodded, hoping that Grant would not waste any more of his time. He took a seat at the chair facing Grant's desk, holding the briefcase tightly in his lap.

"Would you like a drink?" offered Grant, "or a cigar perhaps?"

Harrison raised his eyebrows. "Surely there's a law against smoking in a place of work?"

"There is, but that would be the least of my worries if we were ever found out." Grant smiled.

"I'll pass on the drink," said Harrison dryly. "I'd rather just get on with what I came for. But I need to see the goods before I part with any money. Ten thousand deposit plus three thousand per visit is an awful lot of money."

"It is a lot of money, but maintaining secrecy and security is expensive, as is sourcing and caring for our 'goods' as you put it."

"How many have you got?" Harrison quickly interjected.

"We have four dancers here at any one time, each one truly exceptional."

"I really wanted a bigger choice," grumbled Harrison.

"I'm sure you realise how hard it is to come by quality of this nature," said Grant unapologetically.

"So, let me see them," Harrison demanded.

Grant reached into a desk drawer and withdrew four slim leather-bound folders, offering them forward. "Here are the portfolios. Take your time, but remember you can only see one per visit."

Harrison reached across and eagerly took the files,

anticipation building as he placed them on the briefcase on his lap. With a dry mouth he opened the first folder, involuntarily sucking in his breath as he saw the contents. The pictures were just as he had hoped; in fact they were much better than he hoped. He hungrily scrutinised each photos, his eyes lingering on every shot and every angle, his eagerness growing exponentially as he browsed.

"These are...superb," Harrison stammered, hardly able to take his eyes from the files.

"Take your time," Grant said sagely, "there's no rush."

Harrison nodded, feasting on the photos, his palms sweating as he lovingly caressed and turned each page. Despite his desperation to start, choosing which one to see was proving difficult. The minutes passed, his mind a turmoil of indecision, each of the four subjects being perfect in every sense.

"Trudy," Harrison finally whispered. "I want Trudy."

"A wise choice, Mr Harrison," said Grant amiably. "All I need do now is to relive you of the case."

"The money's all there!" Harrison blurted.

"I'm sure it is," replied Grant smoothly. "Just leave it by the chair; I'll take you to Trudy right now."

Harrison stood awkwardly, trying to conceal the erection bulging in his trousers. Grant led him back into the corridor and further into the building, pausing before a wood paneled door with name 'Trudy' written conservatively on it.

"Here we are, Mr Harrison. I'll leave you to your enjoyment; you can take up to three hours. Do you have any questions?"

Harrison shook his head, desperate to get inside the room.

Grant inserted a pass card into an electronic reader set in the wall and the door clicked open. Harrison excitedly pushed through the opening, any embarrassment about his erection long forgotten.

Inside, the room appeared like any normal small hotel room, with a double bed, chair, and bathroom off to one side. The big difference was that the far wall was made of thick glass, and beyond lay a smaller room furnished with just a couch and a shining steel pole in the middle linking floor to ceiling. Trudy was not yet there. He sat hesitantly on the edge of the bed, staring at the sturdy door set in the far wall in breathless anticipation. A trickle of sweat ran down his forehead and his hands trembled as he waited, unsure of what would happen. Although Harrison was no stranger to lap dancing bars and other establishments catering for male clientele, this was completely different. This place had contacted him; and during the three-month vetting process promised to present him with the opportunity to indulge in his most secret and darkest fantasies.

He dared not take his eyes off the door in the smaller room in case he missed her entrance, wanting to savour every moment of his allotted time. Then door opened and Trudy walked slowly into the room. Harrison gasped. She was truly beautiful; tall, curvaceous, with long auburn hair that flowed past her shoulders to tumble down onto her black silk robe. Trudy returned his stare, gazing hungrily at him as she moved towards the pole and stopped. She stood motionless, her eyes locked on his. Music suddenly started and that seemed to animate her. She started swaying with the beat of the song, her hands unceremoniously tearing off the robe to reveal her nakedness. No bra or panties, just Trudy.

Harrison stood and moved to the glass screen, stopping only when the bulge in his trousers bumped hard on the barrier. She was the most beautiful thing he had ever seen. His eyes travelled slowly from her milky corneas, past thin bloodless lips and down her slender neck to her still pert breasts. The nipples stood erect, twin dark protuberances rising from the greenish tinge of once perfect skin, swinging in time to the music. As he watched she reached up to gently caress her own bosom, her fingers tweaking the tips as she continued to stare at him with lifeless dead eyes. He glanced hungrily downwards over her still un-bloated stomach to the hairiness of her sex. The auburn curls adorning her vulva were a surprise; he had expected it to be shaved but instantly saw the beauty of the mound, the green skin complementing the thick pubic hair like verdigris on copper. As Trudy's thin fingers raked down towards her pouting lips he pressed his face hard to the glass, aroused like never before.

\#

Grant smiled, pouring quality whiskey into two crystal tumblers as Harrison walked into his office.

"Your ninth visit in seven weeks," said Grant cheerfully. "I thought you deserve quality single malt at least."

"Thanks," Harrison murmured, taking the proffered glass.

"You said you wanted to see me?" Grant questioned, returning to his desk.

"I do," Harrison began, taking one of the chairs. "I want to talk about Trudy."

Grant nodded solemnly.

"I want to know more about her; where she came from, what she did, that sort of thing."

"It's all confidential information," Grant replied in a practiced monotone. "We can't disclose that sort of information as it could compromise our whole operation here. Somewhere she may still have relatives or friends, who probably wouldn't take kindly to our business model."

"I understand all that," said Harrison. "I just want some background, something to help me enjoy her dancing more."

"Well, the honest answer is that we don't know much about any of our dead girls. They're all Russian and…"

"Russian?" Harrison cut in.

"Yes," Grant replied, slightly surprised. "Now that the epidemic is under control in the States it's almost impossible to go around capturing any kind of zombie, never mind the specific type we need. We have to rely on countries still struggling with the outbreaks, where society has more to worry about than small scale trafficking. We also need societies which had a thriving sex economy."

"Why?" asked Harrison.

"Because when the dead resurrect as zombies they lose all memory, emotion, and rational thinking. All that remains are the basic animal instincts: to kill and to feed. However, sometimes it seems some zombies may be left with vague recollections of their former life, usually connected with something they did a lot, like a job. Hence a zombie who, say, previously worked as a bus driver, may hang around the bus depot. The zombies we have here will have been pole dancers or maybe strippers in clubs before they died. Hence when the music plays they mimic what they did before. You can't actually teach them to do anything – their minds and consciousness no longer exist. All we do is tap into the remains of some sort of Pavlovian fragment."

Harrison stared in sullen silence at the older man.

"I'm sorry," Grant offered, "but that's how it works."

"Is her name Trudy?"

"It is now," Grant replied.

"What was it before?"

"I've no idea. The smuggled girls arrive with nothing; we

clean them up, medicate them, put them on a good diet, and look after them the best we can," explained Grant.

"What do you mean *medicate them* and *put them on a good diet?*"

"We give them courses of antibiotics and feed them as much raw meat as they need, which is normally quite a lot," Grant went on.

"Raw meat?"

Grant allowed himself a faint smile. "Beef mainly, with a high proportion of nerve and brain matter. There's something in neurological tissue that help the zombies to preserve their basic functions."

"Trudy isn't just any zombie, she's different!" Harrison blurted.

"Yes, she most certainly is," Grant agreed readily. "As I said, un-dead like Trudy are very hard to come by, and even harder to smuggle here. This is one of the reasons why we have to charge so much."

Harrison shook his head and ran his fingers through his thinning hair in agitation. "Look, since I started coming here seven weeks ago I've noticed Trudy change. She's decaying, getting slower, visibly wasting away."

"Yes," Grant nodded. "She's a corpse, and we can only do so much to slow decomposition. Depending on how long the girls have been dead when we get them, we struggle to keep them going more than four or five months. Six at most. They slow down, become catatonic, and literally start to fall apart. Some of our customers like that, but most don't."

"So what do you do after six months?" Harrison said slowly.

"We replace them."

"No," corrected Harrison. "I meant what becomes of them once you no longer want them?"

"Well, we just dispose of them."

"You kill them?" Harrison demanded angrily.

"They're already dead," Grant replied flatly. "We can't just let them go and risk them killing and infecting people. We dispose of them as humanely as we can."

"Shit!" Harrison muttered bitterly.

Grant shrugged his shoulders and drained his glass.

"Would you sell Trudy to me once she's done here?" said Harrison.

Grant regarded him in disbelief. "She's a zombie for God's sake! We couldn't risk that for all the money you could muster. At best we'd both end up in the electric chair!"

"What would I need to do to change your mind?"

"You can't," Grant retorted angrily. "Look, we got a new girl in last week. Why not have a session with her. Free, on the house. You need to move on, Mister Harrison, else your membership here will be cancelled."

"I only want Trudy."

"In which case I'll simply get them to bring the limo round to take you home," said Grant firmly. "Think about what I just said; move on or this will be your last visit."

Harrison banged his fist down on Grant's desk in angry frustration, knocking his still-full tumbler flying. "Fine, call your damned limo then!"

Grant nodded, covertly pushing a silent button under his desk. Despite his lavish spending, he knew that Harrison was the type of client the club should be without.

#

Harrison glanced once again at his watch, knowing he only had another twenty minutes left of his three-hour session. His angry exchange with Grant had nearly cost him his membership and he had been forced to nearly grovel to the old bastard to remain. That had been two weeks ago, and this was his third visit to the secret club since. But it was no longer the same; knowing what Trudy's fate would be was always at the back of his mind, always nagging, always ruining his enjoyment of the wonder who continued to dance and gyrate for his pleasure behind the glass.

He once more looked up at her, staring into her glassy and opaque eyes as she jerkily rubbed herself on the now stained pole. Her eyes were more shrunken now, but they still burned with a hunger he could not resist. The greenish tinges that had patterned her skin had darkened and burgeoned and now the decaying flesh displayed a myriad of greens, from dark olive to bright jade, with fifty-five shades in between. To Harrison each shade was perfect, each adding an organic beauty unrivalled outside of nature. Black veins and weeping sores complemented Trudy's appearance, the corruption serving to heighten the elemental force of her sexuality. He wanted her more than he had ever wanted anything before, wanting to hold her tight, to feel the naked slickness of her decay, to penetrate her dead flesh and fill her with his living seed. The thought of being inside her re-aroused him, but he still felt empty and spent. For the first time he decided to leave before the allotted three hours were up, and reached across to button up his pants.

Once he finished dressing he moved back to the glass to mouth his goodbye. Trudy had already stopped moving; something she always did as soon as he made to leave. She stood there holding the soiled pole for support, her ruined eyes following him. With a desultory wave he turned, holding back the tears, desperate for her not to see his distress. He unlocked the door and stepped into the empty corridor, determined to plead with Grant one last time to spare Trudy. Wiping his eyes he paced over to Grant's office, rapping loudly on the door. He knocked again but no answer came.

Harrison stepped back into the corridor, wondering where the manager could be. He stalked down towards the reception but found that empty too. The corridor stretched ahead in a direction in which Harrison had never been, but he needed to find Grant so he followed it. Turning a corner he saw the corridor continue, closed doors flanking either side except one towards the far end. As he neared the open door he caught the whiff of brewing coffee and heard muffled voices from within. He guessed the door led to some sort of staff restroom.

On reaching the door he saw an entrance foyer which led to a larger recreation space beyond, in which sat Grant and two men, all playing cards together at a table. Hanging in the foyer he noticed two lab-coats on wall hooks, along with two pairs of overshoes, thick gloves and face masks. He guessed they belonged to the two men, probably technicians who must have something to do with the girls. Then he saw something that almost made his heart stop: hanging by a lanyard from the top pocket of the nearest lab-coat was an access card, the same type which Grant used to swipe him through the locked doors.

Ducking back away from the open door he quickly scanned the corridor, blood pounding in his head as he realised he had a golden opportunity. Without further thought he gingerly reached around the door frame to grab the lanyard, un-noticed by the busy card players.

Next he knew he had to find the door to Trudy's quarters, and crept stealthily down the corridor towards four sturdy doors at the far end. Each had a name written on a card taped to the door; first was Heidi, then Jenny, and on the third door he saw the name Trudy. His mind raced. He had neither a plan nor a strategy, all he could think of was trying to bundle Trudy un-noticed out of one of the exits and save her.

With trepidation he held the plastic access card next to the reader, trying to stop his hand from shaking. The red light turned green and a metallic click sounded. In the quietness of the empty corridor the click sounded deafeningly loud and he stared anxiously towards the open foyer door. Seconds passed without anyone emerging from the recreation space and he breathed again. Returning his attention to the steel door he grasped the heavy handle with a sweat-soaked hand and gently eased the door inwards, silently thanking the gods that it opened silently. He pushed inside to a glaringly lit room, tiled from floor to ceiling in white ceramic tiles. The first thing he noticed was the smell, and then the cold. Heavy steel bars formed a cage which split the room into two, the other side obviously the place where Trudy was kept. He guessed she must be still in the room beyond her cell, staring through the glass at the empty bed where he usually sat, looking for him.

Anger quickly overcame his nervousness and he knew he had to get her away. The cage had a door at the side, locked by the same electronic reader, and he swiftly offered the access card up. With a click it opened and without a thought he rushed through, reaching for the next door and flinging it open. Trudy stood by the glass, her naked and disfigured back towards him. Harrison gazed at her, transfixed by her beauty and her torment.

"Trudy," he stammered. "I'm here."

Her head stiffened, and slowly she turned to look at him. Despite the chill in the room Harrison felt a warmth course through his veins as he regarded her magnificence. His eyes travelled from the coppery mound of her vulva up past her the dark mottling of her distended stomach to the blackened pleasure points of the erect nipples upon her now sagging breasts. Finally he gazed up to the bloodless and torn lips which could no longer cover the once perfect dentistry, watching the ruined lips awkwardly curl in the mockery of a smile.

"I want you so much," Harrison offered, holding out his arms.

Trudy slowly stepped forward, jerkily moving towards him. Her smile widened so much that a jagged tear in her bottom lip opened to seep black glutinous blood. Overcome by lust Harrison knew he could wait no longer and unbuckled his belt to step out of his pants. Trudy's eyes lowered as his pants fell to the floor, fixing on his throbbing penis. She staggered the last few steps, never taking her eyes from it, before sinking to her knees in front of the rigid member.

"Oh God!" Harrison uttered, closing his eyes, waiting to receive the loving embrace of her mouth and tongue.

Instead he received her teeth.

Movement
by Laura DeHaan

The receiver cuddled moistly against her ear. Oils from the previous callers' hair and sweat glands licked her skin. Philipa pressed the phone harder to her ear, counting the rings. ... *five, six* ...

"Hello?" Her mother's voice, far away.

"Momma?"

"Yes? Lola?"

Philipa clenched the receiver, the sweat from her palms making it slide in her grip. "No, it's Philipa."

"Oh. Well, when can I hold the baby?"

If I cry now, she thought. "It didn't go so good, Momma."

"Oh." The payphone was old, stealing the inflection from her mother's tone to keep itself alive. "Well, why isn't Jarod making this call?"

If I cry now, she thought. "He broke up with me two weeks ago, remember, Momma? He didn't want–" An unexpected hiccough blocked her throat for a moment. "He decided he didn't want to be a father."

"Well, at nineteen," her mother said. "I remember now. He didn't deserve you, I'm sure."

It was just the payphone stealing the inflection from her tone, stealing it and reshaping it, *he didn't deserve* you, *I'm sure.* "Can I..." *If I cry now.* "Can I come home now, Momma? Now?"

A crackle over the line. "We *had* been expecting you to stay at your apartment. With Jarod, of course. We have that exchange student over now; Anna, the one from Germany. She's still in school, you know."

Philipa felt another hiccough crowd her nose.

"We'll keep sending the rent cheques," her mother said. "You make sure Jarod gives back his keys. I don't want to have to get the locks changed."

"The building super does that, Momma."

"It's still fuss. You sound terrible. You should get some sleep."

"Yuh," she managed to say.

"All right then. Goodbye."

Philipa hung up the phone. *If I cry now.*

She meant to hold it in until she got to her apartment, but a stray hiccough led to a sob when she was only halfway there. Too weak to run, she walked with her back straight and her shoulders high and shaking; minarets caught in an earthquake.

The apartment was dark and echoed oddly without Jarod's things in it. She remembered to hang her keys on the sticky-backed plastic hook by the door instead of dropping them on the now non-existent table. She wanted a cigarette, but Jarod had taken his pack when he left, and how was she supposed to buy another?

She was only sixteen.

Philipa pulled a dishtowel from the rack and blew her nose into the sink. She washed her face, hung the dishtowel to dry with its brethren, and turned to the remaining bookshelf to run her fingers over the figurines.

Jack and Jill. Mother Goose. The Lady of Banbury Cross. "Hi, guys," she whispered. "At least you're still here."

She went to the dresser and pulled out the bottom drawer, where she kept her stuffed animals. Jarod hadn't liked to see them and she'd convinced herself she didn't want them to get dusty during the day, but now she took all of them out: Puddles the Panda, Jake the Giraffe, Mr. and Mrs. Huss. Mandy had mismatched eyes after Philipa's mother needed an emergency button sewn onto a coat. Gregory's fur had been licked off in places by a neighbour's constantly intruding cat. Bog was just a triangular pillow with a face stitched on, but he too joined the others on the bed now.

The row of sad plants on the windowsill reminded Philipa that she hadn't showered for days. She left the damp towels draped over the shower rack, snuggled into her jammies and covered herself with her silent childhood friends.

Childhood, she thought.

She took a fresh dishtowel and placed it over her pillow. Just in case she started crying during the night. She was almost out of toilet paper.

#

In the morning she shook off her stuffed animals, wrinkled her nose at the damp towel under her cheek, and went to start breakfast.

The sad, wilted plants were clustered in the sink.

Did she remember to water them last night? Did she forget to put them back on the sill? She couldn't clearly recall much of the past few days as it was. She stuck a finger into the soil, found it dry, shrugged, and turned the tap on the plants. She replaced them on the sill and made breakfast.

She spent the day at home, reading and rereading a short stack of mystery novels. When she'd memorised each plot twist, she started reading a chemistry textbook. That was even better to take her mind off things, but far more exhausting and she only managed an hour before dropping it in favour of a nap.

When she woke up a few hours later, Jack and Jill were on top of the textbook.

Philipa's eyes scanned the room. Had Jarod come in while she'd slept? He'd given his keys over, though; she hadn't needed her mother to remind her to do that. Did he make an extra copy? No, why would he? She knew his parents were hoping he'd come home, and he had friends he could stay with otherwise. Maybe he'd forgotten something and came to pick it up and left the Jack and Jill on the textbook to...

...not scare her when she woke up?

The plants were still on the sill. She padded to the bathroom, though most of it was visible from her bed anyway. It was a bachelor apartment; everywhere was visible from everywhere.

The towels were still over the shower rack. The curtain was still twitched back. The toilet lid remained cozily resting on the seat.

Unsure what to think, she turned around to leave the bathroom.

"*Haaaaigh!*"

Puddles and Jack, the Husses and Gregory, Mandy and Bog and the pillows too were sitting on the floor, nudged into the spaces between the books.

Philipa tossed a light jacket over her jammies (what had been the point of changing out of them today?) and stuffed her feet into a pair of sandals before grabbing her keys and fleeing the apartment. Worry about it later. Don't think. Go.

Adrenaline palsied her muscles, making the sidewalk jump under her like bubbles popping in a marsh. She stumbled into the closest coffee shop and sat in a little wooden chair by the window, waiting for the tremors to shake themselves out.

Eventually a nervous young man in generic black wrung his hands at her. "Uh, miss, I'm sorry, but we have these chairs for paying customers."

She blinked at him. "My apartment is haunted," she explained.

His face fell. "Oh shit, I'm sorry."

A woman wearing a better cut of generic black bustled over. "Now then, we can't have seating taken up by just anyone off the street," she said brusquely.

"Her apartment's haunted," the young man said.

The woman levelled a look at him. "She's wearing pyjamas," she intoned and circled her forefinger at her temple.

"I can see you," said Philipa.

"And I can still see you," said the woman. "So why don't you pack up your sad little story and your sad little sack of crazy and go on back to whatever homeless shelter let you out for the day."

"I have an apartment," Philipa said.

"Your *haunted* apartment," the woman said.

Philipa looked to the young man, but he had already turned away. She pushed her chair out from the table and stood.

"I hope you get murdered in your sleep," she told the woman.

Philipa returned to her apartment with dusk hanging limply from her cheekbones. The streetlamps, beginning to wake from their daylit slumber, opened their burning eyes and cast their gazes elsewhere as Philipa walked beside them. Even the darkness wouldn't have her, and Philipa cast no shadow in the twilight. When she crossed an intersection, she did so only when the three people in front of her went across, because the stoplight would not turn green for her.

She took the stairs up to her sixth floor, not trusting the elevator to come at her bidding. Her key turned reluctantly in its lock and Philipa opened the door.

There was a mild resistance as the door pushed a clean half-circle of space into the room. Gathered around the entrance were her books, her plants and her stuffed animals all watching the door.

Philipa picked up as much as she could carry, spilling dry soil over her arms. Trip by trip she emptied her possessions into the garbage chute.

She entered her apartment, noting her clothes dangling out of opened drawers, caught in their crawl to freedom. She could hear the shower curtain pulling at its plastic hooks, lapsing into sullen stasis when she went to check on it.

A sudden noise made her jump. It came from the closet, a hollow, plasticky thumping of something trying to escape. The sliding doors juddered and shuddered from the onslaught, the thudding growing frantic, echoing strongly in the spartan room. Philipa put her fists to her ears and mouth, elbows two spiky shields at her defense, and watched plaster float down.

The thumpings slowed but became more powerful, concentrated; the sliding doors were buckling and a wide chunk of plaster gave way at the corner. Philipa ran the eight steps to the closet and wrenched it open.

The baby things – the box of rompers, the pack of diapers, the funny giraffe with the so-soft belly – teetered gently, off-balance, and then fell over at her feet.

Behind her, soft slithery noises of clothes creeping across the floor.

Of course the baby things don't want to be with me, Philipa thought. *I've been the worst kind of mother. But even my clothes? Did I ask too much of them?*

Armful by armful, not bothering to bag anything first, Philipa tumbled clothes and diapers down the garbage chute, letting it clang shut every time. On every return, the furniture had marched closer to the door.

"Good," she told the bookshelf, the dresser, the futon. "Show yourselves out. I can't do everything."

The bathroom items she bundled into the shower curtain, its vinyl whispers accompanied by the rough grunting of wood against wood by the bookshelf in the main room. There was still plenty of space in the shower curtain for the kitchen things too, and Philipa took down the dishes and cutlery and, after a moment's thought, emptied out the fridge as well.

She hesitated over the peanut butter and the canned tuna. Its food was trapped inside, surely she had some power still over it? She stuck her finger into the peanut butter and it burned her. Liquids went down the drain.

She had to drag the shower curtain and its lumpy, jagged contents to the disposal. It was past the hour when residents were encouraged to use the chute, but Philipa knew no one would peek their heads through a crack in their doors to scold her. What use was it to scold a pack mule carrying its burden?

Philipa half expected to not be allowed back into the apartment after that trip. The bookshelf would use itself as a barricade, while the dresser would be ready to shoot its drawers at her if she proved bold enough to fight.

Still, it was not entirely surprising to find the furniture neatly lined up by the door, giving her plenty of room to enter and manoeuvre the bulky items out into the hallway. She left them by the elevators. It was tempting to push them down the stairs, but there were so many stairs with so many turns that Philipa felt they would have an easier time showing themselves out without her blundering behind them.

Work-sweat and worry-sweat itched her neck and knees. Philipa turned on the bathroom faucet – she didn't trust the shiny-smiled porcelain of the bathtub – and nothing came out but a wheeze and a sputter. A fat drop beaded at the mouth and was sucked back inside the pipe.

I should tell the landlord, was her first thought, and then, *but it's childish to complain that the apartment doesn't like me.*

She turned off the lights so the walls didn't have to look at her and lay on the bare floor, trying to touch as little of it as possible. The refrigerator was quiet, ignoring her.

She dozed in a halfish dreamstate and awoke in much the same way, growing aware of a cold band around her middle where her bare skin now lay against the floor, of her shirt rucked up under her chin. Something had a grip on her shirt and was dragging her to the door.

Now fully awake, she screamed and thrashed at the air, sickened by its intrusion. Free of the thing, she scrambled to the lights, which refused to turn on. She reached out for matches and remembered they had been part of her earlier purge. She thought of them lying in darkness bundled up in a shower curtain, smugly unlit, blissfully blind.

"I should have burned you," Philipa said to them, to the apartment, to the diapers down the garbage chute. She picked up the keys from the kitchen counter and left the apartment once more. The key slotted into the lock, but she didn't turn it. "Anyone can go inside you now," she told the door. "They'll think you wanted it, leaving the keys like this. I hope they leave the bodies in here."

She wandered to a nearby park and curled herself around a tree. The bark was rough and bit her; the grass was wet and chilled her. *But only for a little time,* Philipa consoled herself, *because I am a little caterpillar and I am making a cocoon for myself. I am only using things that no one will notice are missing, and since that thing is me no one is going to mind. In the morning I will be a butterfly.*

Barely had the false dawn drawn the first shadows but a robin came along and nipped at the cocoon, crunching and swallowing the little half-formed butterfly inside. The robin was pleased at first, but soon felt a sickness growing inside it, a thing that clipped its feathers and made it stagger out onto the road, where a car struck it and ground its hollow bones into the asphalt.

The car barely noticed, big as it was, but bits of the bird were wedged into the treads of the rubber wheels, which no longer gripped the road so tightly. The car swerved, just a little, there, just a little, just as it was about to go over a long bridge, the only bridge connecting a little island to the rest of the world.

The car swerved and hit a bar which wobbled a rail which, little as it was (compared to the rest of the great long bridge), caused the bridge to crumble, elegantly, into the great deep watery chasm which was the secret passageway to the island.

There was wood in the bridge, and concrete, and thick steel wires and rivets and nuts and these things drifted across the top of the secret passageway (because, after all, it was a secret, and no one was allowed access who didn't know it) and came to rest at the base of this island, far, far down in the sea. The island, of course, was not a floating ball, but a tall thin column whose roots were the molten core of the earth itself; this column could not be eroded by such natural things as time and weather, this column was made up of things unwanted and Philipa, Philipa belonged.

There were people living on the tiny island and now they were separated from the rest of the world, but whether they wept or whether they laughed was not for Philipa to know or care. They were allowed to live on their island because she supported that island; without her they would be lost.

"Lost, lost," sang Philipa.

She was a part of the island now, integral and immortal. In the park, wrapped knees to elbows around the already dying tree, Philipa finally could not be moved.

The Tome
by T.C. Phillips

He ran his hand gently across the tome's cover, his fingertips gently tracing the silver lettering that had been embossed into the pale leather. Something about the book's binding was not quite right. He couldn't quite fathom what it was, but there was definitely something wrong.

The leather perhaps.

It was far too soft, far too pale, for it to have been taken from the hide of a typical beast. No, whichever poor creature had given its hide for this book, it was a sheltered animal.

A kept beast like himself.

Revulsion rose in his throat, and he quickly snatched his hand away. It was an obscene thing, something that should have been destroyed long ago.

But he couldn't bring himself to do it.

Even now and then it sang to him, a sickly whisper that beckoned his trembling hand back to its pages.

A daemonibus docetur, de daemonibus docet, et ad daemones ducit. The cover's lettering was immaculately formed, glowing blood red in the candlelight.

Latin, he thought quietly. Somehow, even through the heavy fog choking his mind, he could recognise the words if not their meaning. *I knew Latin once.*

His hand had returned to the book's cover, and for the first time he actually noticed how alien the appendage had become. A thin crust of brown flakes clung desperately to his skeleton-like fingers, the tops of which were split and bleeding from nails that had been chewed right down to the cuticles.

He flexed his fingers, if only to prove the hand he was seeing was indeed his own. Tiny brown flecks, whether dried blood or excrement he could not tell, showered the floor at his feet. As he watched them fall, panic beat fleetingly through his chest at the thought that he might spoil the tome's cover.

The book, however, seemed perfectly untarnished despite his blood-stained touch.

Hesitantly he reached forth once more, gently testing to see if any mark could be left. When he squeezed his index finger against his thumb, a fresh clot of blood began to form at its tip. Taking a deep breath, he pressed his bloody finger squarely into the centre of the tome's leather binding.

Exhaling, he realised that he needed to open a set of eyes that he never remembered closing. The blood had begun to pool around the finger which still stood upright, stabbing right into the middle of the book's cover. He began to lift it gently, and as he did so the blood that remained behind flowed cleanly off the binding's edge via two, gravity-defying rivulets.

The embossed writing almost seemed to flash defiantly, rousing his anger. He thought briefly of tearing the parchment sheafs straight from the binding, of setting them to the candle's flame. Yet as quickly as the thoughts came, he realised his mistake.

The pain came once again – the same pain that came every time he thought of doing damage to the tome. A demonic heat seared through his skull, causing his left eye to twitch and his vision to blur.

I'm sorry, he thought desperately. Yet his silent pleas came too late and the room turned black as the floor rushed up to meet him.

#

The faltering dreams were of a time long forgotten. Like a series of random photographs, he saw faces he knew he should recognise but their names escaped him.

Amongst all these fleeting images there was a recurring picture – a beautiful woman with grey eyes.

She was screaming in terror, but he didn't know why.

He knew he should have been able to remember her. He should have known why she screamed so, why she was in so much pain. But the harder he tried, the further his recollection slipped beyond his grasp.

The pictures of the grey-eyed woman changed, morphed into

a grey-suited stranger from another time.

Shadows seemed to cling to the stranger, surrounding him with an aura of palpable darkness. In this fevered dream-state, he knew well enough this was a man to be feared.

"Are you hungry, friend?" the stranger asked, the smallest twinge of a smile playing on the corner of his lips. "You must be hungry. It has been so long, has it not?"

The shadow surrounding the stranger grew, devouring whatever light was left. Soon there was nothing left but the stranger's obsidian eyes and the raging hunger within.

The grey-eyed woman screamed again, and the pain of it rang in his ears.

\#

His ears were still ringing when he woke on the cold, hard floor. A warm trickle caressed his upper lip, and he lapped at it with the tip of his tongue. A sharp metallic taste announced it as fresh blood, and the burning pain in the middle of his face revealed its source. When he gently touched his nose, the pain flared again and he realised he must have broken it with his most recent fall.

He regained his feet slowly, the weakness permeating his limbs making it a somewhat difficult task. His stomach growled, and he couldn't remember the last time he had eaten.

Are you hungry, friend? The stranger's voice echoed in his thoughts. *You must be hungry. It has been so long, has it not?*

Not again. The faint echo of his former self tried desperately to claw its way back to the surface of his thoughts. *Do you remember the last time?*

But he couldn't remember the last time. It was hard for him to remember anything beyond the tome and its pages. They were immaculately detailed pages, each containing scores of tiny illuminated figures. And every one of them were engaged in the foulest sequence of obscenities imaginable.

He could dimly recall being initially revolted by those illustrated creatures, wanting to shut the book and be done with it. But the cursed thing kept calling to him, beckoning him back to its sickening mysteries.

Now those self-same images merely fed his mounting appetite.

He really was hungry.

But not hungry enough yet. Not enough to take him from this room, to take him from the book and its tiny obscene images.

Stumbling back to the podium upon which the tome held reign, he thought he saw a movement from the corner of his eye. A quick turn of his head revealed the room to be empty. There was nothing else here, save himself.

And the book.

Grabbing hold of the podium's edge, he rested his tired weight and returned to his place before the tome once more. The cover's silver writing flickered, whether in welcome or warning he could not tell.

He opened the book to a random page; the words really meant nothing anymore. He couldn't read them; it was the intricate drawings that drew his attention.

Yet for some untold reason, he could read this page.

Are you hungry, friend? it read.

#

It seemed like a lifetime had passed since he had last taken these stairs. His world now was the cold dark room of the book, and whilst he hated the thing he could not bear to be apart from it. Even now, only being a mere handful of feet away, he longed to return to it.

But the hunger had grown too great.

As he moved down the carpeted stairwell, pictures of strangers lined the walls. Smiling faces he could no longer recognise.

Not one, save the photograph of a beautiful grey-eyed woman dressed in white.

Like everyone else who occupied the wall, she was smiling and her grey eyes twinkled. The woman had a name, he knew he should be able remember it, but it refused to come.

Besides, there were more important things to attend to. He needed to appease his hunger. He needed to feed and then return to the tome.

As he descended lower, leaving the images behind, the sickly-sweet stench of carrion assaulted his nostrils. *Do you remember the last time?* The thought rose again, bringing with it a touch of wild panic.

As he moved to the doorway at the base of the stairs, a strange noise caused him to hesitate. A constant hum, like the grinding of mechanical teeth, was coming from the other side of the door.

It was an odd sound, constant and throbbing.

Taking a deep breath, he pushed the door inward and the overpowering reek of rotten flesh caused his eyes to water. Blinking the tears away, he finally understood the source of the unexplained noise.

A seething black mass of flies and carrion insects occupied the table in the centre of the room. Like thousands of the tome's tiny illuminated figures, they gorged themselves on the rotting flesh of the table's occupant.

A woman's hand, which bore a simple gold ring, dangled carelessly over the table's edge. It was the only human feature still visible underneath the swarming mass of feasting insects.

"Alicia." The sound of his own voice was foreign to him, and the word had escaped even before he knew the name had surfaced. He couldn't see her face, but he knew somewhere underneath lay a beautiful pair of grey eyes frozen in terror.

From the corner of his eye, a quick movement of shadow drew his attention. Tracing its source he discovered a grey-suited man from another time. The smallest hint of a smile touched the corners of his lips, and his obsidian eyes flashed.

The grey-suited stranger asked, "Are you hungry, friend?"

The Light of a Beautiful World
by Josh English

My patience is wearing thin with you. You've been sitting on that bed for six days now, arms hugging your knees to your chest, whispering the same things:

"We are the light of a beautiful world."

"Logical thoughts are self-defeating."

You stare into the mirror where the TV used to be. These cheap motels insist on putting the television in prime bed-viewing position. I moved them before I rescued you, to free you from distractions. This room is your universe, little girl. You've lost yourself, and you'll stare into that mirror until you come home.

No TV, no phone, no wake up calls, no chance of calling the other victims to rescue you. They can't. I already did. The lights stay on because you can't see yourself in the dark. It's just me in this room, until you come back.

You're only looking at the mirror. You aren't focusing. You used to be that girl the guys dreamed about: small town cheerleader, almost made prom queen, almost made homecoming queen. You even had a major role in the senior musical. Large schools don't have room for one person to fill so many roles, believe me. Hell, my graduating class was bigger than your whole town.

Damn. This isn't about me.

The room lets in the morning fog, but never lets it go. It hangs around, basting us with the heat of our own bodies. Look at yourself. Your bare arms glisten with sweat. You only eat once a day, and then just a few mouthfuls. You're starving yourself. Why?

The guru that seduced you made you eat nothing but rice, tofu, and peas. The smell of real food, a burger, fries, anything, should have woken you up.

"We are the light of a beautiful world."

Bullshit.

You only move when you go to the bathroom. I removed the door, but I don't disturb your privacy, so I don't move to watch. I listen to you pee. You wash your hands. You go back to the bed, fold yourself up, and sit there, not a shred of ego. I get up to flush the toilet and sit back down.

That creeped me out that first day, you know.

Since you didn't eat, I assaulted your ears. You didn't resist as I laid you on your back and wrapped you up in the bed sheet, just like a mummy. Your arms and legs pinned down, pressure all over your body. I slipped the buds into your ears and plugged you into some of the worst music I could find. That part was easy; the world is full of it.

Your parents, when they hired me, didn't question me when I took your CDs and a few stuffed animals from your room. They haven't changed it, you know? You might have grown up, gone to college, but that room looks like a twelve-year-old lives there. What is it with girls and stuffed animals?

"Logical thoughts are self-defeating."

You're right. There's no logic in it. Like horses. I never understood the fascination and I studied these things. I majored in psychology and minored in brutality. The music you hated didn't drive you out, so I played you your favorite songs. All those anemic Disney crap pop anthems played one by one, and your lips continued the mantra.

Yeah, I read lips. Grandma went deaf and finally stopped shouting, but we all learned to listen to her with our eyes. It's useful in this line of work. What does the mantra do? Does the phrase keep you locked away from the world? You're not the first, you know. I've rescued others from him before you ever heard of him.

He's gotten better over the years. So have I. I pulled a couple of kids out of his apartment five years ago. I got them back. He disappeared. You won't believe how pissed I was to find him back here on my turf.

I know my pre-recorded voice interrupts the music, reminding you of when you went to summer camp and the councilors made you sing in the mess hall during lunch to get your mail. You hated it. Your mother wrote postcards and mailed them two days before you left for camp, so you always had a letter waiting for you on that first day. Before you knew who would be the bitch of the bunk, you had to sing show tunes to read a postcard. You were a gangly scarecrow with pink hair then. You almost look the same now. The beautiful young woman has come and gone.

Six hours of music and you don't react. What did that piece-of-shit guru do to you? How did he get you to give up?

There's more stuff for you to listen to. I tracked down your old boyfriend. You've had a few, but I found the one that mattered. The guy you swapped virginities with during the all-night graduation party. He recorded a message for you. Don't you recognize his voice?

No. I unwrap you. Your cotton dress clings to you, like a near-invisible second sweat-soggy skin.

I've figured out why you aren't responding. You stink, and it's not you. It's not your smell on you. Underneath the muggy air and matted hair you stink of that apartment I pulled you from. Didn't he ever let you bathe? I don't like doing this, what I have to do. You have to get clean, and you aren't going to do it yourself. If I toss you in a running shower, you'll just sit there. Damn. I wish I had a woman to help me in these situations.

I'm not afraid of you. I could break your body, and I will break into your head, sap your willpower, and bring you back to the world of the attentive. It just looks bad when my patient has to get naked when I'm in the room.

Hell with it. I roll up my sleeves, pick you up with more force than I need to use, and push you into the bathroom.

"We are the light..."

I shut your mouth with the shower spray. I don't want to hear it. The water raises goose flesh on your arms and runs across your skin like balls in a pachinko machine. I shove you closer to the shower head, drenching your hair under the spray. You hang limp, like a rag doll, but you're not a doll, no matter how that guru treated you. You're a human being. I squirt shampoo into your hands and slap them against your hair. I order you to rub. You obey.

Feel better? Feel like an individual again? Once you do, I can call Mommy and Daddy and they'll come meet you in the lobby and take you home, shuddering from the nightmare he put you through.

I can't put it off any longer. With your arms up, frothing your matted hair, I pull up your dress. I'll wash it in the sink later.

When it's up to your ribcage, I know the plan has changed.

Scars line your thighs and belly, across your back, some old, some look raw and new. I didn't see them before.

This wasn't part of his scheme five years ago. I haven't touched you. What did you manage to do to yourself in those few moments by yourself?

I pull the dress up and off, fighting your arms. You get shampoo foam in my face, my eyes. The dress goes in the sink and I slap water on my face to clear it. I spin you around and shove you under the spray to rinse your hair.

It's still matted, wet, and has flecks of foam when I drag you out later. I don't care. You smell like soap, which is an improvement. You roll onto the bed, arms and legs spread out, eyes looking up at the ceiling. You don't attempt to hide yourself. You don't make any sense.

"Logical thoughts are self-defeating."

"We are the light of a beautiful world."

Damn you. Damn him. You're the victim. Do you expect me to use you like he did? He has eight bastard children by previous victims. If you had gotten pregnant, he would have freed you, tossed you aside. He doesn't like babies.

Strange, though. I kept tabs on those kids he sired in his first enlightenment scam. They're strong, intelligent, brave, healthy kids. The mothers are still slightly damaged in the head, though. If he drugged all of you, those kids would have been sick. You weren't drugged, as far as I can tell. Your parents only want you back. The cops want you stable enough to testify. I want you out of my life.

I grab a couple of towels and wrap them around your chest and hips. Giving you that much respect and privacy is more than he ever gave you. You know that, don't you? You lie there and let me examine the scars. They're not random marks on your skin like I first thought they were. They almost look familiar. If I didn't know better, the small collections were things I could read. Some form of eastern writing, characters, words, phrases, repeated over and over. Some follow the curves of your body, others cut across the landscape of skin.

Somebody had to do this to you. I roll you onto your side. No one can do that kind of detailed work on their own back.

Where did he get this idea from? The last I heard, after he fled he went to Europe. Here you are with words from the Far East carved into your skin. Do you hate yourself that much?

The light bothers me now. It's a sick yellow splashing on ugly walls, an unnatural light in an unnatural space. I need daylight.

"We are the light of a beautiful world."

Shut up! My only clock is the carton of cigarettes I brought for better company. I lose track of time in these sessions.

I sit on the other bed and try to think. I've had nothing but coffee for days, it seems. My stomach is sour; my throat hurts from telling you who you are. I haven't heard another human being's voice but yours, and you don't say anything helpful.

Maybe you need the dark. Maybe childhood fears will bring you back. Yeah, I know about that, too. Your parents told me a lot of things about you.

I turn off the lights, one by one. I feel like the lonely acolyte on Good Friday, extinguishing lights, but I feel great. This will resurrect you. I darken the bathroom, the sink, the three square feet they call a hallway. Finally, I turn off the bedside lamp.

The room is dark. A small red light shines close to the baseboard, illuminating nothing but telling you a wall lurks to trip you. It is a spark. I tap my way to the chair and sit down. Your bed blocks the light. I can hear you breathe. You're still whispering but you don't move. I wait. Something will happen. I can feel it. I'm breaking through.

I rub my eyes, sending rainbow sparklers across my imagination. If I close my eyes, I'll sleep. That's what mankind trained himself to do. I keep them open, watching nothing.

Something moves. I hear a bed sheet sliding against a nylon comforter. Do you think you can go somewhere, little girl?

"We are the light of a beautiful world."

I can see it, floating where you are, lying on the bed. An optical illusion. The brain gets so desperate for light it imagines something to look at to keep the visual cortex busy. The illusion speck is joined by another. Do you see it, little girl?

Something slides in the dark, like fingers down a guitar string, and something heavy, thick and wet slaps against me. I shout and strangle it. It's just the towel I wrapped around you. I toss it aside.

More lights appear. The characters on your skin are almost visible, even from the other end of the room.

"We are the light of a beautiful world."

The lights are almost pure white. The Milky Way, just like the one you marveled at in the clear mountain air, illuminates your stomach, twisting around your buttock and wrapping around your thigh. I've been in this room too long. There isn't enough oxygen any more for the two of us.

It is beautiful. I envy the hours you spent staring at the stars, watching the sunrise. Did I even live? Or did I just stay alive?

You moan, the first sound that isn't a mantra.

The Milky Way undulates as you rock your hips up and down. The bed moves with you. The light gets brighter, spawning radiant streams that play with dust motes.

I try to stand. My knees are weak. This won't stop me. I will save you. You will come back, little girl.

I'm on my feet, hovering over you. I mistake the sparkle in your eye for a reflection. It's not. You buck your hips wildly and scream with raw pleasure. I shroud my eyes. This will wake the people next door. I can't see anything but the light. My arm shines with it. I see my bones as clear as an x-ray.

My ears pop and I turn away, falling to my knees and curling up into a ball. My body shields me from the light and even with my eyes clamped closed and pressed into my forearms I can see the light. I feel it pressing against me, grinding my knees into the crushed shag rug and driving my breath from my lungs.

It stops.

My joints are stiff. They crack as I push myself up and twist around to look at you.

You're gone.

I need air. I need light. I unbolt the door and throw it open.

The walkway is a halogen mockery of dawn.

It doesn't make sense, I say to the morning fog.

"Logical thoughts..." I hear your voice giggle through my head.

I'm crying.

Damn it, little girl, you made me cry.

The Thing Within
by Erin Eveland

She labored, deep in the cave. Sweat couldn't match her push. Screaming would have been a release but they gagged her with a soiled pelt. Hindmilk of the foremilk dribbled down her uneven breast. A stranger to their clan, her rippling belly was spared. Her mate was not.

She had watched her mate, whose arms once wrapped around her in starless nights, immerse into a clay pot of boiling water. His hair tossed about, and then rose to the top, clinging to the bubbles of the foam that came from his cooking flesh in the crock. His bones sunk to the bottom while the meat of her lover rolled over the top of the water, and down again, in a riptide grave. Naked and stricken like the stone she was tied against, she couldn't feel the multiple hands which fondled her, nor taste the scorching swill that entered her mouth. A slap followed when she choked on it, and the regurgitating shock she was surrendering to. But that was then, in the mist of the dawn when they were discovered. Now, it was only cave and the eternal dark. She was the stranger, the carrier of the womb and the thing within. Only the comfort of death was her security.

Her water broke. There was dancing. The mucus plug oozed.

Fattened by the fruits of the pot, they poured distilled grain over her breast and belly, along with the oily broth of her mate's leavings. A weathered woman, half clad in buckskin, kneeled down and cupped her engorged nipple. The woman teased it with her gnarled nails and suckled it with her decaying mouth, burning the labor pains forward.

"The first. The first!" they cried in shouts, as the head of the thing within crowned.

Her tongue flexed the cloth over her mouth and down to her chin, expelling exhausted breath and then a raging scream as the thing within was ripped from its sanctuary. The thing's head passed the opening. Shuddering spasms vibrated her as the rest of the four-limbed creature slipped forth.

They hollered like banshees as the thing was lifted with the umbilical cord still attached to the placenta inside of her. She closed her eyes as she felt her life essence being drawn out. Instinct told her she would die and never see the gray sun that warmed the land, nor her people whose impotency had healed, only to spawn abominations they would not suffer to live. She was not allowed to witness the creatures the women of her clan birthed, but she had seen a forgone world emerging from the animals of the forest and the mutations they brought forth. Before the Great Spirit claimed her, she needed to see the thing within.

Bending to the side, she braced herself on one elbow and buckled her throbbing belly. She swiped the cord into her mouth and bit it in two. Like her intestines of internal fluid and iron, she tasted the cord's discharge and spat it out. Her belly cramped and she pushed on it with her tendon-bound wrist and hands to expel the placenta inside. A man gripped the broken end of the umbilical cord between her thighs and pulled on it as though he were dragging a fish-filled net from the water.

With a speechless wail, the placenta was free. She fell in and out of sight and mind. Like a torrent, she sunk into soothing black waters and then submerged into a salt-watered sight that filled her with the horrors of the cave and the flesh of the thing within, which was being held high for those who could see. In all its infant weakness, the only thing it bore was calamity.

She lay there, hemorrhaging.

They ate the placenta raw. Virgin meat. The purest flesh of all. It would heal the blind, crippled, and impotent clan. And the babe would lead them. The infirm savored the first bite of meat, extracting the givings like the sieve of life, until a bloodthirsty call came from the others to relinquish it.

Left on the earthen floor like a carcass, her bleeding stopped. She could not see the creature being passed hand to hand through the masses, but she thought she heard it call to her with a deep-seated whimper.

Gluttony and drink took the group to sleep. All, but her and the offspring. She could see it clearer now across the cave and in the arms of a leathered woman. It wriggled its way out of the elder's hold easily and came towards her in the darkening firelight, crawling unnaturally in its newborn movement.

Its flesh was covered with downy hair which swaggered as it moved. Even though its limbs were those of a normal child, it didn't crawl, it slinked to her. Its eyes were set wide apart. The bridge of its nose was missing where two wide slits were covered with loose skin which flapped in and out as if it were sniffing her out as it came with a pretentious grin within its wide cheeks. Fear gripped her. She tried to bite through the sinew bonds. Hopeless. Exhausted from the enduring labor, she released a sigh and fell back to wait for her fate.

Did the creature know her, she wondered. She thought best to kill it. Or let it kill her.

The profane, unassuming babe stopped at her side. It smiled, exposing teeth like blades. She could have screamed, she had strength left in her for that, but it wouldn't have mattered. Nothing mattered now without the heart to ward off its attack.

It flapped over her belly where the blood of the afterbirth was starting to dry. It will tear me apart the way it came in, she thought. Two tongues emerged from its mouth. One was like a human child's, but the other was set deep and long, hidden like a reptile's. This one moved across her belly like a snake in water and down to her legs and up to her arms where the blood of birth had stained her.

The mother was clean. The reptile tongue retracted as the

thing's body and mouth moved over her breast and to her face, baring its serrated teeth. Her bound hands lay against her neck, unwilling to fight, nor finding a reason to. She closed her eyes as the thing's mouth grew wider, as if to clamp down on her neck or hands that attempted to cover her face. As the creature's teeth bore down, she felt the restraint of her bonds loosen. She opened her eyes with free hands. She moved slowly to touch the thing, her babe, which was now moving down to her breast to suckle upon her with nothing more than the soft pink lips and tongue like those of a normal infant's mouth. As it nursed upon her, she felt its flesh with her hands. It felt as soft as milkweeds' velvet before the sap and as gentle as a daisy's petal.

She lay on her back. She held her babe and felt the instinct of nurturing, survival, and love overcome her. A child of milk and blood, she thought, as it drained both breasts and sat up, thirsty for more.

The babe slipped out of her arms and she felt an overwhelming loss watching it return to the sleeping elder woman who had held it. Quietly it came. Its reptile tongue protruded forth as if it were diving in and out of air waves until the babe was over top of the elder woman's head. Its tongue swooped and then slid between the woman's lips and down her throat. The babe clamped its razor teeth over the elder's lips. Her eyes snapped open and her body jutted just for a moment before all the fluid she contained therein was drained from her. The mother watched her babe's chest and stomach suck and gulp in contractions as it was filled. Its limbs extended and swelled as it drank. The shagged tuft on top of its head grew into brown golden locks of hair like corn silk. The infant's bones defined within its body, like its muscles, that never knew the will of the hunt and yet looked as though it had spent its lifetime as a predator, with the knowledge and skill sculpted inside.

The babe was finished. The woman's petrified body looked like it had been skewered over a fire until every ounce of fluid was cooked from her.

The babe had grown a foot in height and stood as a little child, before it moved onto its next slumbering clan victim. One by one, the child took the cave people in the same form and grew in measure doing so. Eventually, no one was left but mother and child.

The thing that came from within her womb was standing next to her, not a sun-day old and yet with that of a ten seasons body. A boy. Would he be a man tomorrow, she wondered as he held out his hand to help her stand.

Like a splintered stalk, she stood with his support. They locked eyes and she saw his were the same greenish gray as his father's had been.

"Mother," she said to him.

"Mother," he replied, tilting his head into her chest.

"I love you," she said aloud to herself, knowing that no matter what he may be, he was her child and she would protect him against the old world.

"I love you, Mother," he said, as if he knew.

And together, they departed the cave.

Author Biographies

Kierce Severn was born in 1980 in the most northern town in Florida, Tampa Bay. After inhabiting many towns along the east coast of the United States, she settled down in Charlotte, North Carolina. Her free time is spent writing and reading fiction, and the rest of the time is divided between hunting paychecks and enjoying family time.

Adam Millard is the author of thirteen novels and more than a hundred short stories, which can be found in various collections and anthologies. Probably best known for his post-apocalyptic fiction, Adam also writes fantasy/horror for children. He created the character Peter Crombie, Teenage Zombie just so he had something decent to read to his son at bedtime. Adam also writes Bizarro fiction for several publishers, who enjoy his tales of flesh-eating clown-beetles and rabies-infected derrieres so much that they keep printing them. His "Dead" series has been the filling in a Stephen King/Bram Stoker sandwich on Amazon's bestsellers chart, and the translation rights have recently sold to German publisher, Voodoo Press. Adam also writes for *This Is Horror*, whose columnists include Shaun Hutson, Simon Bestwick and Simon Marshall-Jones. Adam lives in the post-apocalyptic landscape known as Wolverhampton, England, with his wife, Zoe, and son, Phoenix.

Jay Wilburn lives in the swamps of coastal South Carolina with his wife and two sons. He has written and published the novels Loose Ends and Time Eaters. He has a piece in Best Horror of the Year volume 5. Follow his many dark thoughts at JayWilburn.com and @AmongTheZombies on Twitter.

Jim Ryan's true origins are unknown, but some say he has wandered the Earth since time immemorial, periodically challenging other writers to single combat. Or taking tea with them – the accounts differ. He appeared in Myrtle Beach, South Carolina in the 1990's, during which time he was a member of the South Carolina Syndicate Theatre Company. Not long ago, he resurfaced in Charlotte, North Carolina. His recent works include short stories in the <u>From the Dark Side</u> and <u>Farrago</u> charity anthologies and a book of comedic monologues entitled <u>Abduction Etiquette</u>. He continues to act silly in public whenever appropriate.

Lizz-Ayn Shaarawi is a Texan lost in the Oregon wilderness. She's a horror screenwriter and author whose short stories have been featured in numerous anthologies and her screenplays have been recognized by the Austin Film Festival, The Nicholl Fellowship in Screenwriting, and the International Page Awards. You can find her random babblings on Twitter under her username @lizzayn

When not writing **Kieran Daly** spends his time teaching music, performing in piano bars, working out, following the stock market, and keeping abreast of current affairs. He enjoys reading a mixture of horror, post-apocalyptic, literary and commercial fiction.

Rie Sheridan Rose has published 6 novels, 1 short story collection, 2 chapbooks of collected stories, and 5 poetry collections. She has "Drink My Soul...Please" and "Bloody Rain" as individual stories with Mocha Memoirs. Her stories have also been published in Reloaded: Both Barrels, Shifters, A Bubba in Time Saves None, and Abandoned Towers, among others.

Her poetry has appeared in Mythic Circle, Dreams of Decadence, and Abandoned Towers, Penumbra, The Voices Project, and the Metastasis, Boundless, and Di-Verse-City anthologies.

She also wrote lyrics for Marc Gunn's "Don't Go Drinking With Hobbits" CD.

Stephen McQuiggan is the name given to a form of Irish paperfolding where, through a series of complex and intricate folds, it is possible to construct a short bald idiot.

John Grover is a fiction author residing in Massachusetts. He completed a creative writing course at Boston's Fisher College and is a member of the New England Horror Writers Association.

Some of his more recent credits include stories in Best New Werewolf Tales Vol 1 and Best New Zombie Tales by Books of the Dead Press, The Epitaphs Anthology by The New England Horror Writers, The Northern Haunts Anthology by Shroud Publishing, and The Zombology Series by Library of the Living Dead Press. Please visit his website   www.shadowtales.com   or   his   Facebook   page www.facebook.com/johngroverdarkfictionauthor   for   more information.

James Dorr's newest collection is THE TEARS OF ISIS, released by Perpetual Motion Machine Publishing in May 2013. This joins his two prose collections from Dark Regions Press, STRANGE MISTRESSES: TALES OF WONDER AND ROMANCE and DARKER LOVES: TALES OF MYSTERY AND REGRET, and the all-poetry VAMPS (A RETROSPECTIVE) from Sam's Dot/White Cat. An active member of SFWA and HWA with nearly four hundred individual appearances from   ALFRED   HITCHCOCK'S   MYSTERY   MAGAZINE   to XENOPHILIA, Dorr invites readers to visit his site at http://jamesdorrwriter.wordpress.com.

Told once 'You have to be an author, then your craziness becomes eccentric', **Shyla Colt** has always been in love with the written word. Named after Super Girl in the comics, she often mistakes her mortality for super hero status. So, she holds many hats: mother,

Marine wife, and writer are her top three. Writing allows her to explore new venues, face her demons, and touch others. A huge practitioner of paying it forward, and putting in what you get out, she hopes to inspire, enlighten, move, and entertain. You can learn more about her and her work at www.shylacolt.com

Tony Flynn is 25 years old and lives in Dublin, Ireland. A writer of poetry, screenplays and short stories; he is terribly afraid of most everything and therefore has a particular interest in the horror genre. Previous publishing credits include the short story 'Monica' which appeared online in the Autumn 13 edition of wordlegs.com. Other writing can be found via http://tonywritesstuff.tumblr.com

Victoria Dalpe is a writer and visual artist based out of Providence, RI. She lives with her husband, writer and filmmaker Philip Gelatt Jr., in a house only a stone's throw from where HP Lovecraft's childhood home once stood.

John F. Allen is an American writer born in Indianapolis, IN. He began writing stories as early as the second grade and pursued all forms of writing at some point, throughout his career. John studied Liberal Arts at IUPUI with a focus in Creative Writing, received an honorable discharge from the United States Air Force and is a current member of the American Legion. John is a member of Indiana Writers Center and his debut novel, titled *The God Killers* was published this summer through Seventh Star Press.

John currently resides in Indianapolis, Indiana with his wife, son and daughter.

Johannes Pinter is a Swedish film director and horror writer with two novels under his belt. He has been published in the Swedish horror anthologies, Eskapix, "Bländverk", and the upcoming Bonne Nouvelle. He also has a short story in the forthcoming American horror anthology Dark Bits. Web site: johannespinter.se Blog: sleepwalkingskills.blogspot.com

Frank Roger was born in 1957 in Ghent, Belgium. His first story appeared in 1975. Since then his stories appear in an increasing number of languages in all sorts of magazines and anthologies, and since 2000, story collections are published, also in various languages. Apart from fiction, he also produces collages and graphic work in a surrealist and satirical tradition. They have appeared in various magazines and books. By now he has a few hundred short stories to his credit, published in more than 35 languages. Find out more at www.frankroger.be

Leigh Jenkins is a writer hailing from Charlotte, NC where she lives with her husband (and editor) Alan. They have recently welcomed their first child, Martha Elizabeth. Leigh has managed to incorporate two of her loves into her writing- Henry the VIII and Disney. She has authored of a series of alternative history novellas centered around Henry's wives, called The Six Lives of Henry the VIII. The first three in the series are available on Amazon. She is also the Disney Expert for Fodor's and co-authors the travel guide "Walt Disney World with Kids". Leigh looks forward to balancing motherhood with her writing career!

Jim Becker casts a long shadow as dusk approaches. He has written short stories, stage plays, movie scripts, essays, and bad poetry, all of which he compiled in his self-published opus Featherless, Woozy. Beyond the page, Jim can often be found on a disc golf course with his three sons, enjoying baked treats with his wife, or locked in a car trunk on a deserted farm near Nashville, Tennessee.

Mark Taylor is a writer from the South East of England. He has had dozens of flash titles, short stories and novellas published in presses large and small. For the most part his publications are horror. He writes twisted material in unsettling ways. His explorations of the mind have taken him from flash to novel and back again.

His short story collection *The Human Condition* is coming soon from Wicked East Press. In August 2013, his novel Shutter Speed was signed to Nocturnal Press Publications and is scheduled for general release this Christmas. You can usually find him at filingwords.blogspot.com.

Craig Faustus Buck is a writer of many faces having been a journalist, a non-fiction book author, a writer-producer for network television, a feature film screenwriter, a short-story author and now a novelist. Among his six non-fiction books, two were #1 NYT bestsellers--one pop-psychology the other pop-gynecology. His short film, Overnight Sensation, was nominated for an Academy Award. He was one of the writers on the seminal miniseries *V: The Final Battle* and wrote the famous episode where The Incredible Hulk dropped acid.

His agent is currently shopping his first noir mystery novel, Go Down Hard, which was First Runner Up for the Claymore Award at Killer Nashville. Based in Los Angeles, he is on the local chapter boards of both the Mystery Writers of America and Sisters in Crime, and a member of the Writers Guild of America and International Thriller Writers.

Dawn Napier is a thirty-something married mother of three and the author of several novels. Her genres of choice are horror and dark fantasy, but she has also been known to spin the occasional sci-fi yarn. She grew up in upstate New York and Waukegan, Illinois. Her favorite color is red, and her favorite pet is an enormous brown rat named Cinnamon Brown. She used to play the cello.

Tom Olbert lives in Cambridge, MA. He's had a taste for horror and science fiction most of his life. His fiction has appeared in various print and online publications, including Mocha Memoirs. When not writing fiction, Tom volunteers for progressive causes close to his heart, like human rights and the environment.

USAF veteran **Tony Brown** holds a BA in Communications from East Carolina University, has won contests by Art Forum and Union Writers and received honorable mentions in Writer's Journal and Writer's Digest. His work has appeared in Huffington Post's Huff/Post50, Foliate Oak (University of Arkansas), Static Movement Press, Birmingham Arts Journal, Sleeping Cat, Whortleberry Press, Perpetual Motion Machine, Writers' Haven, Notes Magazine, Long & Short Review, In Between Altered States, Bartleby Snopes, Word Gumbo (UK) Leodegraunce, Vapid Kitten (UK), The Write Place At the Write Time, Short-Story Me, Gemini, Down in the Dirt, Blink Ink, Postcard Shorts, Short Story Alley, The Storyteller, and elsewhere. Brown is a former writer for The East Carolinian and numerous North Carolina newspapers and publications, and nationally in Tree Care Industry magazine. He's also the former editor/main writer of Rock & Roll Monthly.

Shaun Avery is a crime and horror fiction fan with stories upcoming in various anthologies and magazines. He would like to apologise in advance for any ideas this story puts in the head of reality TV shows producers.

Marcia Colette discovered her love for reading with John Saul and progressed to works by Bentley Little, Stephen King and Laurell K. Hamilton. Her reading tastes convinced her to write paranormals where curses cause people to shift into spiders, psychokinetic mothers are locked away in attics, and murderous doppelgangers are on a rampage. Let's not forget about the hunky werecheetah coalitions who live throughout North Carolina. As long as she can make it believable, that's all that matters.

Born and raised in upstate New York, Marcia now lives in North Carolina. The best place to find her is at www.marciacolette.com.

J. H. Fleming received her Bachelor's Degree in Creative Writing from the University of Central Arkansas. Her stories have been published by Visionary Tongue Magazine, Evil Girlfriend Media, and Seventh Star Press. Her favorite genres have always been fantasy and supernatural, especially the ones with a darker tone. When she's not writing, she spends her time learning French and piano, playing video games, and watching anime. Find more about her at someplacetobeflying.com, and follow her on Facebook and Twitter.

Ross Baxter has been published in print and Kindle by a number of publishing houses in the United States and the UK. After thirty years at sea he now lives in Derby, England. Ross's author page can be found at www.amazon.co.uk

Laura DeHaan is a healthcare practitioner in her hometown of Toronto, Canada. She's a longtime student of the Russian martial art of Systema, is learning German, and considers saag paneer rotis to be her ultimate comfort food. Follow her on Twitter @WritInRooster for publishing updates and the continuing story of the world's most put-upon tourist, Topher Topher.

TC Phillips considers himself to be a novice wordsmith with big aspirations. Hailing from tropical Central Queensland Australia, when he's not too busy sweating profusely he is usually running around after three beautiful young children or completing post-graduate studies in Writing via Swinburne University. Somewhere in-between all that he also manages to squeeze in working as a workplace trainer.

Primarily preoccupied with speculative fiction in all its forms and manifestations, he loves writing horror, historical fiction, sci-fi and fantasy. You can track his everyday encounters with the wonderful world of the written word on his website www.cobblestonescribe.com.

Joshua R English lives in Portland Oregon, the Great Metropolitan Rain Forest, with his wife and a ghost of a cat. When neither writing nor writing about writing, he plays classical guitar, codes a little bit, and counteracts a sit-all-day lifestyle by lifting heavy things. A small portion of his life can be seen at joshuarenglish.com.

Erin Eveland is a Michigan author, writing in the realms of dark fantasy and horror. She never had the dream to write since she was a child. She was never going to be a writer. Period. The accident happened one winter day when a simple idea struck her, spilling into many stories thereafter. She has published short stories while concluding her first novel. Links to her works can be found at http://erineveland.net/.

Eden Royce is a native of Charleston, South Carolina whose great-aunt practiced root, a type of conjure magic. She now wishes she'd listened more closely.

Her stories have appeared in various anthologies by Kerlak/Dark Oak Press, Sirens Call Publications, and Blood Bound Books to name a few. Besides writing, blogging, editing, and reviewing indie authors, her passions include roller-skating and listening to thunderstorms. She lurks around darkgeisha.wordpress.com and edenroyce.com

Thank you!

Thank you for purchasing a Mocha Memoirs Press, LLC contemporary story. Please check our other titles. Visit our website at http://mochamemoirspress.com.

www.ingramcontent.com/pod-product-compliance
Lightning Source LLC
Chambersburg PA
CBHW050026030726
47506CB00001B/132